The
FEMINIST
AGENDA
of Jemima
Kincaid

Also by Kate Hattemer

The Vigilante Poets of Selwyn Academy

The Land of 10,000 Madonnas

The FEMINIST AGENDA

of Jemima Kincaid

Kate Hattemer

ALFRED A. KNOPF
New York

THIS IS A BORZOI BOOK PUBLISHED BY ALFRED A. KNOPF

All rights reserved. Published in the United States by Alfred A. Knopf, an imprint of Random House Children's Books, a division of Penguin Random House LLC, New York.

Knopf, Borzoi Books, and the colophon are registered trademarks of Penguin Random House LLC.

Visit us on the Web! GetUnderlined.com

Educators and librarians, for a variety of teaching tools, visit us at RHTeachersLibrarians.com

Library of Congress Cataloging-in-Publication Data
Names: Hattemer, Kate, author.
Title: The feminist agenda of Jemima Kincaid / Kate Hattemer.
Description: First edition. | New York: Alfred A. Knopf, 2020. | Summary: In her last few weeks at Northern Virginia's elite Chawton School, eighteen-year-old Jemima Kincaid works to upend its patriarchal traditions and, in the process, finds the freedom she has always sought.
Identifiers: LCCN 2019005183 (print) | LCCN 2019007973 (ebook) |
ISBN 978-1-9848-4914-4 (ebook) | ISBN 978-1-9848-4912-0 (trade) |
ISBN 978-1-9848-4913-7 (lib. bdg.)
Subjects: | CYAC: Feminism—Fiction. | Private schools—Fiction. | Schools—Fiction. | Social change—Fiction. | Friendship—Fiction.
Classification: LCC PZ7.H2847 (ebook) | LCC PZ7.H2847 Fem 2020 (print) |
DDC [Fic]—dc23

The text of this book is set in 11.75-point Dante Monotype Pro.
Interior design by Trish Parcell

Printed in the United States of America
February 2020
10 9 8 7 6 5 4 3 2 1

First Edition

For Lucy, Emma, and Rebecca:
sister goals, sister ghouls

CHAPTER 1

"It's nice to meet you," I told Old White Dudes #19 and #20.

Every alumnus looked the same. Sure, there were minor variations. Paunches were small, medium, or large. Hair was nonexistent, receding, or artificially puffed. Smiles were indifferent but polite (good), paternal and doting (meh), or lecherously smirky (gag).

But everyone qualified as Old and White and Dude.

I shouldn't have been surprised. I was at the Senior Triumvirates, Past and Present reception, and the all-boys Chawton School hadn't merged with Ansel Academy for Girls until 1978. They'd combined campuses and mascots (Angel Tigers, rah rah rah!), but Ansel had lost its name, *as in a marriage,* the commemorative plaque says. Chawton is a snooty private school in the snooty suburban enclaves of northern Virginia. It neighbors George Washington's plantation, which should tell you something: it's steeped in history, history of a certain type. The history of Old White Dudes running shit.

OWD #19 had moles. I bet someone clipped OWD #20's nose hair. I bet not him. "A pleasure," said #19.

"The Chawton boys are lucky these days, eh, Davis?" said #20.

"Sure are," said #19, looking me up and down.

With the instinct born of eighteen years of being a girl in this world, I crossed my arms over my chest. "Why do you say that?" I said as politely as I could manage.

Which was not all that polite.

OWD #19 put a spotted hand on my upper arm. I shook him off and took a step back. "Hundreds of adolescent boys," he said. "Not one female among us—remember, Richard?"

"*Do* I."

"We could spot the Ansel girls playing field hockey from the maintenance tower—"

"Naturally we'd convene there—"

"Those gym suits they wore!"

I glared at them, my arms still crossed. OWD #19 chortled. "Your male classmates are very fortunate," he told me.

"Smile, dear," OWD #20 added. "It's not all doom and gloom."

"This is *my* face," I began, "so don't tell me—"

"Hello, hello!" Gennifer Grier appeared at my elbow, beaming at the OWDs. "I am so sorry to interrupt, but, Jemima, we're needed at the silent auction."

I gave them a cursory nod and stalked after Gennifer. They'd put the silent-auction items outside, but in early April the evening air still held an unpleasant nip, and the courtyard was deserted. Gennifer's fake smile vanished. "What's your deal, Jemmy?" she said.

I hated that name and she knew it. "What's *your* deal? Why'd you drag me out here?"

"I had to extract you before you got all three of us in trouble."

"What the hell. This was a ruse?"

"The light dawns."

"I was about to educate those assholes. They told me to smile."

"Yeah, yeah."

"Like they think my function's purely decorative."

"Do you even understand the point of this evening?"

"Of course I do, *Ghennifer*." I said it with a hard, aspirated G, as in *ghastly*. These nicknames weren't new. If there had ever been any love between me and Gennifer, it had been lost long ago.

"We *are* decorative," she said. "We're a blank slate upon which the former triumvirs can write their own memories of Chawton."

Gennifer is what you'd get if you googled "perfect American girl": white and blond and thin. She has perfect teeth, which, like her, are white and straight and polished. Sometimes her prettiness made me think she was dumb. She's not. She is just about the opposite of dumb.

"Come on," she said, "let's pretend we're checking on the silent-auction table."

Andy joined us as we straightened the baskets of fancy shampoo, the placards proclaiming AN AFTERNOON FOR EIGHT AT THE MERCER COUNTRY CLUB and AN ITALIAN COOKING LESSON WITH MASTER CHEF LUIGI DEL CARMINE. "You two hiding?" he said.

"Jemima needed to be reminded how to shut up and smile and nod."

"She's so strident," said Andy, winking at me. "So shrill."

"Fuck off," I said. He grinned. Sometimes he acted like a chauvinistic asshat just to annoy me. And then sometimes he acted like a chauvinistic asshat because he was a white, straight, wealthy eighteen-year-old guy, and chauvinistic asshattery was basically his birthright.

I should note that I, too, am white. And straight. And wealthy, or my parents are. But despite these disadvantages, I do my best not to be a horrible person. I was a feminist before it was trendy.

"I wish we could have a real meeting tonight," said Gennifer. "We have way too much to do before Jamboree."

"Jamboree's eight weeks away."

"Seven," said Gennifer. "And do you *know* how much stuff we have to organize? The election, Powderpuff, prom—"

"Beware," I announced. "Ghennifer Grier has entered checklist mode."

"My checklists have saved your asses all year."

"When I reminisce about my senior year of high school,"

said Andy, gazing into the Commons, where a black-coated swarm of OWDs was doing just that, "it'll be to the soundtrack of you two squabbling."

"Because women don't debate or argue," I said. "They *squabble.*"

"Exactly," said Andy. "They *catfight.* I'm glad we're on the same page, Kincaid."

If he hadn't grinned at me, I'd have picked up that shampoo and hurled it at his handsome face. But he grinned and it was over. That was what happened every time. Andy's magical grin. Not that I had a crush on him or anything like that. He was cute. Of course he was cute. He was Chawton School chairman— captain of the lacrosse team, smart, too, golden-haired and broad-backed—but I steeled myself against all of that, almost by instinct at this point: he was Andy and I was Jemima, and never the twain would meet.

Or rather, we would meet all the time in the bureaucrats' wet dream that was Senior Triumvirate. Meeting after meeting after meeting. But we would never *meet* meet. Like in the biblical sense.

I wouldn't have attended a biblical meeting with him even if a PowerPoint agenda arrived in my inbox.

Probably not, anyway.

Every year, the Senior Triumvirate got their names engraved on this phallic obelisk thing. Andy and Gennifer and I stood by it. Ms. Edison, our faculty advisor, tapped the mike until the OWDs hushed.

"Senior Triumvirate," Ms. Edison began, "is one of Chawton's most hallowed traditions."

Yawn. She went on. Chawton was unique and special. Triumvirate was unique and special. Senior-class ruling body. Major decision-making power. "I'm pleased to introduce this year's Triumvirate," she said. "In the position of Social Committee president, Gennifer Grier!"

Gennifer was wearing a dress so tight it went out for her butt and then back in underneath. The OWDs and I all noticed as she pranced up there.

"And the recipient of the Mildred Mustermann Award for Academic Excellence, Jemima Kincaid!"

I'd been dreading the walk. It's like: *Please look honored, happy, and humble all at once, okay? Oh, and navigate the heels your mom strongly suggested you wear, and be aware that a hundred encrusted alumni are checking you out, but don't be self-conscious, honey!* I like my body until I have to squish it into a pencil skirt.

"And the Chawton School chairman, Andrew Monroe!"

He had the walk much easier. For one, his clothes were built for functionality, not for displaying his body. And he didn't have to worry about looking too pleased with himself, because arrogance in a teenage boy is almost expected—it's *endearing*—whereas in a girl . . .

Gennifer elbowed me. Hard. She's got a bony elbow. I guess my thoughts were showing, because she hissed, *"Smile."*

"This Triumvirate will surely go down in Chawton history," said Ms. Edison. "They spearheaded a new community-service initiative, Senior Citi-Zen, in which Chawton students went to nursing homes to teach yoga and meditation."

I squirmed. Senior Citi-Zen had been a failure. An abject failure. To the tune of one dislocated hip, three nasty bruises, and a whole roomful of old ladies cracking up when I told them how important it was to inhale and exhale. Between wheezes of laughter, one called out, "How else do you think I've lasted eighty-seven years?"

"Furthermore, this Triumvirate organized an excellent senior-class picnic—"

Three kids had gotten suspended for bringing vodka in Nalgene bottles, and Lacey McStern had gotten hit in the head with a Frisbee and had to miss half of soccer season with a concussion.

"—a reenergized Hype Club that provided support to all of Chawton's sports teams—"

People went to football, boys' basketball, sometimes boys' soccer, sometimes boys' lacrosse. The. End.

"—a senior-class Secret Santa circle—"

We forgot to send a reminder about bringing final gifts, so it ended in a maelstrom of hurt feelings. Oh, and dumb old Sam Masterson got Sydney Armstrong a box of eggnog-scented condoms—as a joke, he claimed—but Sydney burst into tears because she thought Sam was implying something about her. The teachers caught wind and banned Secret Santa forevermore.

"In short, we're so proud of this Triumvirate. They had big shoes to fill—yours—and they have truly lived up to the challenge. Please give them a round of applause."

I glanced right and saw Andy awkwardly shifting from foot to foot.

I glanced left and saw Gennifer wrinkling her forehead in perturbation.

I wouldn't get this chance again.

I elbowed her right in the skinny rib cage.

She squealed.

"Ghen," I said, "let's see that smile."

The reception officially ended after that. Some alumni lingered, sharing one more bawdy tale of Ye Olde Chawton, but Ms. Edison, with a relieved and sort of collapsed look, shot out of there, and the facilities staff started bundling the tablecloths and folding the chairs. "Frosting," Gennifer said, drawing Andy and me over to the plundered cake tables. She scraped up a big, gloppy clump from an empty platter. "The perfect ratio. Seventy-five percent frosting, twenty-five percent crumb."

"Gross," said Andy, edging away.

"I've got emotions that need to be eaten."

She licked the fork clean and dove in for round two. I liked this. Gennifer has one of those cute, compact bodies that never bulge or bloat. She paints her nails with clear polish. If she tucks in her shirt, it stays tucked. She keeps travel-sized beauty products and stain remover in a Lilly Pulitzer pouch in her backpack, not because she needs them herself (Gennifer Grier spills not, neither does she smear) but because she likes to offer them around, either with kind concern ("Oh my gosh, Melanie, *here*, use my Tide pen and don't worry about it! I do that all the time!") or with condescending judgment ("Jemima, you seriously need the Tide pen again? You're going to have to start reimbursing me").

I'd never seen her on a frosting bender. "You know what?" she said, her fork diving in for a fourth—fifth?—helping. "We haven't been a very good Triumvirate."

"You got frosting on your nose," I told her.

"We've tried, but nothing's worked."

"Truth," said Andy. "Hand me a fork, would you?"

"Frosting," I said dramatically. "Our only succor."

"Haven't we discussed your use of the word *succor?*" Gennifer said testily. "Didn't we determine it needs to stop?"

"*Succor* means 'help or support in difficult times.' *Sucker* means . . . well, anyway. They're very different."

"Not always," said Andy, licking his fork in a way that was positively pornographic. Gennifer giggled and bit her bottom lip. Yech. Have I mentioned she's dating Mack Monroe, Andy's genetic near copy in the junior class? Flirting with your boyfriend's brother: Isn't that kind of sick?

"You're right, though," Andy said. "As a Triumvirate, we've sucked."

"Sucked?" said Gennifer. "I wouldn't go *that* far."

"Wouldn't you?"

"We've been profoundly ineffective," I said, mostly to cut the sexual tension mounting between Gennifer and the man theoretically on track to become her brother-in-law. "Have we put on *one* successful event?"

"Nope," said Andy. "And we haven't added anything. We're leaving no legacy. We've made no mark on the school."

All three of us fell silent, which, given our personalities, didn't happen much. I mashed frosting around in my mouth. I already had a sugar daze, which made me wonder how Gennifer, outpacing me two to one despite her head start, still stood upright.

"That's depressing," said Andy.

"Seriously," said Gennifer.

"Yeah," I said.

Not all second-semester seniors would have cared. But we did. We were completely different from one another, sure, and we'd earned our Triumvirate positions in completely different ways: Gennifer was the popular socialite and Andy was the charismatic leader and me, well, I was the nerd. But we had something in common, too. We were overachievers. That was why we were on Triumvirate. Gennifer was *super* popular. Andy was *super* charismatic. And I was, well, *super* . . .

You get the idea.

We didn't like sucking. We didn't like being ineffective. And we definitely didn't like the idea of passing into obscurity. Like most of our class, we had college plans lined up. I was heading to one of those New England schools that put the *liberal* in *liberal arts*. Andy had gotten a big merit scholarship to UVA, and Gennifer was going to a state school down south, where, I presumed, she'd run the most selective sorority yet somehow manage to graduate summa cum laude. We were all excited for our futures, but we weren't there yet. We had unfinished business.

"All we've got left is Jamboree," said Andy. That's Chawton's big end-of-year celebration, an all-weekend affair with a bonfire and a Powderpuff game and an alumni reunion and prom. As Senior Triumvirate, we had a lot of shit to do.

"We need a really good theme for prom," said Gennifer.

"Prom is the worst," I said. "Maybe we should cancel it."

"Okay, Jemmy, no—"

"The guys ask the girls. Always. I'm speaking heteronormatively because only heterosexual couples even *go*. The girls wait passively for an invite—sorry, a *promposal*—and the guys get to choose who to ask."

"That's a problem?" said Andy.

I rolled my eyes at him. "It's practically a silent auction."

"The girls still get to say yes or no," said Gennifer. "That's a lot of power."

"What if we change the rules?" I said.

"Let's have, say, a silent auction," Andy suggested. "The girls pose on tables and the guys stroll around and bid—"

"You're a misogynistic cretin," I told him. He bowed. I smiled. I killed that smile so fast, but he saw it. I knew he did.

Damn it.

Andy freaking Monroe.

We straggled out into the April evening. No legacy, no idea. Nothing behind us but a string of failures, nothing ahead but swiftly plunging blood sugar.

"Think," said Andy. "We'll come up with something."

Crispin was at the wheel of our mom's Lexus. "At last!" I cried, belly-flopping in. "My getaway car! Drive, Jeeves, drive!"

"You're always horrible after these things."

"Flee this accursed place!"

He braked. The car stopped. We hadn't even exited the circle. "You going to act normal?"

I slumped back. "Yes, Jeeves."

He didn't lift his foot from the brake.

"Yes. I am acting totally normal. Unscarred and serene after an evening with a hundred Old White Dudes, Ghennifer Grier my only succor."

"You've got to stop using that word."

"It's a good word." Hadn't anyone realized that the more they told me I couldn't do something, the more I'd do it? "The word *succor* provides me much succor."

Crispin shook his head, but at least he started driving. He'd graduated from Chawton six years ago and from UVA two years ago. Now he worked at a consulting firm and lived in our basement, though Mom told me he was moving out. (I'd believe it when I saw it.) "Mom dumped the driving on you?" I said.

"It's a thankless task, but someone has to deal with the disagreeable runt of the litter."

"There's only two of us. We don't count as a litter."

"You had quite a night, huh, Bump?" said Crispin. "You're arguing with literally everything I'm saying—"

"Is that so unusual?"

"—including this very sentence."

"I wouldn't call it *arguing*—"

"Relax. Deep breaths. Tell your old Bip how happy he should be he didn't show."

Crispin had been chairman his senior year at Chawton. He'd gotten a thick, cream-papered invitation to this reception, and he'd recycled it immediately.

"Did your Triumvirate *do* anything?" I said.

"Besides each other?"

"Ew, no details." Though I was sort of intrigued. I weighed my gag reflex against my curiosity, but given the all-too-recent frosting debacle, I chose the prudent path and redirected the conversation. "Were you worried about your legacy?"

"How quaint. No, we were too busy banging."

"All three of you?" I said impulsively. "No—wait—don't—"

"Not at the same time. Despite the Mildred's *repeated* propositions."

I groaned.

"Oh, high school," said Crispin with a reminiscent sigh. "The weirdest time of life."

"Seven weeks left," I said. Sometimes I felt like I had a foot out the door, and sometimes I thought, Can't I just stay? Chawton wasn't the real world. I knew that. It was a bubble, a snow globe, all privilege and academic glory and social hierarchies and free cake. I didn't even like Chawton that much, but without my having had much choice in the matter, it had become my home.

CHAPTER 2

Crispin went out that Saturday night, and my dad was at work, so I had to ask my benightgowned mother to give Jiyoon a ride over to our house. I felt guilty. I didn't like asking Mom for anything, meals or rides or advice or whatever: she offered what she could, I figured, and I tried to provide the rest myself. Mom gets migraines, these hellish headaches that make her curl into a ball and shun the light like a vampire fetus. She's tried a bunch of medications and remedies and therapies and stuff, everything on the market plus some. Nothing's worked. And no one knows what triggers the headaches, so even when she's feeling okay, she has to avoid sugar, screens, cheese, sleep disturbances, caffeine, loud conversation, and excitement. Basically, everything that makes life worth living.

She put a sweater on over her nightgown and I followed her out to the car. "You'd never have to drive me anywhere if I had my license," I pointed out.

"Once your father's schedule eases up, he'll teach you."

I'd had my permit for two years. Twenty-four months. One hundred and four weeks. And my dad had taken me driving exactly once, and a few minutes in, before he'd even let me switch seats with him, he got an important call and we had to go home.

"He taught Crispin right away."

"Crispin was different."

"Well, that's a little sexist."

"Jemima. It has nothing to do with your gender. He just doesn't want to have to replace the brake pads again."

"Who says I'd suck as much as Crispin did? Crispin's not known for his motor skills. Besides," I said, suddenly processing, "*that's* the real reason? I thought he was too busy!"

"That too."

"Crispin could teach me."

"Crispin's working long hours these days."

"*You* could teach me."

"Sweetheart. Be patient. We'll take you where you need to go."

Did having a kid wipe all your memories of being a kid? There was a huge difference between getting a ride and being your own ride. And it wasn't like I was going to absquatulate with the car for a wild road trip to Mexico. I was a nerd. My best friends were from Quiz Team. The closest I had ever come to pot was when I went to a lecture at George Mason last April 20, and I'd spent the whole afternoon thinking that someone was burning rope.

I mean, guys. I was the Mildred.

"Give a girl a fish and she eats for a day," I said into the silence. "Teach a girl to fish and she eats for a lifetime."

My mom sighed and switched on NPR.

Some friends you go places with and some you just chill with, but Jiyoon and I always make stuff. It's funny because alone, we aren't crafty; alone, all we do is read, not out of virtuous self-betterment or anything but because we're lazy and escapist and, I guess, kind of lonely. Together, though, we do weird projects like building a functional scale model of an Archimedes' screw or sewing an Arachne doll that turns inside out into a spider. A few months before, we'd turned *Pride and Prejudice* into a card game called Pemberley, sort of a cross between gin rummy and *The Bachelor*. It was a big hit among the Quiz Team crowd.

"My mom suggested we have chopped salad for dinner," I said to Jiyoon. "That okay?"

"Sure."

We chopped for a while, talking about unimportant stuff like:

Jiyoon: "The only accurate word to describe this cucumber is *flaccid*."

Me: "No. The word *flaccid* belongs in just one context."

Jiyoon: "Feel it, really."

Me: "Limp as . . ."

Together: ". . . a dick."

Cackle, cackle. Dick jokes are funniest when you've never seen a live one. We ate on the spinny stools at the kitchen island. "What makes the perfect prom?" I asked her.

"Not going," she said immediately.

"You like dances."

"Not prom. Prom's about three things. One, the ask. Two, the photos. Three, getting wasted at the after-party, despite graduation the next morning. I will *never* go to prom."

"I bet you'll go next year." Jiyoon was a junior.

She started twirling on her stool. "Not a chance."

I hadn't twirled on these stools for years, but I joined her. Conversation briefly ceased.

"Oh, gross, so dizzy," said Jiyoon. "What was I saying?"

"Prom?"

She clutched her stomach. "Blech."

"Do you need a bucket?"

She put a hand over her mouth and waved me away. While she recovered, I thought about prom. Blech indeed.

"Okay," she said. "When did I get old? Next thing I'll realize I hate roller coasters."

"I already hate roller coasters," I confessed.

"You know? Same."

"Maybe we should bust out the sherry and prunes."

"High-fiber crackers."

"Cottage cheese."

"We should make something old-fashioned tonight," she said. "Like . . . a diorama."

I went with it. "A diorama of when we're aged spinsters, living together, eating high-fiber crackers, hating roller coasters."

"And men."

"We already do," I said.

"Speak for yourself."

"Men hate *me*."

"Uh-huh. Right. Find a shoebox."

We made a gigantic mess on the kitchen table as we turned the shoebox into a parlor suitable for Old Jiyoon and Old Jemima, blue-haired troll dolls who were briskly christened Dotty and Dorcas.

Jiyoon measured the sides of the box for wallpaper. "My dad got another job in Indiana. Three more months."

"Ji! That's—well, great. And not great."

"Yep." Her dad, who does construction, couldn't get work here in Virginia, but when he'd heard there were jobs in Indiana, he'd gone out there with a few other guys from their church. "He hates living in a motel."

"I bet."

She was quiet, her bottom lip between her teeth as she cut gold-and-green-striped wrapping paper.

"It must be hard on your mom," I ventured. "Not to have him home."

"The money is nice. More than nice. Necessary. But my mom gets down. When he's home, she cooks and cleans and, you know, *moms,* but now . . . well, I try to get Hae-Won and Min to help me, but Hae-Won sleeps all the time, she's such a blob, and Min's sweet, he says he wants to help, but he's ten, so how much can you expect? He tries but gets distracted, or I get mad at him because he does a sucky job. . . ." She shoved the wallpaper into the back of the shoebox. "Damn. The stripes aren't straight."

"It doesn't matter."

"Of course it matters." She laughed. "I may have to hide out over here for a few months. That's all."

"Can I—"

I didn't know what to say.

"Can we do anything to help?" I finally said.

"No," she said flatly. "It'll get better once my dad gets back."

Jiyoon and I are best friends, and we supposedly talk about everything. But we don't talk about money. We don't talk about the fact that my dad is general counsel for a corporation you've heard of, and her dad is a construction worker. And my mom has stayed at home since Crispin was born, and her mom is a receptionist at a gastroenterologist's office in Annandale. When Jiyoon and I met, back in elementary school, her mom cleaned houses. That's how we met, to be honest. Her mom cleaned our house.

I'm not like some of the kids at school, going to Antigua for long weekends, getting a Maserati for sweet sixteen. But we have a big house in a pricey suburb; we have three newish cars. If I need—want—a haircut or cleats, I ask and get. When the school put on a dog-sledding trip to Maine, I went. Chawton costs as much as a private college. Jiyoon is on scholarship.

Nobody at Chawton talks about money.

"Seriously, Dorcas," she told me. "Pretend I didn't say anything. Everyone's fine. Like, we're getting *fed*. It's just a little depressing."

"Okay," I said uncertainly. "But tell me if—"

"Will do. New subject." She ripped the crooked wallpaper from the shoebox with perhaps more force than necessary. "Dotty and Dorcas do *not* tolerate shoddy workmanship!"

"We need a couch," I said. "What would you say to papier-mâché getting involved?"

"Do you *know* me? I am always down for papier-mâché."

I found some balloons and stirred up a batch of flour-water paste. A papier-mâché couch, however, was a more intricate project than I'd imagined. "This is going to look like a blob," I said.

"Maybe Dotty and Dorcas want beanbag chairs instead of a couch," said Jiyoon.

"Good call."

I got the hair dryer to hasten the process. "So," I said as I blasted the soggy beanbag chairs. The scent of lightly toasted flour filled the air. "About prom. It needs to be the best dance ever. I don't know whether we need to up our game with the decor, or the theme, or—"

"None of that matters."

"Of course it matters."

"Nope." She motioned down to the diorama. "Look at Dotty and Dorcas. Shitty crooked wallpaper, swampy-ass beanbag chairs, and they still love it, because they get to hang together. Prom's like that. It's who you're there with."

"Right," I said. "You're so right." In the corner of my brain, the hazy outlines of an idea came into being. But ideas are skittish. You can't show them the whites of your eyes. "I love it too," I said, moving the hair dryer even closer. "Hanging together, just Dotty and Dorcas. Shitty wallpaper and all."

Jiyoon sniffed. "Something's burning," she said. "You should turn that off. Now."

CHAPTER 3

It is a Chawton tradition (get used to that phrase) that Senior Triumvirate meets alone. As the school tells prospective parents, the level of autonomous responsibility allowed to Chawton's student government is truly unique.

Translation: they give us a lot of tedious shit to do and they don't have to sit through us figuring out how to do it.

"We need to get Powderpuff going," said Gennifer after school on Monday. She usually ended up running our meetings because she was the only one who prepared beforehand.

"Powderpuff is the reason I wanted to be on Triumvirate," said Andy, stretching his arms behind his head. "I can take charge of that."

"Ugh, Powderpuff," I said, even though I was distracted by the pleasant bulge of Andy's biceps. He'd taken off his tie and rolled up his sleeves. He had nice forearms. Lean, tanned, golden-haired—

"I'll assign the girls to teams," said Andy.

"Don't forget dealing with jerseys and fan gear," said Gennifer, who is a walking to-do list. "And you have to organize the fund-raising competition, find faculty refs, appoint senior guys to coach—"

"I'm appointing myself," said Andy.

"Fair," I said sarcastically. I was ignored.

"And I'll survey all the guys in our class to see which team they're rooting for."

"I hate Powderpuff," I said.

"I thought you hated prom," said Gennifer.

"I do."

"Is there anything you don't hate?"

"It's all so . . . problematic."

Powderpuff is the biggest event at Jamboree. The senior girls play football: the Angels vs. the Tigers, since our school mascot is the Angel Tiger. Everyone gets so into it. The guys all support one team or the other, cheering or literally cheerleading, and the alumni love it too because it's a lifelong allegiance, which team you root for. There's even a big secondary competition over whether the Angels or the Tigers get the most donations to the Chawton Annual Fund.

"You think it's sexist?" said Andy.

I knew what I would write if I were doing an op-ed for the school paper. *A mockery of female athleticism. A throwback to an era when the idea of girls on a football field was a hilarious reversal of gender roles.* But I knew this, too: If you were going to call something out, you had to be like a chess player. You had to think a move ahead. *It's not a mockery*, they'd say. *The girls are serious about winning. There are practices, a playbook. It's like any other sport.*

I wasn't satisfied but I didn't know how I'd rebut the rebuttals, and so my pawns held fast and my queen mused, silent and still, behind her army.

"It's the twenty-first century," said Andy. "If it were sexist, someone would have gotten rid of it already."

"So are you playing?" said Gennifer.

"Me?" I said.

"You play soccer," said Andy. "You'd be good."

"But it's so . . ." I struggled for the right word. *"Problematic,"* I said again.

"Lighten up, Jemmy," said Gennifer.

"As the newly appointed head coach of the Tigers," Andy said, "I'm drafting you, Kincaid."

He smiled at me and I felt a rush of warmth, a cozy and anticipatory stirring, like when you get home and you smell dinner before you open the door and that's when you realize how hungry you are. Like there were good things in store. What if I let go and got excited for Powderpuff? What if I dropped the Jemima Kincaid, Angry Feminist thing for like three seconds and . . . and had a good time?

Pleasure was a feminist choice too.

"Fine," I said, rolling my eyes. "I'll play. Also, I had an idea for prom."

"I brainstormed a few themes in history," said Gennifer. She flipped around her notebook to show us. *Hawaiian Hoopla. Ivy League Gala.*

"No, no," I said. "We don't need a theme. We need to change the dance's very structure. We'll call it the Last Chance Dance."

"Well, we're seniors, so by default—" began Gennifer.

"Listen. You make a secret list. Of anyone you've got a crush on. Anyone you've ever crushed on. And then you get matched."

"Just the guys, right?"

"What?"

"Like, the guys write down who they like. The girls see who put them and choose their favorite."

"No, no. Everyone submits a list. And if any of the choices overlap, you both get notified."

Andy grinned and put his hands behind his head again. "Nice. So say I put Gennifer, because she's hot, and then it turns out she's *always* dreamed of me, turns out she thinks I'm Lust Incarnate, God of Sex, which, of course, I am—"

"Shut *up*," said Gennifer, giggling.

"—and she's only dating my brother because, genetically speaking, that's as close as she can get—"

She gave him a naughty little smile. "I bet you two have a lot in common."

Barf. "Anyway," I said loudly, "in your hypothetical situation, Andy, yes, you and Gennifer would be informed you were matches. But say you'd put me as well. Obviously I'm not going to put you, given that I wouldn't touch you with a ten-foot pole—"

"What if I said I could touch *you* with a ten-foot pole—"

Gennifer slapped his arm. "Bad boy."

"Nobody would ever know you'd put me," I continued. "And your embarrassing crush on someone totally out of your league would remain cloaked in secrecy."

"As if," said Gennifer.

"What if someone doesn't get any matches?" said Andy. "That'll happen, right?"

"Well, then, they can just find a date the usual way. But we'll encourage people to go broad. Put anyone they'd even consider. We'll give everyone, like, a hundred slots."

"Honestly," said Andy, shrugging, "I think it's a great idea. Change it up around here."

I was quiet. Now that I'd made my point, I needed to lie low. If Gennifer didn't take some ownership of the idea, she'd never agree to it. She looked between us, her eyes narrowed to slits. She pursed her glossy lips. I found myself staring. How did she get the lip gloss to stay on? I always end up eating mine. Especially if it's fruit-flavored.

"Do you have an ulterior motive?" she asked me.

Yes. Giving girls control over their own lives. Balancing the power structure of dance invitations. Smashing the patriarchy. The usual. "Not at all," I told Gennifer. "I just think it'd be a fun twist. It could jump-start some relationships."

"True," she said.

"I think the class'll be into it," said Andy. "As long as they're assured it'll be anonymous. We can't be the ones sifting through the lists, making the matches."

"But that'd be the best part!" said Gennifer.

"We'll do it online," I said. I'd thought about this. "We'll have a program that encodes each name as the lists come in, and it'll pair the codes and only decode the ones that match."

"You can write this program?" said Andy.

"I'll ask Paul Cunningham. He's a junior. You know him?"

"I still think we should do it ourselves," said Gennifer. Ha. She was in. Now that she was worrying about the details, I knew she'd bought the big picture. "Don't you think there's room for discretion? Like, if two people match who'd be *gross* together—"

"Let's talk decorations," said Andy quickly. "What's Last Chance decor?"

"Ooh," said Gennifer, diverted. Andy quirked a smile at me, and I smiled back without even meaning to. That was the effect he had on me. And on every other girl at Chawton, I hasten to add.

"How can we visually evoke the idea of chances?" said Gennifer.

"Garlands of lottery tickets," I suggested.

"They'd look like trash hanging from the ceiling."

"I mean, most dance decorations do."

"We could use actual trash," said Andy. "To conjure the theme of desperation."

"You two are hopeless." Gennifer slammed shut her notebook. "I'll discuss it with Social Committee. Meeting adjourned."

★ ★ ★

Wednesday Quiz Team practice was my favorite time of the week. I got to hang out with my friends *and* show off. The two spices of life, as far as I'm concerned.

Mr. Peabody was our coach. He had me, Paul, Jiyoon, and Jonah playing Ashby, Zachary, Greg, and Cilla. We were neck and neck right till the end, when Paul got some computer-science toss-up that the rest of us had no clue on. That reminded me. I needed to ask him to code the Last Chance Dance site. Preferably in private, since Triumvirate had decided it would be best if nobody knew who'd done the programming. It'd be a tiny bit of extra security for all that sensitive data.

"I have a favor to ask you, Paul," I said as we walked out. Jiyoon was with us, but she was extremely trustworthy. "On behalf of Senior Triumvirate."

"Does this have something to do with Powderpuff? Because I hate that shit."

I was surprised. Paul wasn't the most dynamic person. He was laconic, understated, dry. Him saying *I hate that shit* carried way more clout than someone saying it who was bombastic and bilious and prone to hyperbole—e.g., me.

"Why?" asked Jiyoon.

"I hate school spirit. For the same reason I hate professional sports. They're ways for people to hide."

"Did you have a traumatic experience with pro sports?" I said. "Puking at a football game or something?"

"Never mind, if you're only going to mock it."

"You mean," said Jiyoon, "if you bury your identity in an

institution, you don't have to worry about what your identity actually is."

"Exactly!" said Paul.

They kept talking. I was annoyed. It was like I'd lost my chance to participate because I'd made that one dumb joke, and now I had to trudge along and watch them bond via a cool intellectual discussion about identity and groupthink and nationalism and subsuming the one to the many. I would have been all about that discussion.

When we reached the junior parking lot, Jiyoon was flushed, neat circles high on her cheeks. "So," said Paul, turning to me, "to what do I owe this pleasure?"

"Huh?"

"The favor? With Powderpuff or whatever?"

"Not Powderpuff. Even better. Prom." I explained the Last Chance Dance.

"Ah," he said. "And you want me to build the website."

"Right."

"That's a terrible idea."

"Do you even get it? Traditional dances force girls into passive roles, and—"

"The idea's cool. But only a moron would put information like that into a website."

"It'll be a secure website."

"Anything can be hacked. Anything can be leaked."

"Nobody at Chawton knows how to hack."

He raised an eyebrow.

"Come on. Can you do it?"

"I *can,* sure."

"Will you?"

He hesitated. "Maybe he needs a minute to think about it," said Jiyoon. Reasonably enough, I guess. "How old's your car?" It was the jankiest one in the lot, a maroon Honda Civic that would have been put down long ago if it had been a dog.

"Prudence?" said Paul. "She's nineteen."

"She's been on the planet longer than we have," said Jiyoon.

"I think about that a lot, actually. The impermanence of humans. Compared to things."

"We think we're so much more sophisticated than machines, but which lasts longer?"

They were at it again. God. I checked my phone just to have something to do. Under normal circumstances, I loved this kind of talk. Shooting the philosophical shit. "You're *that* teenager," Crispin had told me once—the week I was into Nietzsche, I think. But now it annoyed me, the way Paul and Jiyoon were so into it, so into each other. They were having an Intellectual Discussion Party and I was definitely not invited.

"Ideas, thoughts," Paul was saying. "They last longer than anything. Us or cars. But they're also the most insubstantial." He did this quick, jerky shoulder thing. The two of them beamed at each other. When Paul smiles, he gets a whole mess of lines spooning his mouth. Maybe because he's so superlatively skinny. Possibly malnourished. He has all these food allergies, so usually for lunch he has something weird from the salad bar, like an entire compostable plate of artichokes.

But Paul is cute. You look at him and think he's a spindly

nerd, and then you look again and see his gray-blue eyes, which always match the sky, and his foot-long eyelashes, and that tiny smile. I watched him flash it at Jiyoon, and I watched her dimpled one shoot back to him, and I thought, They're cute *together.*

It had never occurred to me.

"I have a great idea," said Jiyoon. "You should teach Jemima to drive."

"What?" Paul and I said at the same time.

"It'd be perfect," said Jiyoon. "You need to learn and Paul has a car."

"How about he teaches *you* to drive?" I said.

"It'd be pointless," said Jiyoon. "I wouldn't have a car even if I learned. You, though. If you knew how to drive, we'd be free. We could go anywhere. We could go to California."

"Or the soft-serve place," I said.

"Or there."

It was indeed a great idea. How could we convince Paul? What was in it for him? Men love explaining to women how much they know about engines, right? "You'd get to mold me from raw clay," I told him. "You'd be the first person in the world to see me control a motor vehicle."

"You've never driven a golf cart?" he said.

"Never."

"A lawn mower?"

"Nope."

"A bumper car?"

"Yeah, but I kept crashing."

"Nobody knows what'll happen if she touches a steering wheel," said Jiyoon.

"It'll turn into a toad, probably," said Paul.

"That's if she *kisses* a steering wheel," said Jiyoon.

"We'll have to find out," said Paul, and they both turned bright red.

There is something supremely awkward about watching your best friend flirt. Maybe even more so when it's mutual. It's like when your parents kiss. You want it to happen; you just don't want to be there when it does. "Well, well!" I said, feeling like Old Great-Aunt Dorcas, taken aback by the coquettish habits of the younger generation. "Think about it, Paul. You've got a willing student if you want one. And meanwhile . . ." I hated to bring it up again, but Gennifer would eviscerate me if I didn't get confirmation. "The website?"

"Fine," he said, ripping his eyes from Jiyoon. "I'll do it." You could tell he still thought it was a terrible idea. "But I don't want anyone knowing I'm doing it. I'm just a contractor. This is your thing."

CHAPTER 4

Once a week, though not on set days because Chawton goes by an insanely complicated rotating block schedule, the explanation of which I will kindly spare you, we had a Town Meeting for grades nine through twelve. Sometimes Triumvirate ran it and sometimes Mr. Duffey did, but we always sat on the stage.

The faculty chose the Mildred. That was the only position that was, in theory and practice, filled by both boys and girls. Social Committee elected their own president, who was and ever would be a girl because boys never joined Social Comm. And the Chawton School chairman, elected by the whole school, was always, *always*—as the name implies—male.

Always. Ever since, according to the aforementioned obelisk/penis, 18-freaking-92. Of course, no girls had attended Chawton till the merge with Ansel in 1978, but even in the past four decades there hadn't been a female chairman. A few years back this super-cool senior named Maria Lovelace had started a petition to change the name to *chair*, but it was quashed. Rumor had it a few influential (read: deep-pocketed) alumni played the tradition card. "It's like *mailman*, or *man-made*," they said. "Everyone knows what it *means*."

And honestly . . .

Here goes Jemima Kincaid baring her soul . . .

I couldn't imagine a girl chairman.

Let me explain.

The senior class wanted a good leader: intelligent, likable. And it was hard for a girl to seem both. For a brief time in maybe fifth or sixth grade, before anyone had figured out the code, there were smart girls who were popular and popular girls who were smart. But then you had to choose your dominant wing. Fast. You chose your friends; you chose who you dated, and whether you dated. You chose your clothing. Did you raise your hand in class? Did you volunteer to do the torque problem on the whiteboard? When you got specially recommended for the Model UN conference, did you go? Did you join Social Comm or Quiz Team?

I'm not saying the popular girls *weren't* smart—look at Gennifer—but they weren't *known* for it. If you were a girl, you couldn't have two reputations at once.

The chairman needed both. There was a spark you got when you were both beloved and respected, when you were popular and you deserved it, intelligent and you knew it, clap your hands. Call it whatever you want—mojo, moxie, charisma, that je ne sais quoi—the chairman had to have that spark.

Example:

Town Meetings can be extremely boring, because when certain teachers get a captive audience, they take monotony to heights heretofore unreached by mankind. (Humankind. You know what I mean.) As Triumvirate, we did our best to combat the boredom. At homecoming, when the Spirit Week themes were announced, Andy disappeared while we were talking about Twin Day and Hat Day and Nineties Day, and right as Gennifer said, "Thursday will be Pajama Day," he strolled back onstage. In a rainbow-unicorn onesie. The auditorium exploded. Everyone was screaming and laughing, and Andy started doing this floaty, New Agey dance—it was dreadful—and everyone got even more hype, and Gennifer and I just stood back and laughed and laughed. Finally Mr. Duffey walked over and said, "That's enough."

Andy straightened. He said into the mike, "Yeah, so wear your favorite pj's on Thursday! But just like mine . . ."

Everyone was already smiling at the punch line.

"They've got to be something you actually wear to bed."

He was Chawton's darling.

That never could have happened if he hadn't been a guy.

For one, girls aren't allowed to wear onesies to school. They're deemed immodest. Because, you know, distracting female bodies pose a huge educational barrier for the poor boys. And if a girl had done that zany dance, either it'd have been sexualized or it'd have been stupid, depending on the girl. "She's hot," people would say. Or "She's weird." That morning, leaving Town Meeting, everyone was jostling one another, still in high spirits. "Andy is so out there." Voices dripping with admiration. "He's such a . . ." They couldn't even finish. No words. Shake head. Smile, smile, smile.

What they meant, of course, was this:

Andy Monroe is so, so freaking cool.

Right after that dance—still in the onesie!—he tapped the mike and said, "Next announcement. The Service Club is hosting a winter-coat drive on behalf of the Coalition for the Homeless."

A girl wouldn't be allowed to bridge both worlds, the silly and the sober. To be taken seriously, she'd have to act serious, and her seriousness would make her unelectable—just as a lack of seriousness would. It was a quintessential catch-22, and we couldn't even call it out, because it sounded like an excuse. *Well, I could be that cool, if I were a guy. . . .*

We couldn't say it, but we felt it. We felt it as surely as we felt the weight of our bodies, because, like gravity, it was a truth about how it worked, this world we knew. Girls didn't even consider running for Chawton School chairman because, as girls, we knew, we knew deep in our bones, that we would always lose.

"Hey, guys," said Andy. "I've got a few announcements about Jamboree."

There was a whoop. Mr. Duffey tensed his lips. Earlier he

had told us that we needed to cut down on unnecessary audience interaction, since Town Meeting had been getting lengthier all year. Unsurprising, given that the longer it dragged out, the shorter third period was.

"Juniors," said Andy, "start thinking about next year's Chawton School chairman position. Anyone can run, of course. Applications are in Ms. Edison's room, and soon you'll start campaigning, debating, bribing, all that good stuff. The election will be held at Jamboree."

Andy's pants looked good. From, um, the rear.

"An announcement for juniors and seniors only"—a boo from the freshmen and sophomores, who had recently figured out the cut-third-period-short thing and adopted it with the zeal of youth—"but with Jamboree comes prom. You probably think I'm about to tell you the theme's something dumb like Hawaiian Hoopla or Ivy League Gala." Everyone laughed but Gennifer. "Nope. This year it'll be called the Last Chance Dance. Juniors, you're invited, of course. But there's something special for seniors."

He explained the rules: go to the website, enter names, get matched. Even from the stage, I could sense the excitement sweeping the auditorium. The whispers. The giggles. The knowing looks. Everyone was eyeing the crushes they'd had all along, while also trying not to be obvious about eyeing them, while also trying to see who they were getting eyed by. "Nobody'll know if you don't get matched," said Andy, "because it's all private. But to better your chances of a match, I'd suggest putting anyone you'd even *consider* getting with. Lower those standards." Everyone laughed.

"They love our idea!" Gennifer whispered to me.

"Cool idea, right?" said Andy, right on cue. "Gotta say, I want to take credit, but it was one hundred percent the brainchild of Jemima Kincaid."

That was a surprise.

"So when you get with the guy-slash-girl of your dreams? Thank *her.*"

Credit! I'd never expected credit. I blushed and tried not to grin too hard. Gennifer grabbed Andy's arm when he sat down between us. "You forgot to tell them when chairman applications are due," she said, and I knew she was jealous.

Mr. Duffey started a long spiel about lunch cleanup. "Thanks," I whispered to Andy.

"You deserve some acclaim," he said.

"It was a group decision."

"You want me to go correct the record?"

I giggled. Yep. Straight-up giggled. "That's okay."

"So Kincaid *does* want something besides academic glory."

That was the time for a witty riposte, but my mind went blank. I gave him the slit-eyed look, the one that's like, *I am so annoyed at you!* Not! *Tee-hee!*

Andy turned to gaze diligently at Mr. Duffey. He seemed to be concentrating hard.

Me? I was not concentrating. Not in the slightest.

Because Andy's knee was touching mine.

It was probably accidental. We were in folding chairs, and Andy's not a small person—he's six-one or six-two, with muscular lacrosse quads, and I, I mean, I'm not your petite pint-sized cutie pie either. Lots of leg and not a lot of space is what I'm trying to say. It was an accident. Right?

No. He had to have noticed. The pressure was not incidental. Was it a subtle hint that I move over, à la the classic airplane-armrest situation? But he was in *my* territory.

If it had been anyone else, I thought, I'd have just moved my leg. Like when you realize that the chair you're bumping is actually someone's foot. You're like, *Oops, let me awkwardly withdraw, let's pretend this never happened, cool.*

But I didn't want this to have never happened.

My knee liked it. I liked it. Despite his khakis, despite my tights, the contact was sending my stomach into flutters, my breath into quivers. All I wanted was for Town Meeting to last all third period. Or all day. Or forever. *Keep talking, Mr. Duffey. Please, explain to us how to deal with lunch detritus. What can be composted? What can be recycled? What, alas, must be placed in the trash? Go into detail. Wax eloquent. Don't stop.*

We had Latin class right after. The class was small, a dozen or so, the survivors of the four-year forced march across the Alps of Latin grammar. It was the one class Jiyoon and I had together. Juniors could only take Latin IV if they were super good at Latin (Jiyoon Kim) or if they'd gone to a classical elementary school that had pounded so much Latin into their still-developing brains that it actually would have been embarrassing for them to be on level, despite the fact that they still translated more like a trouser-wearing Gallic barbarian than a properly togate Roman (Mack Monroe).

"Jemima!" Victoria said when I walked in. I jumped. Victoria Heinle was not known to speak to me. "I just wanted to say, I *love* your idea for the dance!"

"Oh," I said. "Thanks!"

"Same," said Lacey.

"We're already talking about who we're going to put," said Larchmont. "There's really no limit?"

"Nope," I said. "Like Andy said, put a lot."

"But not *too* many," Victoria told Larchmont and Lacey. "You don't want to be a skank."

"Well—" I started, but Mrs. Burke cut me off.

"Ladies and gentlemen," she said, "the bell will ring imminently." It rang. We instantly fell silent and opened our books. Mrs. Burke taught at Ansel Academy for Girls before the merge, and she's been at Chawton ever since. She is an institution: a purple-spectacled, maroon-lipsticked, bejeweled, brilliant, borderline-terrifying institution.

"Miss Kim," she said, "translate. Start at line forty-seven."

"'But what does it matter to me that Troy has fallen,'" said Jiyoon, "'if I'm still waiting, waiting just as I was while Troy stood?'"

"Hmm," Mrs. Burke said, which is what she says when she

has no corrections. "Ovid's Penelope, eternally waiting. The plight of women in the ancient world. And in the modern world as well, of course."

Victoria waved her hand in the air. "Not with the new prom system," she said.

"Wishful thinking, Miss Heinle," said Mrs. Burke. "Mr. Monroe, translate the next four lines."

"Wishful thinking?" I said, feeling defensive. "It's going to change—"

"And tuck in your shirt," Mrs. Burke added to Mack.

"Yes, Mrs. Burke," Mack said, shoving in his shirttail in a literally half-assed way. "But I think Jemima has something to say." Mack's translation must have been particularly shitty, because he usually did everything possible to avoid listening to me talk.

"She sure does," I said before Mrs. Burke could tell him she didn't have time for Miss Kincaid's irrelevant observations. "I just think the new prom system makes it so girls don't have to wait around for guys to ask them out. It gives girls choice. And power."

"Your naivete is amusing," said Mrs. Burke without a trace of amusement. "This so-called new system will have zero effect on the gender dynamics at this school."

"Wait and see," I said.

"I will," said Mrs. Burke. "The outer trappings may have changed, but we live within a patriarchy as solid and as implacable as that of Ovid's day. Or, for that matter, of Penelope's. Now translate, Mr. Monroe."

"I agree with Jemima," said Mack. What? This was unprecedented. Probably he hadn't even *done* the translation. "Girls have just as much power as guys now."

"That's not at all what—" I said.

"Ancient ladies, sure, they couldn't vote or stuff. But modern girls have it pretty good. They can vote and own stuff and work and run for president."

I was waving my hand so hard I was creating a breeze. So were Jiyoon and Victoria and Larchmont.

"Nowadays girls have it better than guys in a lot of ways," said Mack. "At least *girls* aren't accused of sexual assault all the time."

"Maybe guys should stop assaulting us, then," Jiyoon snapped, and pandemonium broke loose. Mrs. Burke struck her ruler on her desk. No one listened. She struck it again.

"Quiet!"

We settled down, which is a testament to the fear Mrs. Burke inspires. In her ponderous old-lady voice she said, "The level of critical thought and insight present in this room is truly abysmal."

Cool. Thanks.

"You are wrong, Mr. Monroe, and you are wrong, Miss Kincaid, and I would wager that every one of you who so impolitely shouted a hasty opinion is wrong as well. I suggest you garner more life experience before expressing such generalizations on the fortunes and misfortunes of women." She lifted her penciled eyebrows to survey the class. "Any questions? Or shall we proceed with our *work*?"

I considered saying something, but I didn't dare. Neither

did anyone else. She'd subdued us as surely as Caesar had those Gauls.

"Good. Now. Translate, Mr. Monroe."

I sat back and didn't look at anyone but passive Penelope, moaning and groaning in elegiac couplets. After class, Jiyoon waited for me at the door. We widened our eyes at each other. "What a cluster," I said.

"Mack is a douche," she said.

"So is Mrs. Burke."

"You just don't like being told you're wrong."

"Yeah, no."

"But at least she's got some idea of what's actually going on in the world. And at this school."

"I really think the new dance system is going to help."

"I know you do," said Jiyoon.

"You don't?" The defensiveness roared back.

"I like your white-girl faith in humanity. I'm just not so optimistic myself."

I know it's bad of me, but I hate it when Jiyoon reminds me that I'm white and she's not. I get that she has an experience I can't understand. I just wish she wouldn't rub it in. "We'll see," I said, because that was about all I *could* say.

"Yep," said Jiyoon. "We'll see."

CHAPTER 5

"*L*ift, Jemima!"

"I am!"

"Lift *harder!*"

Apparently it was true: Crispin was moving out of his lair in our basement. I would have been more interested in the details if I weren't so consumed with wondering how his furniture looked like plastic but felt like marble. I'd practically gotten a hernia trying to pick up a coffee table.

"Where did all this stuff come from?" said Mom.

Crispin was only in his sophomore year of life, but he'd somehow amassed the amount of furniture you'd associate with a titled dowager. "Yard sales, Mother dearest," he said airily. "Thrift stores. Antique shops. Some pieces here will be worth a lot one day."

I was struggling up the stairs with the complete works of Proust. "Have you even read these?"

"I'm sure I'll get to them eventually."

"Do you know how heavy they are?"

"Do you know how sophisticated they make my book-shelves look? Bump, here's a tip: Books are the perfect accessory. They're functional *and* decorative. They position you as one of the literati—the glitterati, if you will—while also—"

"Spare us the theories, Crispin," huffed Dad. He was only carrying a potted plant, but he didn't get a lot of exercise these days. A small mound of dirt fell to the stairs. Mom squawked in dismay and hurried over to sweep it into her hand.

Crispin surveyed the empty basement. "Well, that was easier than I expected."

I gave him a death glare.

The U-Haul in the driveway was packed to the gills. I climbed into the passenger seat and yelped in horror when I saw myself in the rearview mirror. My hair has never met a hair tie it couldn't escape, and sweat only frizzes it up further. I looked like a rat that had been electrocuted in the bathtub.

"How am I supposed to back up?" asked Crispin, squinting at the mirrors. "I can't see a thing." He shrugged. "I guess it's the go-slowly-and-pray method."

"This is the real reason Mom doesn't want you to teach me to drive," I said. "Do you want me to get out and— Oh! Eek! Bip!" I gripped my seat as we whizzed backward.

"Excellent," said Crispin. "No bumps, no screams." He revved the truck and headed down the street.

"Shouldn't you wait for Mom and Dad to follow in the car?" I said, craning back.

"Dad has a call, and Mom got an aura."

That's the pre-migraine signal, the thunderclap of the migraine storm. "Poor Mom."

"Yeah. I thought this might be a bit much for her."

"Dad, though—"

"He wasn't much help anyway."

"Don't you have any strapping friends you can call?"

"I'd never burden my friends with this. Cheer up, Bump. I'll help *you* move out in six years."

"I'm never moving back in," I told him. "Once I'm out, I'm out."

"That's what they all say," he said darkly.

"Are you sure you want to move out, anyway? Do you really want to live in Clarendon? Bro Central?"

"I love bros. Bros are my people."

This was true. His last three boyfriends had all been of the backward-baseball-hat, pumped-up-pecs, UVA-basketball-maniac variety, and his friends weren't much different. "But you're *my* people," I said.

He merged the U-Haul onto 66 East, if *merge* is the word to use when you cut off three sedans and make a semi screech on its brakes. "I'm not dying," he said. "I'm moving. Six Metro stops away. You can come hang out whenever you want. Sit in the leather chair, admire the Proust, consider how lucky you are to be kin to such a well-read young man."

Maybe it was the prospect of hauling the Proust up to his new apartment, but I felt too gloomy to laugh. "You won't be home all the time."

"You survived fine when I was in college."

Yeah. I'd survived. I had read a lot. I'd nagged for rides to Jiyoon's. Mom and I had played double solitaire, an oxymoron that pretty much described our family until Crispin, four years and one bachelor's degree later, came back. Suddenly I could stay up late and not get the postapocalyptic feeling of being the only human left on earth. I could text him from the same room, and he'd read it and smirk at whatever ridiculous thing our parents were doing. I had competition for the tortilla chips, for the washer, for the marginally bigger cookie. We revived our ancient nicknames for each other: Bump for me because that's what they'd called me in utero, Bip for him because that had been as close to Crispin as my toddler tongue could manage.

He got me. He got Chawton. When I'd walked in the door after Jamboree last year, he'd been draped over a countertop, flipping through the *Washington Post*. "So?"

"I'm the Mildred."

"I *knew* it!" He hugged me. "Another Kincaid triumvir."

"I don't know if I want to be on Triumvirate."

"Too late," he said cheerfully. "You're stuck."

"I like being in charge—"

"No kidding—"

"But I'm not into the whole Chawton spirit thing."

"Fake it."

"All year?"

"The thing is, Bump," said Crispin, "you fake it at first. But you'll get consumed by it. And one day you'll wake up and you'll realize you're not faking it at all."

"You're sure you want to do this?" said Jiyoon, poised above me.

"I'm sure." I was lying on a towel on my bedroom floor, my hands above my head.

"It's not too late to back out. If you back out, I get to back out."

"I've been dreaming of this day for months."

"It might sting."

"No pain," I proclaimed, "can be worse than the pain of the patriarchy."

"If you say so." She lowered the foam brush smeared with bleach cream. It made contact. I jerked and giggled. "Jem!" she said.

"It's ticklish!"

"It's your armpit! What did you expect?"

I lay back, closed my eyes, and thought of England while she slathered first one armpit with the chilly bleach cream, then the other.

"Don't move for fifteen minutes," she said. "Can you handle that?"

"If you amuse me," I said.

"I'm glad you're going first. Now I get to be just as annoying when you're doing mine." She heaved herself to her feet. "I've got to gather supplies for phase two."

I could hear her puttering around in the bathroom. "Did you have dinner already?" I called.

"Yeah, we got Bonchon fried chicken. Which is good until you're left with a pile of bones. Makes me feel like a carrion bird." She suddenly loomed over me, flapping her arms and making a deranged vulture face. "Caw! Caw!"

"You should do that bird-of-prey impression for Paul," I said. "It's extremely attractive."

Jiyoon put her hand over her face. "God. Stop. I have to go get more supplies."

"You do not." She'd already brought in old towels and a Super Soaker. "Stay right where you are and tell Great-Aunt Dorcas what's going on."

"Nothing's going on. As I keep telling you."

"And I'm going to keep pestering you until you admit it. I was there. I *saw* something going on."

She shrugged, but I could tell she was repressing a smile. "We were just talking."

"If by *talking* you mean *oozing with sexual energy.*"

She grabbed the Super Soaker and shot me in the face. "Ahh!" I cried, trying to wipe my eyes with my shoulder. "Meanie!"

"Don't move," she said sweetly. "The bleach needs six more minutes."

"Has he texted you?"

"Nope."

"You should text him."

"Nope."

"Oh, come *on,* Jiyoon. Make this interesting."

I meant it. Any sliver of jealousy I'd felt—and yes, I'd felt it; a tiny sliver, but it had been there—was gone. Jiyoon, like me, had never had a boyfriend. Paul was funny and weird and nice and smart and cool. I wanted it to happen.

"I'll renew my efforts on the driving-lesson front," I said. "If I can get him alone, I can plant a subtle hint. See what he's thinking."

"Don't you dare."

"He used to date Katie Bishop, right?" I said. "That sophomore?"

"I think so," she said. Her vagueness was unconvincing. She had clearly done her research.

"She's so annoying," I said. "She always wears those white jeans just so everyone knows she wears thongs."

"Why are you looking at her butt anyway?" said Jiyoon. "You sound like one of those creepy male teachers. 'Your pants don't fit the dress code'—ogle, ogle . . .'"

"I'm just saying."

"Maybe they're comfortable."

"There's no way pants that tight are comfortable."

"Maybe she likes them."

"Look," I said, feeling attacked, "I'm trying to support you. His ex-girlfriend was a bust. He needs a new one. A new one by the name of Jiyoon Kim."

Jiyoon raised the Super Soaker. I instinctively shielded my

eyes, but she was aiming lower. "A lovely platinum," she said, then blotted my armpits with a towel.

I craned to examine my pit hair. It was as luxuriant as before—we'd renounced the razor back in October—but it was now the crusty yellow of a cheap bleach job. "Awesome," I said.

"Phase three," said Jiyoon, brandishing the bottle of blue dye.

I closed my eyes as she began to paint on the dye. "Well," I said, "I have a confession. I was texting Andy last night."

"Who texted who first?"

"He texted me."

"Ooh."

"But it was on Triumvirate business."

"Yeah, sure. Just like it was Triumvirate business for his knee to have sex with yours at Town Meeting. Damn, Jem! Hold still! Do you want blue pit hair or a blue armpit?"

"I *had* to shudder! That was gross!"

"You're the one who had knee sex onstage. Why'd he text you?"

"He had an idea for Powderpuff fan gear, but then we kept talking."

She grabbed my phone and tapped in my pass code, which was her birthday.

"Hey," I protested. "I do have two armpits."

"It can wait," she said, scrolling through the conversation. "Hmm. Interesting. Nice, you let him text last. Playing hard to get?"

"I fell asleep."

"I should have known. No way you intentionally restrained yourself." She crawled to my other side. "Well. That was flirtatious. Definitely flirtatious."

I pretended my smile was due to ticklishness. She knew better.

"You like him, don't you?" she said. "You actually like him."

"No! No."

"Don't lie to Great-Aunt Dotty."

"The way Great-Aunt Dotty lies to me?"

Jiyoon smirked. "Perhaps."

"He's cute," I admitted.

"And he's also Andy Monroe."

That was not the awestruck tone in which most people would have said that sentence.

"What do you mean by *that*?" I said.

"Is he really good enough for you?"

"He's Andy Monroe! Of course he's good enough!"

"Never mind," she said grimly. "You're in too deep to save."

Jiyoon actually had a chance with Paul. But Andy and I would never happen, no matter how many flirty texts we sent, no matter how much our knees got it on. "I'm Jemima Kincaid," I said. "I'm the Mildred. I've kissed one boy ever."

"What, and that makes him better than you? This isn't some game where you get points for romantic contact, where if you kiss someone, you level up—" She broke off, and I knew we were both imagining how to design a card game with that premise. "The fact that he's had a bunch of girlfriends doesn't mean he's better than you."

"It's more the fact that he's Andy Monroe," I said.

She rolled her eyes. "You are truly a lost cause. Okay. I'm done. Let the dye set for thirty minutes, and then it's my turn."

She didn't believe me, but I was right. There was capital in high school. Sexual capital. And you got it with experience. If you were a girl, you could also have *too* much experience, sure, but you didn't have to worry about that if in your whole eighteen years you had kissed only one boy and nobody at school even knew because you met him during a whirlwind, highly romantic weekend at the National Academic Quiz Team Championships in Chicago junior year. And even if he was legit cute—not cute relative to Quiz Team boys but *cute* cute—and even if you and he maintained a correspondence fraught with longing for several months, thereby proving his feelings were true and he hadn't just been trying to get some at the Quiz Team tournament, well, even then. Even then you didn't have much to go on.

Andy and I weren't on the same level. He could have had any girl he wanted—I bet even Gennifer would have traded up—but Chawton boys weren't interested in me. My mom, in the grand tradition of nerd moms everywhere, claimed I intimidated them. Like there were hordes secretly in love with me but I was too menacing a presence. I was *too* attractive. *Too* smart. *Too* fun. Right. Because that made sense.

Jiyoon Super-Soaked the dye off my pits and I flung up my

arms in front of the bathroom mirror. The blue was startling and hilarious and I loved it. "I cannot wait till everyone at school gets an eyeful," I said.

"Even Andy?" said Jiyoon.

"Even Andy," I said.

Convincing myself as much as I was convincing her.

Chawton School

CHAPTER 6

Andy had to switch our Thursday meeting to the evening because he had a lacrosse game after school. *No problem!* I texted. Starbucks, after all, did not subscribe to the Chawton dress code. That evening, after alerting my mother that I'd need a ride, I put on jeans and earrings and a soupçon of makeup. And a stretchy, clingy V-neck.

I tested it by bending over in front of the mirror. I'm well endowed, chesticularly speaking. That is, I have big boobs. I'm not going to tell you the cup size, because if you're skinny, you'll be like, *Ha, ha, I didn't even know they made bras that far down the alphabet!* I've never particularly liked the ol' bosoms—they've always been a source of awkwardness and discomfort, of high-tech swimsuits and higher-tech sports bras, and as for the guys who address all conversation to my chest, let me just say, *Hi, communication orifices up here*—but as I leered at my own cleavage, I suddenly saw their advantage.

Not that my appearance mattered for a Triumvirate meeting.

Gennifer was already there. "You look good," she said suspiciously.

"That's such a surprise?"

She was saved from answering—or I was saved from her answer—by Andy's arrival. "Hey there," he said.

"Hi," I said in a strangled tone.

Why had I worn blush?

Shouldn't I have anticipated I'd be able to take care of that on my own?

It had been a full week since the Patellofemoral Fornication Incident, alias Kneegate, as Jiyoon and I had deemed that fateful Town Meeting after determining that *knee sex* sounded way too Teutonic and gross. I was still hung up on it. There'd been another Town Meeting on Tuesday, and my stomach had gotten so churny beforehand that I'd almost thrown up. But Gennifer had ended up sitting between me and Andy. Talk about a cockblock. A knee stymie. Okay, that was awful. There had to be a better pun—

"Jemima," said Gennifer. "Jemima! Hello. We're trying to get started here. Is the prom website ready to go live?"

"That link you texted us looked good to me," said Andy. "Nice work, Kincaid."

"I did nothing," I told him. "It was all Paul."

"You hired the contractor," said Andy. "That's not nothing."

"Is it ready?" Gennifer said sharply. "Should I email it out?"

"Oh, um, Paul wants to do one more test or something?" I said. I'd checked in with him after school, but in my current state, the details were hazy. I needed to get it together. Nothing was happening with Andy. I sat up straighter, hiked up my shirt, and licked off some lip gloss to tone down the try-hard effect.

Andy was staring at me.

And I was licking my lips.

What was *wrong* with me?

"The site should be ready by early next week," I said, frowning in my best impression of Dorcas the Octogenarian Troll. "Let's get it out promptly so people can start making their lists."

"Sweet," said Andy. "Who's on yours, Kincaid?"

"Why would *you* care?" said Gennifer.

"It's called polite conversation."

"Moving on," she said, rolling her eyes. "Social Comm is developing decor ideas to fit with the Last Chance theme—"

Okay.

This was a small table, yes.

Andy had long legs, yes.

But Kneegate was happening.

Again.

I tried to look attentive, but I heard nary a word from Gennifer. I was busy evaluating three possibilities:

1. Andy didn't know it was my knee. He thought it was a weirdly warm table leg.

2. Andy knew it was my knee, but, like a normal person, he considered knee-to-knee contact unremarkable.

3. Andy was doing it on purpose.

But if he was, *why*?

Was it an erotic experience for him (too)?

Or was he messing with me?

AHHHHH!

I wished I'd worn a skirt. And what if he'd been wearing shorts? Mmm. Andy in shorts.

"How was the lacrosse game, Andy?" I heard myself asking.

"Um, hel-*lo*, I was speaking," said Gennifer.

"Great. We won, twelve–nine. And it was warm for once. It felt good to get out there and sweat."

"Oh," I said.

Oh.

"So, to summarize, we're going casino," said Gennifer. "Which isn't totally Last Chance, but it is chance, and that's about as good as it's going to get."

Andy shuffled in his seat. His knee bade farewell to mine.

Damn.

"What's going on with Powderpuff?" Gennifer said.

"I hate that name," I said. "Like we're supposed to stop after each play and powder our noses."

"It's a tradition," said Gennifer. "Andy, you're working on teams?"

"I've talked to all the guys," he said. "They're all assigned to either Team Tiger or Team Angel."

"What about the girls?" said Gennifer.

"We're almost done," said Andy. "Some are more obvious than others. Kincaid, for example, is very much a Tiger."

"I thought it was random," I said.

"What am I?" said Gennifer.

"Hmm," said Andy. "Now, this takes some thought." His eyes raked her. She duck-faced and posed with her hand on her hip.

"It's not random?" I said again.

They ignored me. "This is a tough one," said Andy. "Some of you could play for either side. I'm going to have to say . . ."

Angel, I thought fervently. Angel.

"Tiger."

Gennifer hmphed. "Looks like we'll be playing together, Jemmy."

"Guess so, Ghen."

She flipped her binder closed. "That's it for now, right? Chairman apps are due in a week. Do we have a second candidate?"

"Wait, we have a candidate already?" I said. "Who is it?"

"According to the Triumvirate Handbook, we're not supposed to know until the application deadline," said Gennifer.

"But you know!"

"We should tell her," said Andy to Gennifer.

"You know too?"

"Because it's—" said Andy.

Gennifer, unwilling to be scooped, cut him off. "It's Mack."

"*Mack?*"

They both nodded.

"Your brother? Your boyfriend?"

Mack was the *worst*.

"That's the one," said Andy.

"Well," I said, "this reeks of corruption."

Gennifer shoved away her skinny vanilla latte. "Jemima, do you wonder why you don't get told stuff? You turn everything into a big deal. Everything. A qualified junior has chosen to run for chairman. And?"

"Mack Monroe is one triumvir's brother and another triumvir's prospective life partner—"

"They're never getting married," said Andy at the same time as Gennifer said, "We're not even engaged yet."

She glared at him.

"And," I said, "he's running for the highest office in the land, unopposed! Yeah, that's not at all fishy!"

"Chill," said Gennifer.

"We need to rustle up another candidate!" I said. "Make an announcement in Town Meeting! Target juniors we consider promising! Have teachers make recommendations!"

Gennifer raised a finger. I shut up. Such is the power of Gennifer Grier's gel-manicured hand. She opened her binder. "Allow me," she said. "Triumvirate Handbook, chapter four, section one-point-three: 'Candidates for chairman shall nominate themselves. The Triumvirate shall make it widely known that they are soliciting applications, but neither need nor ought concern themselves with the identities of the candidates. The chairmanship shall rest upon the premise that the cream rises to the top.' "

She thwacked it shut.

"Applications are open for another week," said Andy, conciliatory. His knee nudged mine.

"May the cream," said Gennifer, "rise to the top."

CHAPTER 7

I had spent all of Saturday in Maryland at a rec league soccer tournament, and I was exhausted. The house felt deserted. My mom was probably asleep. I showered, pulled on sweats and a ratty tank, and inhaled cold leftover sausage, an entire sleeve of saltines, and three grape Popsicles that had been in the freezer so long that most of their syrup had melted to the bottom of their waxy sleeves. #cleaneating, #fitlife, #blessed, etc.

My phone buzzed. *I'm bored, you're immobile. First driving lesson tonight?*

I considered it while I rummaged around in the freezer. By the time I'd found another Popsicle, this one in a truly advanced state of decomposition, I knew I wanted to go. I sent Jiyoon a quick text.

It's okay if I have a driving lesson with Paul tonight right?

I wasn't sure what I was asking: Was it okay that I wasn't hanging out with her? Or was it okay that I *was* hanging out with the guy she (putatively) liked? I got a row of weeping emojis back, then texts:

No, go ahead

Feel free to spend Saturday night with the coolest guy ever while I sit at home

NO PROBLEM AT ALL

Ha. I knew it.

You definitely like him

You're a total goner

Pause. Typing bubbles.

A single blushing emoji.

I laughed aloud. Got her. Well, I would have to perform some reconnaissance. I texted Paul that I was free.

See you at 9:37, he said.

He pulled into my driveway at, you guessed it, 9:37. By the time I got out, he was leaning on Prudence's hood, wearing his usual hiking boots but some sweet tan skinny jeans and a black T-shirt. I hadn't bothered to change. "Yo," he said. It was clearly an ironic *yo.*

"Yo," I replied, also ironically. "Nine-thirty-seven, huh?"

"I'm against the ghettoization of numbers that aren't multiples of five."

"How manic pixie dream boy of you."

"Gross," he said, making a face. "It kind of is."

I got into the passenger seat. "Thanks for the lesson."

"Yeah, I looked this up, and it's illegal. You have to be twenty-one to teach someone to drive."

"We'll be scofflaws," I said.

"Easy for *you* to say. You don't have a license that could get revoked."

"Rub it in, why don't you."

"However, I'm willing to risk it all. Whoa! Whoa! Wow."

I was stretching. Soccer, for whatever reason, always made my shoulders stiff. "What?"

"Is that a thatch of blue armpit hair?"

"Oh!" I'd forgotten. "Yep. Jiyoon and I dyed each other's."

"Jiyoon did it too?"

"Yep," I said, smirking internally.

"That's so cool. I want to do that to mine. Though that'd miss the point, since men are culturally permitted to have pit hair. Right?"

"Yes! You get it!"

"You two are amazing." He shook his head, apparently overcome by our coolness.

We whizzed down Route 50 in old Prudence, her engine whirring and revving, the wind whistling in through her seams. Most of the cars that I'm in are like sealed pods. "I was texting Jiyoon earlier today," I said. Super casually.

"Oh?"

"Yep." Oops. Now what? I should have thought this through. "She's really funny," I added.

"I am aware." He pulled into the big, empty parking lot of a closed Home Depot. "This'll give us a lot of space to practice. Want to switch seats?"

He got out. I shimmied over with the agility and grace of a warthog. It was weird to be so close to the controls. "I've never sat in the cockpit of a car," I said when Paul got in the passenger seat. "I feel so powerful." Suddenly the windshield wipers started, making me jump. "Ahh! Did I do that? Make them stop!"

Paul reached over and flicked something. "Careful. Power corrupts."

"So how do I make it go forward?"

Prudence, it seemed, was a "stick." Paul explained the mechanics, the main takeaway being that somehow, with two feet, I was supposed to deal with three pedals.

"That makes no sense!" I felt a rush of nerves. Driving was already harder than I'd expected. "Who came up with that?"

"That's how it works."

"That's like having glasses with three lenses," I said. "Or a glove with six fingers. Or—"

"Or a piano with eighty-eight keys. Humans are capable of remarkable feats of coordination. Even you, Jemima. Okay, press down the clutch and the brake, and turn the key in the ignition—"

"Oh my God. It started. I started a car."

"Now *slowly* let out the clutch as you *slowly* push the gas— no, *slowly*!"

The engine revved and then, with a grisly cough and a jerk forward, died.

"That's called stalling," he said. "Let's try again."

"I'm getting good!" I said thirty minutes later. I had successfully started the car three times in a row, and the grinding sound that came from letting out the clutch too fast was nowhere near as loud or frequent as it had been. "I actually think I can master this."

"Me too," said Paul, who had gone slightly gray. "If my clutch holds out that long. But I need a break. This is emotionally fraught."

It really was. I relaxed back into the seat. "I bet Jiyoon would be good at this," I said. "She's very coordinated."

"I hadn't noticed," said Paul. I gave him space to continue—Just admit you like her, I thought, so I can make this happen—but his eyes had closed. I took the opportunity to send a surreptitious text.

What if I tell him you like him? I bet he'd be in

She responded within seconds.

NOOOOOOOOOO don't you dare

A knife emoji came in, and then another. Okay, so maybe not. I wrote, *Can I just ask him if he likes you?*

Dorcas you're a bumbling idiot

Keep your mouth closed and don't mess this up for me

"Are you revived?" said Paul.

I quickly locked my phone. "I'm ready!"

"Let's drive in first gear. You're going to start the car and then give it a bit more gas, and it'll go."

"I'll be actually driving?"

"Indeed."

"Where should I go?"

"Um, the other side of the parking lot?"

"My maiden voyage!" I said, because my mouth always tries to make my life as weird as possible. At least I hadn't said *virgin voyage*. Maybe next time. "I mean, cool. I'm excited."

I revved the engine. "I *think* this lot is big enough," Paul muttered. The car hopped forward, and instead of stopping, I gave it more gas. "Whee!" I yelled. We were cruising! Gripping the wheel, I glanced down at the speedometer. Ten miles per hour. Twelve! Fifteen! Scenery sped by the windows: light poles, shopping-cart bays. This was awesome. This was exhilarating. Freedom! America! Road trips! The age of the automobile! I was *driving*!

"STOP!" yelled Paul.

Where had that fence come from?

"BRAKE!"

How had we already crossed the entire lot?

"HIT THE LEFT PEDAL!"

I slammed down my foot. The car careered forward.

"THE OTHER LEFT!"

We jolted to a halt, inches from the fence. The car stalled.

"Oops," I said. "I think I forgot to put in the clutch."

"Among other errors," Paul said grimly.

We sat there in silence.

"Okay," I said finally. "Maybe I can try again? A bit . . . slower?"

CHAPTER 8

The standard Chawton male aesthetic is Banker in Basketball Shoes, which is a natural consequence of the guys' dress code: shirt, tie, khakis, whatever shoes they want. The girls' dress code is different. More complicated. You have to have a collar, which is obviously a subtle attempt to keep us from wearing those V-necks that V basically at the pubic bone, and you can't wear jeans, and all skirts have to be knee-length. What that means is that ninety-eight percent of the girls wear loose plaid shirts over pants that could have been sprayed on. The teachers are supposed to enforce a not-too-tight rule, but hardly anyone dares.

Me, I don't like the Lumberjane in Jeggings look. I like dresses. They're the greatest hoax in history. You look all suave, and meanwhile you're literally wearing a bag with holes for your extremities.

One night back in August, Jiyoon and I had gone to Unique Thrift Store and bought XXL men's shirts and patterned sheets, and we sewed swaths of sheet to the shirt hems so they'd be long enough for the dress code. We made me three shirt-sheet dresses: one white with a plaid bottom, one light blue with roses, and my favorite, a pale pink uber-preppy shirt, complete with tiny reptile, that got a skirt made of *Power Rangers* sheets. Jiyoon is brilliant with a sewing machine. She fixed the thread when I'd irredeemably snarled it, and when I was going to leave the bottom edges loose to unravel, she hemmed them up. She hemmed up the sleeves too. "There," she said. "Now, to quote every magazine ever, cinch with a wide belt."

I did. I admired myself in the mirror. "Don't you want some for yourself now that you see how great they look?" I asked her.

"I'll stick with my uniform." Jiyoon wore khakis and pastel polos every day. She looked fine. Unremarkable, but fine. "I prefer to let my personality attract attention. Not my clothes."

"You prefer *no* attention," I said, slightly stung at the insinuation that this was just one big *Look at me* move. Jiyoon just shrugged, and I shrugged, too, because I loved my new dresses. And three days out of ten, which was how often I could wear them without seeming unhygienic, I felt, and thus looked, amazing. I noticed this a while ago: how you look and how you feel are directly correlated, and what we've been told, what women are supposed to believe, is that looks come first, that looking good makes you feel good. Nope. It's the opposite. When I was in my shirtdress-belt-Converse ensembles, I felt so offbeat and oddball and awesome that I looked awesome too. It goes *that* way. Feeling is the independent variable, the *x* axis. What, in the end, determines it all.

I met Jiyoon outside her history class on Monday so we could walk to Latin together. "I just checked with Ms. Edison," I told her, "and Mack's still the only candidate."

She crossed her eyes and stuck out her tongue for half a second: short enough that no one saw, long enough to get her point across. *"You'll* be gone," she said. "We poor juniors are the ones who'll have to get through a year with him in charge."

"I hate that the election's unopposed," I said. "The House of Monroe, they're a freaking dynasty. They're downright Haps-burgian."

"Though with better chins," Jiyoon pointed out.

"The problem is, who'd run against him? He's got it locked up. I wonder . . ." I trailed off. We were navigating the busy hall-way, but everyone was so devoted to chatting and/or Snapchat-ting in their five precious minutes of freedom that I didn't think we had eavesdroppers. "I wonder if I could persuade someone else to run."

"Aren't you supposed to stay out of it?"

"Minor corruption to fight major corruption. That's ethical, right?"

"Debatable."

"Do you have any ideas? It's your class. Who'd be a good chairman? Give me some names."

She didn't say anything.

"What about Jonah?" I said. Jonah was on Quiz Team, but he wasn't the polarizing kind of nerd. He was blandly handsome (strong jaw) and blandly smart (good grades). He was into political science, and he could hold a reasonable yet tedious conversation about anything with anyone. I was meh about Jonah. So was everyone, I think. "Jonah might have a shot."

Jiyoon still didn't say anything.

"What?" I said.

"*What* what?"

"You got all pissy."

"Don't even go there. I literally said nothing."

"Yeah, but—"

We'd arrived at Latin. We were standing outside the door. Jiyoon said, "Don't put words in my mouth."

"God. I put nothing in your mouth."

Mack sauntered up. "Who put something in Jiyoon's mouth?"

"Fuck off," Jiyoon and I said simultaneously.

He chortled and went inside.

"Okay, Ji, what's your deal?"

"Jonah. *That's* who comes to mind?"

"Well, who else is there?"

"If you don't know," she said, "I'm not going to tell you." She went into the room.

I lingered outside, but even my desire to avoid Jiyoon wasn't enough to risk being late to Mrs. Burke's class. She surveyed us as the bell rang. "Tuck in your shirt, Mr. Monroe," she said. "Miss McStern, are you wearing pants or pantyhose?"

Lacey blushed. I, and everyone else, looked at her lower half. It was true that the garment in question was tan and very tight. "They're pants, Mrs. Burke," she said.

"Stand up," said Mrs. Burke, "and let me see the rear."

Jiyoon kept a studied and purposeful gaze on the whiteboard, but everyone else gawked at the spectacle of Lacey spinning for Mrs. Burke's inspection. I couldn't take it. "Mrs. Burke," I said, "shouldn't this happen out in the hall?"

Mrs. Burke's heavy gaze moved to me. Lacey began to sit, but Mrs. Burke, without looking, lifted a warning palm in her direction. Lacey froze. "Are you telling me how to do my job, Miss Kincaid?" said Mrs. Burke. "A job I have done for forty-six years?"

Yes. "No."

She waited.

"I just think it's weird to do this in public."

"Dress is a public act. Miss McStern, did you choose these so-called pants to wear in public?"

"Yeah," said Lacey, "and I swear, they were in the pants section at Amer—"

"Does it matter?" said Mrs. Burke. "You should have the good sense to dress yourself in a manner befitting the standards of this institution, eschewing"—she coughed—"alleged *pants* that betray every curve and contour of the lower half of your body. Detention."

Everyone got very quiet. Detention wasn't the worst punishment—you sat in a quiet room doing homework for an hour, so honestly it was kind of the *best* punishment—but it wasn't assigned often. Especially not to seniors.

"Learn to dress modestly," said Mrs. Burke to the whole class, "and we won't waste time on such matters. We will begin class with a scansion assignment in threesomes." Every other teacher said *trios,* for obvious reasons, but no one was going to giggle at Mrs. Burke. "Miss McStern, tie a sweater around your waist and join Miss Kenney and Miss Heinle. Mr. Monroe, work with Miss Kim and Miss Kincaid."

Ugh. More proof that Mrs. Burke was a sadist. The desks groaned as we scooched them together. "Well, *I* lucked out," said Mack with his lazy grin. He was Andy but blockier: broad shoulders, a square face. Furthermore, he lacked all intellectual curiosity and could, in fact, be described as a blockhead. "How about we split up the work? Jemima does half, Jiyoon does half, and I'll supervise."

"How about you get us a dictionary?" said Jiyoon. "That requires brawn, not brains, so you should be able to handle it."

"Jiyoon Kim with the zinger!" He stood and bowed. "Let it never be said that Mack Monroe can't take orders from a lovely lady."

He strolled to the bookcase, stopping along the way to flick Tyler Donner's pen out of his hand (Tyler grumbled good-naturedly) and to cover Lola Camarena's eyes while growling, "Guess who?" (Lola squealed like she'd gotten a pony for Christmas). Mack was popular. God knew why.

"That was gross, what Mrs. Burke just did," I said to Jiyoon.

"It's like she knows women are oppressed, but that doesn't stop her from oppressing them herself."

"You're always calling out girls' clothes too."

"I am not."

"You were just trashing Katie Bishop's white jeans."

"What about white jeans?" said Mack. He flicked the dictionary at me like a Frisbee. I lunged to keep it from sailing into Larchmont's head. "I'm a fan. If that's the question."

"Yeah, it wasn't," said Jiyoon.

"You're salty today," Mack said. "I like it."

Jiyoon grabbed the assignment and started marking syllables, but I couldn't let it rest. "Ji. Come on. I would never make a girl spin around in front of the class while I inspected her ass."

"Weird," said Mack. "That's, like, the main reason I'd want to be a teacher."

"You're a creep," said Jiyoon. "And I didn't say you'd do that, Jem. But I hear you hating on girls' clothes sometimes."

"Only if they're totally too much!"

"Don't get defensive."

"I am not getting defensive!" Hashtag irony.

Mack leaned back, enjoying the show. "Want to know what *I* think?" he said. We both snapped, *"No."* "The dress code is sexist. Reverse sexist. Boys have to wear ties and girls can basically wear anything they want."

"There's no such thing as reverse sexism," said Jiyoon. "And, as we've just seen, girls *can't* wear anything they want. Because they're going to get spun around and told they're distracting. Or immodest. Or too much."

She was glaring at Mack *and* me, which was completely unfair. He was a troll. I was a feminist. "Stop lumping me in with him and Mrs. Burke," I said.

"Stop acting like them, then."

"God," I said. "What is this even *about?*" She'd had it in for me ever since we'd talked in the hallway before class. "Is it because of . . . the election thing?" I couldn't spell it out, not when the one and only candidate was right there listening.

"Maybe you should have remembered I go to this school too," said Jiyoon.

"That's why I was *asking* you about it!"

"This conversation is off task," said Mrs. Burke from behind me. I jumped. I hadn't even smelled her perfume. She craned over our paper, which had about three pencil marks, and shook her head. "Disappointing. I expect better. Unless you too would like a detention."

Forced isolation sounded pretty nice about now, but Jiyoon and I shut up and marked dactyls and spondees. Mack contributed nothing.

CHAPTER 9

Andy posted the Powderpuff teams and cheer squads the next morning. Gennifer promptly upstaged him by emailing the senior class the Last Chance Dance website. Within seconds it became the only subject of conversation. Groups of girls hunched over their phones.

"But what if he puts me, too?"

"You like *him*? Um, how long has this been a thing?"

"I'm not that into him, but I need to know whether he's into me."

The guys walked around all casual, but when asked, they'd say, "Yeah, I'll put in a few names." Or "Might as well, right?" At lunch, Greg and Zachary said they had already decided their picks. "Not that I'll get any matches," said Zachary. "The only other guy who'll put guys is Robert Oliver, and no way am I going to put him."

"All I want is one match," said Greg, gazing at Ashby's chest.

"That's so sweet!" cooed Monique. "You're only putting one girl?"

"Uh, no," said Greg, ripping his gaze from Ashby's mammary organs to look at Monique like she was a grade-A nitwit. "I'm putting thirty-three. It's called the law of probability."

"Oh," said Monique, visibly deflating at further evidence of the male adolescent's stunted romantic development. "Jemima, you're the mastermind. You must know who *you're* putting."

"Nope," I said, "and I wouldn't tell you if I did."

Jiyoon probably could have guessed who I was putting, but she was sticking to the other side of our lunch circle. We hadn't talked since Latin class the day before. This was how we always fought: we snapped and snarled and had it out, we ignored each other for a few days, and then we suddenly got over it and never mentioned it again. We were deep into the ignoring phase, and I was trying hard to focus on other things so I wouldn't get too upset. I missed her.

Luckily, there were other things to focus on. The senior class was made of pursed lips and buoyant cheeks, as though we were keeping ourselves from bursting. Coy glances, enigmatic smiles, and again and again: "Who are you putting? Who are you putting?"

"This is the most exciting thing to happen in the history of Chawton," Haley Rawlings told me before econ.

"You guys are the best Triumvirate ever," said Melanie Richards.

"Wasn't it your idea, Jemima?" said Haley.

I smiled modestly. "Triumvirate is a team."

"Yeah, but—" The bell rang. Ms. Margolis started hollering about opportunity costs. I basked.

In the scrum leaving econ, Melanie said, "You're a Tiger, right? Can I get your number? I'm organizing Powderpuff practices, and you should definitely be in the group chat."

She handed me her phone. Standing on the shore of the hallway, the rest of the class streaming past us, I felt weirdly conspicuous. Like we were arranging a date.

Or maybe I had dates on the brain.

Not that Andy would ever ask me on a date.

He did have my number.

But he wouldn't text. He'd say something in person. *You want to hang out sometime? You want to grab food after the meeting? You want to take our knee contact to the next level and bear my adorable babies?*

These daydreams sustained me through an English class that exceeded all precedents of boredom and annoyance. We were in the middle of reading *Jane Eyre*, mired deep in the Land of Plot Summary. Once we actually finished the book, which at this rate would be in July, we'd sail across the Sea of Halfhearted Class Discussion (with frequent sallies back to the Land of Plot Summary, for provisions), and if we were lucky, we might make it to the Merry Isle In-Class Essay. Some English classes, I swear, are an insult to reading.

During last-period calc, Melanie texted the group chat:

Andy talked to Simms and got the turf field. 7 p.m. TONIGHT! We need ALL OF YOU!

The thread exploded with emojis, exclamation points, and openmouthed selfies. I didn't respond, but I was in.

The turf field was on the edge of campus, next to the woods, and by seven the sun was low, gilding the trees with a rich, eggy yellow. It was the perfect spring evening. It had been sunny all day, but now there was a nip to the air, just enough that my whole body longed to run. The girls milled around the fifty-yard line, a vivid flock of neon shorts and patterned headbands and T-shirts sloppily chopped into tanks. I shoved my hair back into a ponytail, bunned it, and tied on a bandanna. "You are *ready*," said Tyler Donner, Andy's co-coach and the quarterback of the Chawton football team.

We'd been going to school together since seventh grade, but this may well have been the first time Tyler Donner had ever acknowledged my existence. "You bet," I said.

Or, to be fair, the first time I'd acknowledged his.

"Huddle up, Lady Tigers!" called Andy.

"You know the basic rules, right?" said Tyler.

"Nope!" yelled about six girls, collapsing into giggles.

"Oh, come on, we do," said Jessica Landover, who was probably the best athlete in the class, male or female. She'd be playing lacrosse for West Point next year, which was (as the laxers say) sick. "We're trying to advance the ball down the field."

"You can throw it or you can run it," said Tyler, "or both."

Tyler and Andy gave us an overview. About half the girls

weren't paying attention, texting and redoing their ponytails and kicking up bits of turf instead. The rest were serious, decked out in Chawton athletic gear, hands on hips, intently nodding along.

I was one of the serious ones. I had never played football, and although I enjoyed my uncle's annual Super Bowl party, that was one hundred percent due to guacamole.

"So basically," said Melanie, "it's a glorified game of tag."

Tyler looked insulted. "It's a lot more complicated than that."

"Yeah," said Haley, nudging Melanie, "it's tag *and* fetch."

We all laughed. Even Tyler and Andy. "Let's run some plays," said Andy, "and see if you think it's so easy."

Here's the thing, though: it *was* easy. Football's complexity is a hoax. Behind all the starts and stops and strategy, behind *offensive* and *lateral* and *rush*, it's tag plus fetch. It's the easiest thing in the world.

And—surprise!—I was good at it.

In the first few plays I wasn't that involved, just lining up and trying to block the girls storming Jessica and whoever Andy told her to throw to. But then she missed her mark and the ball squirted toward me and I scooped it to my stomach and darted around Kayla Wu and leapt over Brittany Bowling, and suddenly I was in the clear, the backfield opening before me. Andy blew his whistle, and he and Tyler had a quick conference.

"Come here, Kincaid," said Andy. "Let's try a few plays with you in a more central role."

I could barely meet his eyes. I reminded myself that he didn't know about my daydreams. "Got it," I managed.

"Run a buttonhook," said Tyler. "You remember that one?"

"Of course she does," said Andy. "This is Jemima Kincaid we're talking about."

"The girl who never forgets anything," said Tyler.

My first thought: Oh no, what *is* a buttonhook?

But I do have a good memory. I rewound, found it. As I jogged back to the line of scrimmage, as Andy blew his whistle and Jessica balanced the ball between her fingertips, as I tensed to run, my eyes darting all over the field, Melanie shifting in response to me, the last spears of sunset golden and the shadows dark and deep, the goalposts stark white against the twilit sky, I thought, Is *that* what my name means? "Hike," called Jessica, and I ran. *One Mississippi. Two Mississippi.* Sprinting up the field, Melanie keeping pace. You walk around with a hazy idea, but you don't often get an unfiltered glimpse into the truth of how others see you, how they hear your name. *Three Mississippi.* Did they hear Jemima Kincaid and groan? Or did they hear it with respect? What did they think? What did I *mean*?

Four Mississippi, and I reversed, hooked the buttonhook, and left Melanie in the dust. Jessica bulleted me the ball, and I basketed my arms and caught it and took off down the sideline. Christina was speeding at me, but I shifted gears. She dove. I leapt. She missed. I took another few steps free and clear before Andy whistled. He looked exhilarated. "Donner," he said, "the Tigers have their running back."

You stop wondering whether something's sexist when you're having that much fun.

Andy had the keys to the light box. He double-stepped

up the bleachers to turn the lights on. "Staring much?" said Gennifer.

"Me?" I said. He was wearing these silky white shorts, and I could see the muscles tense in his calves. "What?"

"You're just *ogling* him, aren't you?" said Gennifer.

Under normal circumstances I'd have brushed her off, but I met her eyes and smirked. "In my humble opinion, that's an ass worth ogling."

She laughed, loud and startled. I laughed too. It felt like we were on the same team. "What's so funny?" said Melanie.

Gennifer didn't tell her.

Andy flicked on the lights, and the field was suddenly a movie set. It was all-American. Football under the lights, happy kids running around in gleaming, gorgeous youth. The weird thing, I think, was that all of us knew it. We saw ourselves from the outside. We were high school seniors! Look how young we were. Look how old.

Gennifer was my defender on the last play. We'd planned a quick handoff from Jessica to Melanie, but Melanie got double-teamed. I'd been going long as a ruse, but I blinked through the lights to see the ball spiraling through the air, and I leapt for a catch that better have looked as spectacular as it felt. Andy let loose a quick, joyous shout. Gennifer didn't have a chance. I ran it all the way to the end zone.

"That's it for the night," said Tyler. He high-fived me, and so did Jessica. Girls laughed, laughed, laughed, smacked each other on shoulders and butts. "We're gonna crush the Angels," said Tyler. "I knew I was right to choose Tiger."

"You were *assigned* Tiger, dude," said Andy, winking. He flipped his car keys from hand to hand. "Hey, Kincaid, you need a ride home?"

Andy braced his hand on my seat to back out of the parking spot. "That was fun," I said.

"Because you're good at it," he said.

"It would have been fun under any circumstances. Running around, being outside. Though maybe not quite so *much* fun." I was prattling, because that's what I do when I'm nervous. "I do like being good at stuff."

Andy drove the way most teenage boys do, with a cartoonish nonchalance. "Of course you do. You're Jemima Kincaid."

My name again! What did it *mean*? We were at a red light. I tried to relax. I felt tense and ungainly, like my body didn't fit within my skin. "Well," I said finally, *"you're* Andy Monroe."

A truly inane comment, but he nodded sagely. "Andy Monroe and Jemima Kincaid—"

That *and*! Was it a significant *and*?

You know you're far gone when you're parsing conjunctions.

"—drive together through the night."

Oh. Just the beginning of a sentence.

"It's this one, right?"

He pulled up in front of my house. One light burned in the kitchen. I wiped my sweaty hands on my shorts. "Thanks for the ride. My mom was relieved not to have to get out of bed."

Without warning, he put his hands on my head—like

earmuffs, I thought—and mashed his face into mine. His tongue made one wrong turn onto my cheek and another onto my lower lip before it found my mouth.

I jerked away.

"I have to go," I said.

"Hey, wait—"

"I just . . ." I was already opening the car door. "I have to go, see you, thanks, bye!"

CHAPTER 10

"You *what?*" said Crispin.

"I huddled on the window seat in the kitchen—"

"No. Before that."

"I have to tell you again?"

"Yeah. Because it's not computing. Someone as masterfully hot as Andy Monroe kisses you, and you dive away? That goes against everything our family stands for."

"I'm pretty sure Mom and Dad wouldn't—"

"It goes against everything *I* stand for. I didn't raise you to be this person."

"You didn't raise me!"

"Did my shining example mean nothing?"

The first stage of Andy Monroe Kissed Me had been shock, and, debilitated by it, I'd made the mistake of texting Crispin. He'd called me immediately.

"Bump," he said more gently, "don't worry. You'll have another chance. If you want it. *Do* you want it?"

"What I want is some warning!" I said. "I'd have handled it fine if it hadn't been such a surprise."

"You had no signs this was coming?"

"No!"

"No?"

"No . . . well . . ."

Kneegate I. Kneegate II. The ride. The dark car. *Andy Monroe and Jemima Kincaid.* I'd known. But I'd thought I was fooling myself. I'd thought it was my imagination, if only because I'd wanted so badly for it to be true.

Before the guy at the Quiz Team championships had kissed me, we had discussed it at length. It was late the last night of the tournament, and we were sitting on the floor behind a cart of folding chairs in a forgotten corner of the hotel lobby. He said, "May I ask you a question?" I figured it'd be about my mnemonic for the complete list of Nobel Prize winners since 1901, and I wasn't sure whether I'd be able to bring myself to give away team secrets, even though I was majorly crushing, but instead he said, "I like you sort of a lot," and I said, "That's not a question," and he said, "Well, the question is, well, despite the distance between us, and obviously with you in DC and me in San Diego there's not really, like, long-term potential, at least not unless we're thinking *really* long-term, like maybe college, maybe, but, anyway, I mean, I like you, and I'm wondering, as a theoretical question, what would you do if I kissed you?"

I internally freaked out, but I kept my cool, or what little cool I'd started with. We talked about it for a while. For a long while. Once we concluded that a kiss was an acceptable—if not entirely rational—act, he said, "Okay, I'm going to do it now," and he wiped his hands on his jeans, and I was like, "Oh God," and he said, "It won't be that bad," and he put his hand on my jaw, and his mouth on mine, and when I saw his eyes close, I even remembered to close mine. It was wet (which I guess is what you'd expect when one wet thing hits another) and it was squishy (ditto, mutatis mutandis), and beyond the wet squishiness, it mostly lacked sensation.

I was relieved when it was over. Though for months afterward, I'd think about it when I called up Mr. O on the pink telephone, or whatever awful euphemism for female masturbation you want to use since all the nice simple ones like *jerking off* are definitely not gender-neutral. I had always considered it weird that I'd fantasize myself back to an event that had registered approximately 0.0 on my personal Richter scale of turn-ons, but that didn't stop me—

"Well?" said Crispin.

"Sorry," I said. "Just thinking."

"Was it a good kiss?" said Crispin. "Or did you launch yourself inside before you could tell?"

Good? It was horrifying. Andy's tongue was long and slithery and hard—ugh, it was *muscular*—and thinking about it, I raised my fingers to my cheek, to the corner of my mouth, and I shivered.

Horrifying.

"I have to go," I told Crispin. "I have a phone call to make."

So to speak.

I had texted Crispin instead of Jiyoon because Jiyoon and I were still ignoring each other. Fortunately, our internal get-over-it clocks tended to run at the same speed. Rapprochement occurred during Quiz Team practice. We were on the same team, and there was a question about the former attorney general who had helped Airbnb with their antidiscrimination policy. I said "Eric . . ." but blanked on the last name. "Holder," said Jiyoon. We fist-bumped. I felt my body loosen. Being back on good terms with her was like taking off an uncomfortable bra. I hadn't realized how the fight had been digging into my skin.

Mr. Peabody stepped out of the room, and I don't know if it was the nice weather or what, but everyone got in a rambunctious mood. Greg rooted through Mr. Peabody's Costco carton of Jelly Bellies and pitched nasty ones at Monique, who shrieked and said, "You know I can't even *see* a buttered popcorn without mouth-barfing!" Jonah yelled, "1877!" and about four of us yelled back, "Rutherford B. Hayes, Lucy Webb, William Wheeler!" We do these study conglomerates where a bunch of us memorize the same list, and we'd just done the presidents and their dates and spouses and vices. Vice *presidents,* that is, not vices like "cheeseburgers and interns" or "Nicorette and tricolon."

Jonah shouted, "1957!"

"Dwight D. Eisenhower, Mamie Doud, Richard Nixon!"

It was rowdy, in a Quiz Team kind of way. Ashby started talking about what she'd just read on Wikipedia. "All mammals flirt," she proclaimed. "It's a basic signifier of sexual interest. Mandrills shake their blue butts at each other, and—"

She was drowned out by Greg and Vivek hooting, scratching their armpits, and shaking their butts. "Ashby!" Greg cried. "Ashby! I'm signifying my interest!"

"Oh my *God*—"

A buttered-popcorn Jelly Belly sailed through the air. Paul rolled his eyes at me and Jiyoon. "There's no need for booty shaking," he said under the din. "You know what's the best way to flirt?"

In the history of tricycles, there had never been such an obvious third wheel as I in that moment. "What?" said Jiyoon.

He set his hand confidingly on her forearm. "This."

"What?"

"Arm touching. Simple and effective."

Jiyoon touched *my* arm. Jiyoon! No! Wrong target! "Like this?" she said.

"Does it feel natural, Jemima?" Paul said.

"Um, I can't tell," I said. "I'm hardly a flirting expert. Try it on him, Ji."

She slit her eyes, just enough so I'd see she resented me deeply, but moved her hand to Paul's forearm. He grimaced. "Remember planking?" he said. "Well, your hand's planking on me. Keep it relaxed."

I glanced around. The rest of the team was either imitating monkeys or loudly proclaiming their exasperation with monkeys.

"Try again," said Paul.

Jiyoon touched him. He jumped. "Ouch! That was a claw!"

"I'll leave you guys to it," I said as smoothly as possible. I don't know if they even noticed as I edged away. "Shake that monkey ass, Jemima!" yelled Greg, and, with my team hooting and hollering, I obliged.

Mr. Peabody returned to simian chaos, but he's a passive dude. Plus, he liked us. "Er, shall we wrap up?" he said. We played a few more questions, and then he unplugged the buzzer system. "I hope you're all prepping for our last tournament. Who's got phyla?"

"Me," said Jiyoon.

"Supreme Court cases?"

"I'm on it," said Greg from the floor, where he was picking up Jelly Bellies. And eating them. I averted my eyes.

"World rivers?"

"I will fall upon that sword," I said.

"You're still hosting the end-of-season party, right, Jemima?" said Ashby.

"Of course." Traditionally, the senior captain throws a party on the night of the last tournament.

"Are we going with that idea we had on the bus?" said Greg.

"Gourmet s'mores," I said. "I'm on it."

"Gour'mores," said Greg. "Gour'mores! That is so catching on."

"Not if I can help it," Paul whispered to Jiyoon, touching her arm.

She and I walked out together. "Well, well," I said quietly. "A flirting lesson, huh?"

"He's just looking out for me," she said. "It's a major life skill."

"Uh-huh," I said. "So selfless. Come on, Ji. He has a major thing for you."

She blushed. She couldn't hold back her smile. "You really think so?"

"You're just asking so I'll say it again."

She deftly kicked me in the back of the knee. I crumpled, but then chased her down and got her back as we left the building. "Truce!" she called. "We're even!" It was a glorious spring day, sunny and windy and blue and green.

"I heard last year he was dating a college girl," I said.

"What's that supposed to mean?"

I wiggled my eyebrows. "Experience."

"Ew. Jem. Grow up."

"Just saying, he may well be a guy who knows his way around a—"

"Stop! Ew! Stop!"

I shut up, but not before a lascivious lip lick. For two people with minimal experience, Jiyoon and I joked about sex a *lot*. We were basically thirteen-year-old boys.

"What's new with Andy?" said Jiyoon. "Speaking of"—she licked her own lips—"*experience.*"

"Nothing, really."

"More knee boning?"

I couldn't help cringing, which meant she won. We both laughed. "Yeah, no," I said, trying to sound casual. "I don't know. It was probably nothing."

I know. I know. My best friend. I hadn't told her about the kiss. Now I had an opportunity and wasn't taking it. I blamed the post-fight shakiness, the gnaw of insecurity: Did she even *like* me? But more, I think, was that I—yes, I, Jemima Kincaid, Lady of the Big Mouth—liked the secrecy. The whole experience, Andy's mouth and mine, was still lurking in the two-toned darkness of a car at night. It was shards of streetlight, smears of shadow, and once I told Jiyoon, the lights would go on.

"We have a Triumvirate meeting tomorrow," I said. "Andy and Gennifer are still totally okay with sitting back and letting Mack run unopposed."

"He's an asshole," said Jiyoon, staring out into the circle. We'd found an empty bench to wait for our rides.

"I just wish . . ." I thought of Jonah. He was quiet, self-assured, respected. He really could have a chance. "I just don't like Mack."

Jiyoon only nodded. I couldn't tell what she was thinking, and I didn't want to ask.

CHAPTER 11

I was breaking the rules, but Mack could not be allowed to run unopposed. I had to give it a shot. I barricaded myself in my room and found the phone app on my phone, which took longer than someone over thirty might presume. I couldn't text. Screenshots would be incriminating.

"Hello?" said Jonah.

"Can I run an idea past you?"

"Sure."

"I think you should run for chairman."

Jonah, not one to express surprise, said, "Why?"

"To foil the heir apparent in his nepotistic grasp for power," I said. "Obviously. Did you know Mack's running unopposed? Plus"—maybe I should have started with this—"you'd be a great chairman."

"I decided a while ago not to get involved with student

politics," said Jonah. "No one cares about the issues. It's all popularity."

"That's, like, *all* politics," I pointed out. I was in Mrs. Burke's Latin class; I'd read Caesar. "Come on, Jonah. You're the only junior with a shot in hell of beating Mack."

"I'd lose," he said.

"Not necessarily."

"I'd have a better platform. I'd make a better speech. I'd out-debate him. And I'd lose."

I woke up Thursday morning on the wrong side of the body. The weather was arctic—good one, April, you got us—and I should have worn pants but every pair made my thighs/butt/calves/crotch look lumpy/flat/mannish/camel-toed. My floor was strewn with discarded clothes. I knew I was buying into the utterly corrupt idea that my body *should* look a certain way, like it wasn't enough that it literally carted around my soul, and that made me even angrier. I ended up putting on my favorite shirtdress, even though I'd worn it two days before. I Febrezed myself. At least I'd smell like a mountain breeze.

Of course, wearing a shirtdress when it's forty degrees means that all day you'll get inundated by "Aren't you cold?" comments. "Not at all!" I kept saying in an airy voice, forcing my teeth not to chatter. My classmates were wheeling like vultures in down jackets, waiting for the first sign of weakness.

"Bare legs?" said Gennifer before Town Meeting started. "You must be freezing!"

"I'm quite warm, thanks."

"Is your lip gloss blue, then? Why would you wear such a thing?"

She leaned in and I drew back. A lip-gloss aficionado like Gennifer Grier would easily discriminate between a regrettable fashion choice and the lack of blood in my capillaries.

"Hey hey hey," Andy said into the mike once the student body was gathered. "A few reminders for you from your Senior Triumvirate."

Wild cheering, which was either universal adoration or a delaying tactic.

"Seniors! Submit those Last Chance Dance picks! They're due a week from Sunday."

I still hadn't even thought about who I was going to put. Well, I'd *thought* about it. But I hadn't decided.

"I know there've been some concerns," said Andy, "but rest assured, your secrets will be safe. The program is fully encrypted, and it does all the matching. Once again, ladies and gentlemen, this is all thanks to the behind-the-scenes work of Jemima Kincaid."

I quickly assumed a humble smile. I hoped it telegraphed *Your obedient servant, J. Kin*, rather than the truth of it: *I live for the applause, applause, applause.*

After a last call for chairman applications, which were due at noon, Andy sat down so Madame Babineaux could babble about the summer Paris trip. "You don't have to keep giving me credit," I whispered.

"But I want to."

Nudge. There it was. His knee. My knee. If I'd tried to kiss someone and they'd sprinted off in horror, I'd never make a move on them again. I'd possibly never make a move on *anyone* again. But chalk one up for male confidence: he wasn't wrong. That knee, it did something to my insides. How was it that my whole body reacted so fast? Imagine the mechanics involved: the nerves sensing the nudge, the information shooting to my brain, my brain going *Oh God* and *Yes* and *What does it mean, is it on purpose, does he like me, why did he kiss me, will he kiss me again?* and all the while busily liquefying the muscles in my legs and sending a pounding, roiling warmth through my gut. My eyes half closed. My tongue felt large and stupid, like I'd just eaten cantaloupe. I was on fire and melting at the same time, which didn't even make sense, God, I was basically a Roman elegiac poet, mixing my love metaphors left and right—

"Ack!"

Gennifer had pinched my arm. "You're onstage!" she hissed. "Look like you're paying attention!"

Andy shot me an amused look. An amused, knowing look. The air between us bristled with static, and his knee pressed into mine.

★　★　★

Have you *seen* a freshman boy lately? It's kind of hilarious. Some are normal-sized, sure, but lots have pituitary glands that have just not kicked into gear, so these baby-faced, toothpick-limbed five-footers are jockeying for fish sticks and garlic bread with seniors who have to shave every day or else they get dress-coded. Always good for a laugh, the lunch line in this place.

The juniors and seniors get to eat outside. I, of course, was frozen, a blotchy and begoosebumped mess, but I wasn't about to eat with the fetuses in the caf. The usual Quiz Team crowd had gathered in the courtyard. Jonah gave me an awkward nod as I joined them. "Look," Greg said, "I can make my tongue into a *W*."

"I'm trying to eat!" protested Ashby.

"So's Greg," said Zachary, "which is worse."

I winced and stepped back. Enough that my field of vision opened, and I could see Andy with his friends across the courtyard. Laughing. Looking impossibly cool. His clothes were flawless, a gingham button-down with the sleeves rolled up, pants that actually fit. Not many high school guys know how to wear pants. Andy's khakis sat at the perfect point on his hips, just slouchy enough that an adult wouldn't have gotten away with it. He had this cool clasping belt, not try-hard cool but just like, *Hey, need a belt, let me grab this one, and*—

". . . happened," said Jiyoon.

"What? Were you talking to me? Sorry, I was totally zoned

out on . . ." I accidentally glanced across the courtyard, and Jiyoon followed my gaze.

"Andy's crotch?" she said.

"The prom poster behind him," I said with dignity.

Jiyoon smirked. "Nice try. Hey, though. Guess what. We're hanging out on Saturday."

"You and me?"

"No, loser," she said, grinning. "Why would I do that? Me and *him*." She jerked her head to Paul.

"Oh my God!" I said. "Whoa! He asked you out?"

"Stop shouting, okay?"

"Ji! You have a *date!*"

"It's not a date. We're just chilling. We were talking before APUSH, like always, and he said he was trying to fill up his weekend so he'd forget he should be studying for the AP exam, and I was like, 'Well, we should hang on Saturday.'"

"You did the asking? Queen."

"It's not that big a deal."

"Were you worried? That he'd think you were, like, forward?"

"*Forward?* Is it 1902?"

"Okay, come on. You know *I* think it's great. But even now, it's not normal."

"Well, here's Paul," she said, sounding impatient. "Let's ask him what he thought."

"Yo," said Paul. He'd put some sort of gel in his hair and shoved it up to get an upside-down V thing. It reminded me of modernist architecture. Maybe an international airport.

"I'm concerned that your ironic *yo* is becoming a real *yo*," said Jiyoon.

He laughed. "You may have a point. *Greetings*. What's up?"

"Jem was just saying you might have lost respect for me when I asked if you wanted to hang out," she said.

"That is *not* what I said!" I felt like people kept willfully misinterpreting me.

"Hmm," Paul said, looking at Jiyoon. "It was mildly surprising. But that was because I was gearing myself up to ask the same thing. It was like when you're playing football and you're out deep and the ball's coming at you and you're like, Okay, I got this, I got this, it's mine—and then right as you're reaching up, someone darts in front of you and grabs it. You kind of forgot that anyone else could even see the ball."

"Interception!" said Jiyoon.

"Except you're on my team," said Paul. "So I was very happy because (a) it got caught and (b) I didn't have to catch it, which means (c) I didn't drop it."

They both had dopey smiles. I could imagine Paul telling this same anecdote at their wedding.

"That's awesome," I said heartily. "Well, I'm glad the ball got caught."

"Aren't you cold?" said Paul.

The question was innocent, and I *was* cold, but that was kind of the last straw. It was that question on top of the fifty other times I'd been asked it, and on top of Ji calling me out, of my being misunderstood yet again. On top of Andy looking unattainable across the courtyard. On top of the twinge of jealousy I'd felt at the crush-addled looks on my friends' faces.

"No," I snapped. "I wish everyone would leave me and my clothing choices alone."

Jiyoon laughed. The kind of laugh that's made for a point.

"What?"

"It's ironic."

"That I'm wearing what I want to wear and nobody'll shut up about it?"

"Sorry," said Paul. "I was trying to be nice."

"Is this about girls' clothes again?" I asked Jiyoon. "Because I think there's a difference between wearing a dress that's maybe a bit too summery for the weather and wearing shorts that, like, reveal to the world the Antarctic Circles of your butt hemispheres."

"Yeah," said Jiyoon, "you kind of have a problem."

"I get it. I should have worn pants today."

"No. Your problem is, you kind of hate girls."

"Are you kidding? I'm the Jeminist!" That had been my middle school nickname, back before it was cool to be a feminist. "I'm all about girls!"

"It's not your fault," said Jiyoon. "It's called internalized misogyny. Men don't even have to do anything because women hate women all on their own."

"I am a woman. I obviously don't hate women."

"It's a real thing," said Jiyoon. "It's like we're all swimming in the sea of gender bias. And until we actively start confronting the fact that we don't want to breathe this water—"

"We have gills now?"

"Look, don't make this into a joke. Unless we start being like, 'What the eff *is* this water and why do I have to swim in it?' we're going to be just as misogynistic as anyone else."

"Wow," said Paul.

"It makes sense. If sexism's everywhere, it's going to infect everyone. Same thing with racism, homophobia, ableism . . ."

"So are you racist?" Paul asked Jiyoon. "Against yourself?"

"When I was eight, I told my mom I wished I was white because Asian people weren't funny," she said. "Or, say . . ." She paused, looking off into the distance, but then shrugged, a *What the hell, I'll go for it* shrug. "For example. Recently. I assumed a certain Asian American person couldn't get elected to a student-government thing. Or, maybe, I thought they shouldn't run. Like, *should* an Asian really be the voice of the school? I don't know. I doubted that."

"But of course they could," said Paul. "And should."

"Yeah," said Jiyoon flatly. "I'm sure everyone agrees. I'm sure Asian kids topped the list when people were like, 'Who should run against Mack?'" She looked right at me. "Didn't they, Jemima?"

Oof. I opened my mouth, but nothing came out. It was then that Gennifer Grier chose to sashay over to us.

"Wrong side of the courtyard," Greg called. "Cool kids are over there."

She ignored him. "Jemima, we've got an emergency meeting."

"I'm sort of in the middle of something," I said.

"Well, you'll sort of have to finish it later."

"An emergency meeting? What could possibly qualify as an emergency? This is student government we're talking about."

Gennifer kicked out her foot and shot out her hip and said, "Senior Triumvirate is hardly your standard student government. I know you have to argue about everything, but can't you stop wasting time? Lunch is almost over and we really need to meet."

"Okay, okay . . ." I turned to Jiyoon. "I'm sorry," I whispered. "I'll text you."

"I'm afraid you'll have to cover some unexpected duties," Ms. Edison told us.

"We can handle it!" said Gennifer. With her feet on the rung of her chair, she looked like a pert, petite bunny rabbit. Andy, meanwhile, was slouched. He hadn't even said hi to me when I came in. Screw him, I thought. My knee stayed firmly under my own desk.

"So much that we thought would be unnecessary this year," sighed Ms. Edison. "Scheduling the chairman debate and open forum, prepping the candidates with campaign rules—"

"Candidates?" Gennifer said sharply. "But the deadline was at noon!"

"You told me there wasn't anyone else," Andy said to Ms. Edison.

"I talked to you after I checked my email, but I didn't see there was an application slipped under my door."

"I thought we agreed to accept online applications only!" said Gennifer.

"We never made an official amendment to the handbook."

"Who's the candidate?" I said.

Ms. Edison handed Andy a large yellow envelope. "I'll leave you to it. We need to get the debate and open forum on the school calendar ASAP, so please let me know those dates."

She left the room. Chawton tradition. Andy tore open the envelope, even though Gennifer was brandishing a letter opener she'd taken from her Kate Spade zipper case of school supplies.

"Who is it?" she said.

He glanced at it. He raised his eyebrows. He glanced at me.

"Well?" said Gennifer.

He paged through the sheets of paper.

"Who?" said Gennifer.

"Ask *her*," said Andy.

"Me?" I said.

"You don't know?"

"I don't know."

"Damn." He looked at me searchingly. I felt nervous, like I was trying to cover up a lie. Even though I hadn't told one. "You really don't know."

"Who *is* it?"

"It's Jiyoon," said Andy. "It's Jiyoon Kim."

CHAPTER 12

"Who are you putting for Last Chance Dance?" Gennifer asked me after Powderpuff practice on Friday afternoon. The jerseys had come in, and we were in the athletic hallway sorting them by size.

"Why would I tell you?"

"It's called *we're friends*?"

"We are?"

Gennifer flipped a shirt into a neat fold. She could have starred in a Banana Republic training video. "Wow, Jemima. Way to be a b." She peered at my stacks. "Could you get your corners straighter? Nobody wants a wrinkled jersey."

"Personally, I don't give a cat's pebbly shit about wrinkles in my athletic gear."

"Just tell me who you're putting."

"No!" Not a chance I'd confide in Gennifer, who only wanted

data for her own Machiavellian purposes. I'd filled out the website the night before, and I'd put just one name.

You know who.

He was at the other end of the hallway, stacking the cones we'd used at practice. Gennifer saw me looking and I quickly turned away. "Who are *you* putting?" I asked to change the subject.

"Not telling."

"Wait." Now I was curious. "What about Mack? Isn't he taking you to prom?"

"Obviously," said Gennifer. "He's my boyfriend. But I still get to have my List."

Her tone made it significant, capitalized the *L*. "Your List?"

"Don't tell me you haven't made one—but no, you've never been in a relationship, have you, Jemima?"

I ignored the jab, because (a) why should it be a jab anyway, amirite? and (b) *List* seemed ungoogleable, and I wanted to know. "Please, enlighten me. What's a List?"

"Guys I'm allowed to do and it wouldn't count as cheating."

"*What?*"

"O-*kay*, chill with the slut-shaming—"

"I'm not slut-shaming. I'm just surprised. You and Mack have discussed this?"

Did all girls have a List? That's what I wanted to know. I should have had a boyfriend before senior freaking year. Or at least a friend with boyfriends. I would never be normal because there was so much about normal I didn't know.

"Andy!" Gennifer hooted down the hallway. "Come here!"

Andy strolled toward us. He was wearing shiny red shorts. His hips swung, and golden hair burnished his calves. "Little Jemmy here," said Gennifer, "has never heard of a List."

"Who's on yours?" said Andy.

Gennifer—she actually did this—licked her bottom lip. She held her tongue between her teeth and smiled at Andy. It was a flirting move I'd never seen in the wild, and it was appalling. And effective. The mood shifted instantly to something tense and loamy and fraught. Then Gennifer broke it. "Jim Halpert."

We both laughed. The tension was cut. "I'd do him," said Andy.

"And Spider-Man."

"Ew!" I said. "In that suit?"

"Presumably he'd be out of the suit for the main event."

"I can't with this conversation," I said. "You guys go on. I'll be sorting jerseys, trying not to heave." Joking about sex with Jiyoon was fun precisely because neither of us had the faintest clue what we were talking about. It was different with Andy and Gennifer. It made me think about how they'd *had* sex. I mean, probably. And that made me think about them doing it, which might have been gross if I'd been able to picture it, but I didn't even know what sex was. Not really. I was a naive kid. I moved down the hallway.

But I heard Gennifer ask Andy, "Have you submitted *your* picks yet?"

"I have."

That eighties power ballad was running through my head, except with *sex* instead of *love*. *I want to know what sex is. . . . I want you to showwww me. . . .*

"And? Tell me one of them."

"I can't."

I imagined jumping to my feet in the hallway as I belted out the song. *I want to feel what sex is. . . .* Then I'd do a slow twirl and dramatically point at Andy: *I know you can showwwww me!*

"What do you mean, you can't?" said Gennifer.

"I only submitted one," said Andy.

WHATIFITSME

That was my brain.

"Now you really have to tell me."

COULDITBEME

Andy laughed. My ears burned. "Never."

I felt a nervous cascade in my stomach. I was blushing in this really awesome way that makes me look like I have a bad case of hives. Of course it wasn't me. He was the chairman and I was the Mildred.

But he'd kissed me.

What if—

I couldn't take it. I scooped up an armload of jerseys so I could escape to the locker room, but I knocked my elbow on the door handle, right in the funny bone. I barely suppressed my scream. "Kincaid?" said Andy, and I looked up. Blushing, blotchy, eyes watering in pain. "You need a ride home?"

I hate it when movies fade out. Like, right when they collapse onto the bed, the camera pans to the nightstand, where the water in the carafe is getting all ripply. *Significantly* ripply.

There was no bed (and who has a carafe, anyway?) and there was—spoiler!—no sex, but I'm not fading out. Because fade-outs make real life weird. They make you think you'll feel different during the whatevering, like the light will get soft and your sensations will too, but you're still a body, you know? You're still yourself. So even as Andy Monroe's hand is raking through your hair and it feels weirdly amazing, all the same you're like, Oh God, dried Powderpuff sweat is probably coming off all gritty in his hands and he must think I'm so gross. And then his tongue is in your mouth and it's super hot and you're also very aware that if you don't manage to unbuckle fast you may well experience strangulation by seat belt.

But I'm getting ahead of myself.

Andy had been quiet as he pulled out of the parking lot, and although I was dying to be cool, I have a dumb habit of compulsively chattering through awkwardness. "It'll be interesting to see everyone's reactions to the chairman candidates," I said. We'd announce them at Monday's Town Meeting. "I doubt anyone knows Jiyoon's running."

"Probably not, if you didn't know," said Andy. "Aren't you guys best friends?"

"Yep."

"That's weird she didn't tell you."

"Yep."

I'd texted her when I'd found out. *Yay! You are my hero!* She'd sent back a single smiley, and we hadn't talked much since. I was pretty sure she was mad at me for assuming she wouldn't run, and I was mad at her for being mad at me. I hadn't even gotten a chance to explain myself. I'd assumed she wouldn't run because she hated student government and Chawton spirit, because she'd never done anything to put herself out there, and maybe a tiny bit because she was a girl. It had nothing to do with her being Asian American and everything to do with her being *her*.

"She's a great candidate," said Andy. "Should be a tight race."

"Are you being sarcastic?" I said.

"Nope."

I didn't totally believe him. Mack had it locked up. Jiyoon *was* a great candidate, and just like Jonah would have lost, she would lose, for all the same reasons and more.

But tonight, I thought, was not about arguing.

"Mack's a great candidate too," I said, keeping my voice light. "He's got a lot going for him."

"Are you secretly a nice person?" said Andy. "Because this feels weird."

"I'm always nice!" It was one of those giggly protests girls are supposed to do when they're teased, and Andy smiled. It must have made him feel at home.

He swung into my driveway. "Well," he said.

"Well."

We lunged.

We went *at* each other.

It sounds so animalistic, but that's the only way to describe it. The warmth of his mouth, the wetness, his bumpy tongue, his smooth lips, I needed it, all of it. I got it. But I wanted more. I wanted to touch more of his back, I wanted him to touch more of mine. I felt constrained by my hands' surface area. I wanted to be all hands.

So I slid my hands under his shirt, all over his back, because if you can't grow giant hands, you at least want high-quality contact with what you *can* touch. Actually feeling skin rather than shirt . . . the difference was huge. Once, Crispin told me he always splurged on cheese, like he bought Parmesan actually made in Parma, because after you'd had the real thing, you knew the difference. That was shirt vs. skin. Shirts were reduced-fat mozzarella shreds, but skin, Andy's skin, it was buffalo mozzarella, it was milky and tender and smooth. It was the real thing.

Cheese. I let out a laugh. It went right into Andy's mouth. He said, muffled, his words going right into *my* mouth, "Wasso fubby?" His hands didn't stop.

"Nuffin."

He had a hand on the back clasp of my sports bra, which—horrors—was slightly soggy from Powderpuff. And—double horrors—this was the bra whose hooks had rusted off, the one I safety-pinned and pulled on over my head. Andy fiddled with the clasp, clearly perturbed, used to working his unhooking magic in one suave pinch, and I was torn: Should I give him instructions? But wouldn't that make me seem . . . forward?

I wasn't about to slut-shame myself. Even if Jiyoon did think I hated women or whatever. I'd prove her wrong. I opened my mouth to tell Andy how to take it off—

But I didn't want him undoing the safety pin. Because (a) who wears safety-pinned undergarments—like, if your degree of chestitude requires high-tech clasping sports bras, at least keep them in good shape—and (b) I had legitimate safety concerns for my back.

"This thing is like a vault," he muttered. He hopped out of the car. I felt a whooshing collapse of disappointment. It was over. But he opened up the back door and said, "Come on. A flat seat. Tinted windows."

It crossed my mind that getting in the back might make me look like a—

STOP INTERNALLY MISOGYNIZING YOURSELF!

I switched seats. He unceremoniously tugged off my T-shirt. His mouth went slack and his eyes went hungry as he stared at my breasts spilling out of that mangy old sports bra. I felt sort of like a hamburger. But in a good way.

I took action before he could discover the safety pin and shimmied out of the bra the way I always did—i.e., gracelessly. "Whoa," he said.

"What?" I said, embarrassed by all my spilling flesh.

He lifted my arms like I was a rag doll and glanced from armpit to armpit. "Whoa."

"Oh," I said, "yeah. Yeah. It's blue."

He dropped my arms. "Just keep them down here and I'll try to forget I saw that."

I knew he was joking, but I drew in a breath to say, *Screw shaving! Screw beauty standards!* I had blue armpit hair, but Jiyoon thought I was sexist. It hurt. That was the truth. When I could drop my defensiveness, I knew she had a point. I had a lot to learn. But it hurt.

But I didn't start my rant, because Andy covered my mouth with his.

I promised not to fade out, so here goes:

I took off his shirt.

We kissed.

He squeezed my breasts, which was weird at first—visions of stress balls danced in my head—but suddenly turned the corner from weird to good. He ran a hand up and down my side, again and again, and I cupped his shoulders and buried my hands in his hair and flattened them against his back.

He started teasing the waistband of my leggings. He slid two fingers under it and gave my whole body a shock of warm, fluid gold. I'd been self-conscious about the way my stomach flabbed out over the leggings—beauty standards, I know, I *know*—and those thoughts didn't disappear when his fingers went underneath, but they didn't seem so important. A moan started way back in my throat. The way our mouths were soldered together, he must have felt the vibrations. My body went limp and tense all at once. Man. It was something.

He put his entire palm flat on my crotch, over my leggings. "You like this, huh?"

I tried to act nonchalant. "Sure."

I could *feel* the ooze between my legs. My reproductive system seemed to be working just fine, lubing up to get something large stuck in it. Amazing. It was amazing. It'd be so easy to have sex, I realized. And it wouldn't have to be a big deal. I guess how people talk about it, it's a major turning point, like you're one person and then you get a penis stuck in your vagina and you're another person. But at that point, as he slowly rubbed me, as I forgot to kiss him, my back arching, these mewling noises coming from someone, someone who seemed to be me, the idea of one turning point seemed stupid, simplistic. Sex had to be a spectrum. What was this, if not sex? What was this, if not one turning point in a long series of them? It was new. It was incredible and strange and human and animal. Earlier I'd wanted to be all hands but now I was all crotch. It was my entire being. I wasn't even aware that my foot was falling asleep, that my hair was all tangled in the seat belt holder. Not until he stopped.

He did stop. Abruptly. He was squinting at his phone. "Listen, I have to get home. Mack needs the car."

"Oh."

"You okay?"

"Yeah, yeah!"

We yanked our T-shirts back on, not meeting each other's eyes. I stuffed my bra in the waistband of my leggings. "See you, Kincaid," said Andy.

"Right." My tongue was thick in my mouth, and my eyes felt like they wouldn't open all the way. "Right. See you." I stumbled into the house.

I lay in bed, fingering my phone, and thought, I should text Jiyoon.

I didn't.

I didn't want to think about what had just happened. Or analyze it, or discuss it. I wanted to be all over Andy and have him all over me. Not thinking. Just *doing*.

It's funny how as an intellectual, or a wannabe intellectual, whatever I am, you're supposed to have a passion for thought and analysis and discussion, but the best times are still when you're just in your body, in yourself. When you remember your body *is* yourself. Sometimes I labored under the misconception that the true Jemima Kincaid was incorporeal, that I was a mind in a carrying case, but really, I was this soft stomach. I was these strong legs. I was these floppy wild boobs, and I was these fingers that didn't text Jiyoon. I was the arm that drilled the football downfield. I was these lungs, these kidneys, these arteries and veins. These cells. This heart.

Chawton School

CHAPTER 13

When Crispin moved out, Mom had said, "Wouldn't it be nice if we had a family dinner once in a while?" That's how she talks. She'll want a roll and she'll say, "Jemima, would you like a roll?" She'll want to play Boggle and it'll be "Remember how much fun we used to have playing Boggle?"

This time, at least, we heard what she meant, and Crispin was coming over for dinner on Sunday. When I went down to the kitchen, Mom was dressed, with gold earrings and real shoes. She was sautéing kale. I peeked in the oven and saw a whole chicken, hunched over, ass up. It was vaguely sexual.

Then again, these days I found everything vaguely sexual.

"I'm home every night, and you never cook for me," I said.

"Jemima."

"I'm just saying." Words of wisdom: when you hear yourself saying *I'm just saying,* you should really just stop saying. "Sorry. Forget I said that. Should I set the table?"

"Please. And do you want to use the nice silver?"

Do you want to? That's more Momspeak. She also asked me if I wanted to put out a tablecloth and cut the baguette. I did want to. I wanted to very much.

One night, when Crispin had first moved back home, I was reading on my bed, and he came in and sprawled across the foot and told me about college. I think he was missing it. He said, "Mainly what we did was hang out on people's beds." Fancying myself funny, I quirked an eyebrow. He said, "Well, sure, but mostly it's just friends, hanging out and being annoying. You pile onto someone's bed and talk about nonsense and real stuff all mixed together."

We chilled on my bed for forever. We decided whose toes were more agile and he gave me some terrible advice regarding my crush on Evan Ratzheimer (namely, that I should cry "I've had enough!" and crawl across the lunch table to bite the buttons off his shirt). We talked about real stuff too. "There are two rules in this household," said Crispin. "One is 'Don't upset Mom.'"

"What's the other?"

"You know. You grew up here."

"Oh. 'Don't upset Dad.'"

It blew my mind that there was someone else who got it. Crispin had left when I was just a middle school twerp, and I hadn't realized until he came back that the specific experience of growing up in this house was something we shared with each other and no one else. Crispin, adult Crispin, my pal, my brother: he was the best surprise of my life.

Mom got all flushed and happy the second he came in. Her thin shoulders seemed to fill out her delicate cardigan. "Mother *darling!*" said Crispin, winking at me as he hugged her, and the thing about Crispin, he says that and it's one hundred percent a joke and also one hundred percent serious. Meanwhile, holding the silver knives from the sideboard, I got teary. It was probably the general overwhelm—Andy school Jiyoon Andy Quiz Team Triumvirate Andy Andy AHHH—but wow, I was emotional.

"Hi, Bip," I said, and dove in for a hug.

"Whoa—hi—watch it with those knives—good to see you too, Bump."

Mom appraised him like he'd been on a yearlong sea voyage. Like she was overjoyed to see him but also felt it necessary to do a quick once-over for scurvy or worms.

After dinner, Dad returned to his home office and Mom said, "Kids, would you mind if I lie down? This was a lot."

"We'll clean up," said Crispin. "Thanks for dinner."

He hugged her again. When he hugged me, it was a party. He lifted my feet off the floor. But he hugged Mom like china, like a bird. Like something he could break.

He took up position at the sink and I brought him dishes. "I wish you still lived here," I said. "It's great you moved and all, but . . ."

"I know what you mean. This house."

It was too big. We were like burrowing rodents, Mom and Dad and me, each with our crannies, emerging only to forage for food.

"But I do have to go soon," he said apologetically. "I'm meeting Thomas."

"Who's Thomas?"

He flicked some dishwater at me. "Just a friend."

"Sure."

"A friend plus."

"I knew it. How'd you meet him?"

"I beamed a signal for intelligent life out into the void."

"Like the Drake equation? Or like Tinder?"

"I object to this interrogation." He was trying to act annoyed, but I knew he was chuffed, probably because of that thing where you can handle any amount of vicious teasing about your crush as long as it means the two of you get mentioned in the same sentence. "Actually," he said, "it's kind of a problem. We didn't *know* we worked at the same company until after . . . well. But we do."

Crispin's consulting firm is huge, so I could see that happening. "Why's that a problem?"

"Because there's a policy against dating internally. Needless to say, we're ignoring that." He set the last pan on the drying rack and checked his phone. "Excellent. I still have enough time to get some groceries."

"Oh. Well, bye, then."

"Not so fast," he said, heading to the pantry.

"I thought you were going grocery shopping."

"I am. Right here." He unfurled a reusable bag and threw in a box of Triscuits and a carton of raisins. "What's new at Chawton?"

"A lot," I said. "Jiyoon thinks I'm misogynistic."

"Are you?" he said, poking around in the pantry.

"What? No. No!"

"I mean," he said, "I was pretty homophobic for a while there. It happens."

"You love gay people."

"You bet I do," he said. "Now. But I used to be super judgy of other gay guys. I hated it when they acted, like, *too* gay. Like when they did that swishy walk, or wore tight pants, even. I took pride in being the gay guy everyone treated like a straight guy. That's why I rushed. Just to prove I could get into a frat if I wanted." He scanned the nutrition facts on a box of Rice Chex. "When the system's telling you you're not normal, of course you're going to want to identify with the people who are."

"So because the system hates women, I secretly want to join in?" I asked. It was so messed up. Especially because it rang true. Did I want to be the girl who acted like a guy? Did I pride myself on not being like other girls? Kind of. Yeah. "Ugh," I said. "I'll think about it. New topic. You took neuroscience in college, right?"

"Yeah." He ripped open the cereal box.

"In the human brain," I said, "is there a sex faucet? Has that been discovered yet?"

Crispin choked on the handful of Rice Chex he'd stuffed in his mouth. "Back up."

I thought he'd know what I meant. "When you started, like . . ."

"Yes . . ."

"Was it just *on* all of a sudden?"

"Are you having sex?"

"This is totally hypothetical. Come on. I'm the Mildred."

"My year," he said darkly, "the Mildred's libido was almost *too* functional."

Why I was asking: I had been fine before. I'd been capable of interacting with males without wondering what it'd be like to be alone with them in the back seat of a Jeep Grand Cherokee. Now—well, there was a faucet, and it had been turned on. I couldn't stop thinking about sex. The guys I saw on TV. The guys in my classes. The guys teaching my classes, which was more than mildly disturbing. Even when I was alone in my room, not a single guy in sight, I'd find myself cupping my *own* breast. Just, like, doing a Taylor series approximation with my right hand, feeling myself up with my left.

"Say there *is* a sex faucet," I said. "How would one go about turning it off?"

"Death?" said Crispin.

"Thanks."

He rearranged the groceries. "I don't know about any sex faucet, except the one called puberty. But listen. Think about what you want."

"What I want?" I wanted everything. That was the problem. I wanted to live through all the R-rated scenes I'd ever seen, and the ones I'd squeamishly closed my eyes through. I wanted a boyfriend. I wanted Andy.

Oh, and I wanted to win our last Quiz Team tournament

and I wanted A-pluses in all my classes and I wanted to learn to drive and I wanted Jiyoon to beat Mack. I wanted Jiyoon to respect me again. I wanted to be *just* like the other girls. I wanted the Tigers to win the Powderpuff game, preferably with me scoring the winning touchdown.

I used to be content, damn it! Damn it. Life was a lot easier when I didn't want so much from it.

"I'm going to make you tell me what's going on," said Crispin. "I've got to bounce now. But think about what you want, Bump. Think carefully. And then, only then, take the steps you need to take to get there."

CHAPTER 14

Half an hour after Crispin left, Paul texted me to see whether he could come by at 9:17 for a driving lesson. It was ridiculously irresponsible of me, given incomplete homework, uncrammed-for exams, etc., but when I saw his headlights in the driveway—at 9:17, natch—I jogged out. "Hi."

"Yo," he said. "Shh."

"What? I have to be quiet? Why do I have to be quiet? Are you—"

He put a finger to his lips. I shushed. He swung out onto the road and I relaxed into Prudence's somewhat grimy passenger seat. Paul had the radio set to the classical-music station, basically background music as far as I was concerned, though as we started whizzing down Route 50, the windows whistling wind above the shiny strings, it sounded pretty good.

"And that," said the plummy voice of the announcer, "was Bach's glorious Concerto for Two Violins, played by—"

Paul jammed off the radio. "What'd you think?"

"About what?"

"Bach's glorious concerto or whatever."

"You're into classical music?"

"No. Not yet. But I believe in the exposure theory. The more time you spend around something, the more you like it."

"If there's anything I've learned from three years of Latin class with Mack Monroe, it's that the opposite is true."

He shrugged, and I felt the same chagrin as when I'd derailed his and Jiyoon's philosophical discussion with a joke. Why did I have to be the way I was? "How's the Last Chance Dance site working from your end?" he asked. "Still good?"

"Seems so."

"I've checked a few times and it seems bug-free. Lots of data coming in. It's all encoded, obviously. But I still can't believe people are submitting such personal information."

"We're used to it. We give the internet personal information all the time. Passwords, credit-card numbers, mothers' maiden names, Social Security numbers—"

"How often are you putting your Social Security number into a website?"

"When I'm asked."

Paul banged himself on the forehead. "We need a modern home ec course. Not how to bake biscuits but how to navigate the internet without ruining your life."

"I'd take that."

"You'd fail that."

"I'd get a Chawton F—a B-minus."

The Home Depot parking lot was empty except for a few orange carts. We switched seats, and I started Prudence without stalling. I did it three times in a row.

"You're actually getting good," said Paul.

"Always the tone of surprise."

"Try a loop around the lot. A slow loop."

We set off. I could do it! I could operate a car and traumatize neither myself nor my passenger! "I can't wait till my dad sees this," I said, hanging a beautiful turn around a pole—

"Whoa!" said Paul, his arm snaking up to the grab handle. "Whoa. Whoa. That was an extremely tight turn. No, don't look at me!"

"Was it really too tight?"

"Eyes on the road, Jemima! Okay. That's better. It's just that Prudence enjoys having both of her mirrors."

"You know what this reminds me of?" I said when we came to a halt.

Paul, who had gone a faint green, swigged from his water bottle. "What?"

"Puberty."

He spurted water all over the glove compartment.

"Controlling the car, but not knowing where it is?" I said. "Not knowing how to make it do what you want it to do? It's dead-on when you pubesce, if that's a word—"

"Not one they taught in SAT prep."

"—and you're like, I know my body—I've had it for thirteen years! And then you walk into a doorframe or sit on a doughnut or wake up to discover large boobular protrusions on your very own torso and it's like, Nope."

"I wouldn't know what you mean," said Paul, "having never been awkward, clumsy, or self-conscious in my life."

"Oh, please. You? You of all people?"

He shook his head. *Jemima Kincaid: Unfiltered.*

But I didn't think he meant it in a bad way.

"How was last night?" The question just fell out. I'd been dying to ask him, especially since harassing Jiyoon by text had yielded nothing more than that it was *fun* and *cool*.

"It was fun," said Paul. "It was cool."

"God. The two of you. A match made in hell. For me, I mean."

"Once the filter goes, it's gone," remarked Paul. "She didn't already tell you all about it?"

"No." I knew it wasn't a law that you had to tell your best friend everything you were doing. I hadn't told Jiyoon a thing about Andy. But I still felt betrayed. "We've been weird lately."

"Because of the chairman thing?"

"You know?"

"She told me."

"Yeah. Exactly. She didn't tell *me*."

"Why don't you take another lap?" said Paul.

Carefully, I drove the perimeter of the lot. We were both quiet. When I stopped and shifted back to first, Paul said, "I'm not in this friendship, obviously. So I don't want to speak out of place. But maybe you guys should talk."

"Yeah."

"My mom's always warning me that things get weird with friends at the end of senior year. It'd be a shame if you two—if your friendship got hurt."

"What did you think when Ji told you she was running for chairman?" I said.

"I thought, That's so freaking ballsy," he said. I drew in a breath to launch into my well-worn diatribe on using terms for male genitalia to mean "brave," but before I could start, Paul said, "Sorry. I'm trying to stop equating balls to positive attributes."

"Do you think she has a shot?"

"Who knows? She's Jiyoon. She's the shit. If anyone can take down that dickhead, it's her."

"Can I do another lap?"

"Go for it."

I drove. And I felt so, so weird.

Sure, there was a warm squiggle of pride for my best friend, for the way Paul's voice got reverent when he said, *She's Jiyoon.* She deserved a guy who thought she was the shit.

But most of my feelings were ugly, unshowered, bed-headed, zit-creamed feelings.

Like: Does Paul think *I'm* the shit?

Like: What does *he* see in her that *I* don't?

Because I didn't think she had a shot in hell of taking down Mack. She was brilliant and hilarious and creative—I adored her, obviously—but to most of Chawton, she fit a type. She was a Quiet Smart Girl. A Quiet Smart *Asian* Girl, as she had pointed out. Not saying I'd have won a chairman election last year, but I had more . . .

Charisma?

Electability?

Whiteness?

What was *wrong* with me?

"I have to be all proud of her," I said. I felt that pressure behind your eyes when you're not crying but your voice gets thick. "And I *am* proud." I really was. "I want her to beat Mack so hard he's embarrassed to come to school. I want her to, like, rub his face in the sand of the arena. I do." I really did. "But I wish she'd told me."

"I got you," said Paul. "I'd feel the same way."

"Really?"

"Really."

"Oh."

"Want some water?"

"The same water you backwashed when I said *puberty*?"

"It's less than five percent backwash."

"Sure. I'd love some water."

I drank. He grinned. I grinned. "I think you're ready for the road," he said.

"What?" I bounced in my seat. "A real live road?"

"Okay, chill. Remember the three *D*s of driving."

"*Defensive, Deliberate,* and *Definitely not freaking out under any circumstances.*"

"Take note of that last one." He directed me to the edge of the parking lot.

"Watch out, Virginia!" I cried.

"We'll just go on the access road to the strip mall. It'll be empty this time of night. Barely different from the parking lot." He sounded like he was convincing himself.

"Oh boy. Oh boy oh boy oh boy."

He took a deep breath. "Look left, look right, look left, and turn out of the lot."

I made the turn and shifted to second. Whee! I was whizzing along at a pace I'd never dreamed possible!

"The speed limit's twenty-five, so you might want to speed up."

I looked down. I was going eleven.

"And shift to third—nice." His voice was relaxed, but he had both hands soldered to the grab handle. "Okay, stop sign coming up, so you'll want to—"

"Stop?"

"Delete that question mark."

I stopped. I shifted to first. I looked both ways and turned right. Paul set a hand in his lap, which I interpreted as a major victory.

Two right turns later, we returned to the lot. I leaned back, exhausted. "What'd you think?"

"You were good."

"Really?" I said, even though I'd said that about twenty times that night. I needed affirmation these days.

"Really." He yawned. "Let's go home. Get out. I'm driving."

CHAPTER 15

It was late when I got home, after eleven, and Jiyoon was all about her eight hours, so I figured I'd leave her a long voice mail, like a podcast with an audience of one. I was mentally scripting it while her phone rang, so I was thrown for a loop when she picked up.

"Huh?" I said. "What's going on?"

"Uh, you called me? And I picked up?"

"Right. That's how this works. Hi. Why are you awake?"

"Can't sleep."

"Where are you?" She sounded muffled.

"In Min's coffee-table fort." She giggled. "My life is pathetic. I'm lying under a table that's draped with a *Star Wars* sheet. Every time I shift position, I get stabbed in the back by a stormtrooper."

"You're a candidate for Chawton School chairman. That's not pathetic."

"Ah," she said. "That's why you're calling."

"*And* you're dating Paul Cunningham."

"Well, I don't know about that."

"He says, quote, 'She's the shit.' Which, you know, I heartily second."

I hoped this was the end of our low-key fight. It was a good sign she'd picked up my call. Communication had not been hopping the past few days.

"Hmm," she said.

I took a deep breath. I had to do it. "I want to apologize," I said. "I'm sorry I didn't think of you. For who should run against Mack. You were right in front of my face. I should have thought of you." I had the urge to explain myself further, all the stuff about how I had assumed Jiyoon and student government went together like peanut butter and spaghetti Bolognese, but I had googled "how to apologize for being potentially a tiny bit sexist/racist" before making this phone call, and the internet had been very clear that I should not, under any circumstances, excuse or justify my behavior. "I'm sorry," I said again. "I think . . . I know I have a lot of privilege. And sometimes I don't see it."

She was quiet.

I waited.

Sometimes with Jiyoon you had to wait.

At last she let out a huge whoosh of breath. "Thanks for apologizing."

"Yeah, well . . ." There was an awkward pause. "I've got a lot to learn."

"We all do," said Jiyoon—rather graciously, if you ask me. "It's a messed-up world we live in."

"Can I tell you how proud I am of you, though?"

"For dating Paul?"

"Ha! You *are* dating."

"Neither confirm nor deny."

"We'll come back to that. No, though, I meant because you're running for chairman. I'm so freaking proud. You're going to smash him. Do you have a battle plan yet? A platform? Rhyming slogans?"

"Ha. Right. I can't even sleep. I feel like I've jumped out of a plane. There's the way I'm supposed to act, the Asian Girl on Scholarship act, quiet and respectful and good at math—"

I snorted. Jiyoon sucks at math. She was in geometry with a bunch of freshmen. And I wouldn't even start debunking *quiet* and *respectful*. She laughed too. "Well, that's what people think! But I've left all that behind. Or I will have, as soon as they announce the candidates tomorrow. I've plunged into an abyss."

"For the sake of Chawton," I said. "To save us all."

"Yeah, yeah," she said. "The lofty ideals are seeming kind of distant right now. But whatever. Too late to back out. I'm in it."

"To win it," I said firmly. "And now we have important matters to discuss, Ji."

"I hope you're referring to my rhyming slogans."

"'Your future is grim if you don't vote for Kim'—no. Back to Paul. What happened last night? And you know what I mean. Did anything *happen*?"

"It was fun," she said, and I could hear the happiness lacing her voice. "It was cool."

On the way to school, four hours of sleep later, my head lolled against the headrest. Mom was post-migraine and hadn't gotten much sleep either; I'd developed a sense for it, I guess, based on the sallowness of her cheeks, how much light was or wasn't in her eyes. We zoomed down 66 in a hazy, tired bubble, the sunrise behind us. I half closed my eyes. It was a clear, cool morning. The only clouds were in a narrow band a few inches above the horizon. I had this—this what, mirage? hallucination? vision?—that we were driving toward a lake, a calm lake that was actually the strip of pale blue sky beneath the clouds. What if we were driving toward a lake, Andy and I? A lake surrounded by cloud-trees? We'd dump our stuff at the cabin and go on a pine-needle-strewn hike, and he'd put his hand on my side to steady me when the terrain got rocky, and he'd say things like "What about Chawton has been the most difficult for you?" and "When should we tell everyone that we're together?" And when we got back to the cabin, we'd be tired and hungry, but even more than rest or food we'd be longing for each other—

"Have a good day, honey," said Mom, and I realized we'd pulled into the circle.

"You too, Mom. Feel better. Get some rest."

"I will. Love you."

"Love you too."

Andy announced the candidates at Town Meeting. The audience reaction was just as I'd expected: Ho-hum, Mack Monroe's running, what a surpr—wait, *what? Who?*

I clapped demurely from my perch onstage.

"The candidates will debate next Thursday," Andy said. "Meeting adjourned."

General brouhaha ensued. "Jiyoon Kim!" I heard in the crush leaving the auditorium.

And "Against *Mack!*"

And "Which one is she, again?"

Before calc started, Monique whispered to me, "Has this ever happened before?"

"What, that two people have run for chairman?"

"Oh, Jemima, quit it. You know what I mean."

"That one of the chairman candidates has a vagina?"

She winced. "Must you?"

"What, use a medical term for a body part that over half the population—"

"Mr. Ulrich," said Monique. "Has a girl ever run for chairman before?"

Mr. Ulrich is a teacher who comes off as personable in front of a class, but when you try to interact with him one on one, he's super awkward. Nonetheless, he was the right person to ask. He'd been teaching at Chawton longer than we'd been alive.

"I was wondering the same thing." He was capable of

chatting because he was behind the lectern. The Lectern That Giveth Social Skills. "The position's been open to anyone since the merge with Ansel, but only once, in 1999, did a female student take it upon herself to run."

"What happened?" said Monique. "I mean, obviously she didn't win, but—"

"There was a bit of a scandal," said Mr. Ulrich. "This student, she was quite the rebel. She fought many a battle with the administration. Piercings, dyed hair, et cetera."

"What was the scandal?"

"Quite sad, really. It came out that she'd, well, gotten involved with someone. And they'd, well . . ." Wow. Mr. Ulrich was literally squirming. "I wouldn't want to gossip, but this could be considered a cautionary tale. . . ." He took off his glasses and cleaned them vigorously with his tie. "She became with child."

"A chairman candidate got knocked up?" said Tim Beanie. Most of the class, I saw, had stopped their other conversations to pay attention to Mr. Ulrich.

"Most unfortunate," he said. "And although it was taken care of . . . well, she was not the ideal representative of the school, the faculty thought. And so her candidacy was aborted." He brought a hand to his mouth to cover his nervous titter. "I assure you, the pun was unintentional."

On Wednesday after school, I skipped Quiz Team for Powderpuff. This took some serious self-justification, given that I was

Quiz Team captain and our last-ever tournament was in two weeks. I told myself it was because I was the Tigers' first-string running back and thus essential for practice, but I knew it was because I wanted to get a ride home in that Jeep.

It ate at me, though, as self-justification tends to do. I stomped out onto the field and stood alone while all the other girls milled around looking sun-kissed and gorgeous. The grass only looks so green, I thought, because of a noxious dose of fertilizer. And my classmates, seniors in May—they were beautiful, sure, but they knew it. That was the problem. The rot of self-awareness, of self-congratulation for beauty and youth and privilege and promise, when they hadn't done anything to deserve it—

Andy blew his whistle. We were split into groups for drills. "What about Kincaid?" asked Tyler.

"Oh," said Andy, "she can go wherever."

Excuse me?

I skipped Quiz Team for *this*?

Andy went with the other group. I ran the drill grimly, receiving a handoff from Jessica, evading Melanie to run ten yards down the field. I knew what was going on. We had learned about it in psychology the year before. It was called hedonic adaptation. Whatever pleasures you have, you get used to them. Like, a few years ago, I went on a wilderness trip with Chawton Outdoors, and by day three I'd have killed for a shower. When I finally got one, I felt like I was living in a fantasyland. Was this real life? Whenever I wanted, I could seclude myself in a clean compartment, have gallons of hot water dumped all over me, step into a soft towel, daub on sweet-smelling ointments—oh, the hedonism!

Then the adaptation. I got used to it in two days.

Once, not long ago, I'd have been content with Andy's presence. I'd have been content to be on the same field, to glimpse him out of the corner of my eye. But now that I'd been introduced to new pleasures, the old ones were no longer enough. Andy had become a necessity for me. Bread, not cake.

In the parking lot, after we'd cleaned up from practice, Andy caught my eye. He raised his eyebrows and jingled his car keys in his pocket. I nodded. We didn't say much on the twilit drive to my house. He pulled into the driveway and turned off the car.

"Finally," he said.

CHAPTER 16

Crispin was having a housewarming party that weekend. "I'm invited?" I said when he called me. "Oh my God, Bippy, you're finally treating me like a real adult, this is so great—"

"Um, clarification. You're invited to the pre-party."

"What's that supposed to mean?"

"It'll be really fun!" Too much enthusiasm. I smelled a rat. "Come over beforehand, hang out with your beloved older bro. . . ."

"Ah," I said grimly. "Come help you prepare. Come vacuum your couch cushions. Come get ushered firmly out the door before your real friends show up."

"Glad we're on the same page," said Crispin.

I grumbled awhile for the sake of my reputation, but I have low standards. Mom dropped me off at the Vienna station on Saturday, and I zoomed past the befuddled tourists, rode to

Clarendon, and marched to Crispin's high-rise, all the while pretending I was commuting to my high-powered, world-saving job in DC. Never mind that it was Saturday and I hadn't left Virginia and I was wearing Keds with a romper. I felt extremely grown-up.

Crispin, in what appeared to be swim trunks and nothing else, opened the door.

"Hey!" I said. "Wow! It smells so good—"

Then the heat struck.

"Is the AC broken?" I said, fanning myself. "It's got to be ninety degrees in here!"

Crispin skipped over to the fancy Nest thermostat. "Eighty-two, actually."

I was already sweating. "Have you called maintenance?"

"You must not have read the invitation," he told me.

"I didn't get an invitation."

"The theme is global warming."

"You're having a *global-warming* housewarming?"

"Hence the temperature!"

"That's so tasteless!"

He poked at the Nest. "This little guy was going haywire, but I've managed to override all his warning settings. Here's hoping we hit eighty-six by the time the real guests arrive." For the first time, I was happy to not be a real guest. "I got this idea back when the leasing agent told me heat was included. What do you think of the decor?"

I looked around. He'd loaded up on tropical plants, and he'd garlanded blue crepe paper under a poster of a polar bear so it sort of looked like it was swimming. "My vision," he said, "is for the futon to be the focal point of the party. It represents the melting polar ice cap."

It was white, I guess. "What's to show it's melting?" I said. "Shouldn't you put some pans of water under it?"

"I knew I invited you for a reason."

The heat was getting to me. I sat on the ice cap, plucking my romper from my sweaty back, and said, "I hope you told everyone to come in swimsuits."

"Of course. The dress code is Doomsday Beach Party."

"Is Thomas coming?"

"Why else do you think I'm having a party?"

I added *throwing a party* to my mental list of the extra things people do because of crushes. "Have your bosses found out yet?"

He grimaced. "No, but this could be the night. I think the work people I've invited have been carefully vetted, but you never know. . . ."

Jeopardizing your job: another thing to add to the list. "Be careful," I said.

"Yeah, yeah. So, Bump. Your first challenge, should you choose to accept it—"

I smiled. That was how Dad had always given us chores as kids.

"—is to help me arrange these glass panels against the walls."

I thought about it. "Oh. The greenhouse effect."

"You got it."

"I still think this is super tacky."

"Does it help that I'm collecting donations for Greenpeace?"

"Actually?"

"Thomas's idea. He said everything you're saying, except with more profanity."

We propped up the glass panels. To be honest, it looked like it'd be a fun party. If, that is, the festive mood wasn't shattered by the ever-present reminder of apocalypse. "In a global calamity," said Crispin, "you probably wouldn't care about a perfectly clean bathroom, right?"

"Bip. You're having people over. You've got to clean your bathroom."

"Your challenge," he began, "should you choose to—"

"Not a chance."

"Well, keep me company, then."

I sat on the edge of the tub while Crispin dumped cleaning solution into the toilet. "Cleaning tip number one," he said. "Use enough Mr. Clean that the fumes make you dizzy."

"I'm already dizzy, it's so hot in here."

"'It's getting hot in here,'" he warbled. "Stop whining. Chat. How's everything at school?"

"Busy. Quiz Team, Triumvirate, exams—"

"You sound like a talking college application. You know what I'm asking about."

"Haven't the foggiest." I did, of course.

He grimaced as he used the toilet brush on the inside of the bowl. "I've lived here three weeks. How is this possible? Okay. Come on. Andy, kissing, sex faucets. Tell me everything."

"We made out. In his Jeep. Twice."

"Well, shit," said Crispin. "The good kind of shit. Not . . ." He wrinkled his nose at the toilet bowl. "Start at the beginning."

"I haven't told anyone about this. I haven't even told Jiyoon."

"All the more reason to tell me."

It sounded like I took some persuading, but I didn't. I'd been thinking all day that I'd tell Crispin. I'd been thinking that even before Wednesday, when Andy and I had moved to the back seat and taken off our shirts with no discussion, and Andy had taken off my bra and draped it like some sort of beached sea creature on the passenger's headrest while we rolled around and panted and felt each other's skin and sucked each other's necks and built up a slidey, glidey layer of sweat. He worked his hand up my shorts and teased the elastic of the built-in underwear—there was that un-Jemima mewl again, uncontrolled—and finally he set a few fingers over the fabric, right where I was pounding for him. "Wet," he said, and I mumbled, "That's *your* fault," and he let out a half laugh before he resumed kissing me.

But fair's fair, I managed to remember before those fingers on my underwear stole all my capacity for rational thought. I girded my courage and moved my hand to the silky athletic fabric draping *his* crotch, which, as I guess I might have expected, was bulging. Oh. God. I mean, I knew it would be hard, but, like, purely in terms of physics or physiology or whatever, how was this possible? I'd been expecting a water balloon—something that, when prodded, would give—but this, well. This didn't give. All that slang, *boning* and *screwing* and so forth, suddenly made a shocking amount of sense. And when Andy let out a quick breath as I tentatively moved my hand along the bulge, which, upon manual inspection, was revealed to have a rather predictable cucumberesque form, it *all* made sense. A shocking kind of sense. Sex, that is. I got it. This was why Helen of Troy. This was why teen pregnancy. This.

The car windows steamed. I'd always thought that was a dumb movie cliché, but no, they actually steamed.

I gave Crispin a highly censored outline of the above while he, riveted, knelt by the toilet.

"You're severely lacking in details," he said. "Any clothes off?"

"Shirts. And, er, an undergarment. My undergarment. The topmost one."

"Was there exploration of the nether regions?"

"Ew, must you—"

"Sorry, do you prefer 'Did you touch his dick, did he rub your—'"

"Stop!" I slid all the way into the tub and drew shut the shower curtain.

"I'm just trying to get the story straight!"

"You're my brother!"

"Which makes me the perfect person to tell. As a guy who's, one, your kin and, two, gay, I'm so far from interested in you that it's totally nonweird to tell me."

"When you put it that way . . ." I opened the curtain.

"Well?"

"A bit. But the nether clothes stayed on."

"So far, anyway," he said. I had to hide in the shower again. "Hmm. Do you want advice? Or did you just want me to listen?"

"Advice," I said.

"Emerge, then."

"I'm thinking you should leave the shower on during the party," I said as I drew back the curtain. "To mimic rain-forest conditions."

"I'm paying the water bill, so no. Listen. Here's my advice. Have fun. But be careful."

"We're making out in his car, not sleeping together."

"You'd be surprised how thin the line is. Not that, though. Didn't I tell you to think about what you want? Is this what you want?"

"It's exactly what I want."

"Then there's some stuff you need to know."

"I've had sex ed. Condoms, consent, blah blah—"

"Repeat this after me," he said. "There's no such thing as a tease."

"I know."

"Repeat it. Seriously."

"There's no such thing as a tease," I said.

"Teases are a concept men invented to make people feel like they owe them sex. And you don't owe him anything. Even if he's up and ready to go. Still listening?"

"Yeah."

"You can stop whenever you want. You don't have to be polite. Keep thinking about what you want. Every minute. And if that changes, change what you're doing."

I wondered what had happened to Crispin that was making him so serious. "Okay."

"Just be careful. Be careful about your . . . your heart, Bump."

"Isn't it men who have heart attacks during sex?"

"Very funny," he said, rolling his eyes. "Come on."

"Andy and I—it's a purely physical transaction," I said. "No strings, no feelings. And that *is* what I want. I'm not expecting him to ask me to prom, or ask me on a date, or *like* me. . . ."

Crispin shook his head. The bathroom was moist and sparkling, the surfaces faintly steaming in the warm air. I followed him to the kitchen. "There are always strings," he said, washing his hands. "Your feelings are always going to get involved. I'm saying, be careful. Do what you want. But you won't be able to stop your heart from getting mixed up in it."

He shrugged and made a production of dunking the paper towel into the trash. Like he'd gone shy. And Crispin, my brother, my loud and ebullient big brother, he never went shy.

"At least," he said, "that's my experience."

CHAPTER 17

I had the attention span of a gnat. This was unfortunate, because life demanded concentration these days. But I couldn't stop thinking about Andy. There was the intense kind of thinking (daydreaming, cruising his social media, lying in bed before I went to sleep), and there was the background kind of thinking, when I'd be doing something else—trying to do something else—and he'd be there, like a humming refrigerator, like clinks and chatter at a coffee shop.

Jiyoon and I were sitting on the floor by our lockers. We had sweatshirts over our school clothes with the hoods all the way up. It was that kind of Monday morning. "I know it's stupid," she said, "but I'm already nervous about the debate."

As Andy had announced, it was scheduled for Thursday's Town Meeting. "You're going to be awesome."

"I prepped a lot this weekend, but I don't know, does prep even matter in this situation?"

"Of course it does."

"You know what I mean."

"Yeah. Mack won't get votes because he's ready for the job."

"He'll get votes because he's Mack."

"And you'll get votes because you're Jiyoon *and* because you're ready for the job."

"As many votes as I'll lose because I'm Jiyoon?" she said.

I glanced over, but with her hood up, all I could see was the tip of her nose. "I guess you can't know," I said, and she shrugged, and I couldn't think of anything else to say, so we sat there in silence. Our hoods and the early morning reminded me of the monks we'd learned about in European history, the ones who sat in monasteries and copied Latin manuscripts and basically single-handedly saved classical civilization from extinction. I would have taken that life. I bet you got a lot of sleep, in between novenas and sharpening your quill. I bet the weight of heavy wool, not to mention original sin, made you not even *want* sex. You wouldn't even have to worry about it. You wouldn't have this tantalizing, painful glimpse, stuff in the back of a car that you weren't even sure would happen again, and you wouldn't ever think about someone so much that it felt like worrying a bump on the inside of your mouth.

"Did you submit your Last Chance Dance picks?" said Jiyoon.

"Last night."

"Without consulting me? Who *are* you?"

The door at the end of the hallway opened. Andy came in this door when he parked in the back lot. But this was only some freshman, straggling along with a gym bag, pillow creases still on his cheek.

"Are you waiting for someone?" said Jiyoon.

"No. No. Why?"

"Because you jump and look down the hallway every time the door opens."

The door opened. I didn't jump, but I couldn't help looking, and there he was.

"Relax," Jiyoon whispered, her voice curling in amusement. "It's just Andy."

Just Andy. But should I say hi? Should I pretend I didn't see him? Should I—

"Morning, Kincaid."

"Oh! Hi, An—um, Monroe."

He loped down the hallway, reaching up to touch the exit sign as he turned the corner. I exhaled.

"I take it I don't need to ask who you put for the Last Chance Dance," said Jiyoon.

I slowly sank down. My legs sprawled all the way into the hallway, nearly tripping a group of freshmen. "Hey!" one yelled.

"Senior privileges," I told them. I tried to get comfortable. I obviously couldn't move now that I'd defended my position, but I was essentially sitting on my neck.

"You're still into him?" she said.

I was thinking about him so often that I'd basically ruined him, the way you ruin a song when you play it for weeks on repeat. "One could say I'm mildly into him," I said.

Now was my chance to tell her about everything: the Jeep, the kissing, the more. I still couldn't figure out why I didn't want to.

Because we always had to be as intense as possible, Chawton had a debate instead of candidate speeches. There were rules and time limits and rebuttal periods, but as with any debate, it all went to shit sometimes, and that was when it was most enjoyable.

Marcela Vasquez, in a skirt suit and heels, strode onstage. "Good morning, students and faculty," she said in her dulcet, competent tones. "As the president of the Chawton Political Union, I consider it a privilege to moderate the debate for Chawton School chairman. Here are your candidates. Mack Monroe!"

The auditorium clapped and whooped while Paul, Monique, and I tapped our fingertips together. "You're my boy, Mack!" yelled some rando, and Mack gave a flip wave. He looked as scruffy as usual. He was in dress code, but his back shirttail was out and his tie was knotted so loosely that you could tell his top button was undone. He wore boat shoes and a smirk.

My stomach roiled.

"And Jiyoon Kim!"

She emerged from the wings. Of course clothes would matter for a girl. She'd hit the perfect note, professional but not try-hard, with slim black pants and a floaty shirt that reminded me of orange sherbet. The applause was substantial. No whooping, but it was solid and sustained. I found myself scratching away tears from the corners of my eyes.

They shook hands. She gave him a polite smile. He barely made eye contact, his gaze already dismissing her, sliding to Marcela.

"Each topic will be introduced by a question to which each candidate will have two minutes to reply," said Marcela. "The candidate who speaks first will then have a one-minute rebuttal period, after which the time will be divided at my discretion." Marcela is going to be either a news anchor or president, because her intellect is fearsome, plus she can walk in high heels and a pencil skirt, which you should film yourself doing if you think you can. She was popular, in a sense. She hung out in the Andy-Gennifer social stratum. In September, though, all those people were decorating the senior lounge, and they put up TV and movie characters labeled with seniors' names. Marcela got Consuela, the Latina maid from *Family Guy*. Mr. Duffey made them take it down, but then it was all white kids up there. I don't know. She said she didn't mind.

"Based on a coin flip, Mack will respond first," she said. "The first topic is tradition versus innovation. As chairman, how would you seek to balance these two objectives?"

Mack stood in a dickish, dick-out way. That was an obvious question at a school like Chawton, but he looked nonplussed, probably at all the polysyllabism. "Um, yeah," he said. "Tradition is what we're about here, but you gotta change too. Otherwise we wouldn't even have computers."

"Profound," whispered Paul.

"But what I'm really about," said Mack, "is a big Chawton tradition. Hype Club."

He got whoops. Chairman candidates always talked about Hype Club, a club for—of all the vastly moronic pastimes—going to sports games and yelling.

"We gotta get more support," he said. "Football, basketball, whatever. Our guys need you." This must have rung a distant bell, maybe to the one time he'd paid attention in history class, because he pointed his finger at the audience and said, "Uncle Mack needs *you!*"

More whooping. "Thirty seconds," said Marcela.

"Hype Club needs gear to rep the Angel Tigers. So we need money. But we have too many *bake* sales around here. You know what I'd have instead? Wait for it. *Bacon* sales."

The audience went wild. Not everyone, but enough of everyone to make me hate Chawton. How was Gennifer dating this slob?

"Time," said Marcela. "Jiyoon? The balance of tradition and innovation?"

"*Balance* is the right word," Jiyoon began. "The long history of Chawton is something we can all be proud of, but at the same time, we have to change as the world changes."

She seemed nervous. She was talking too fast.

"As chairman, I'd keep tradition in mind, but I wouldn't be afraid to innovate."

Kingsley Chabot, in the row ahead of me, yawned. The energy in the auditorium sagged like a cut clothesline. "I applaud the current Triumvirate," said Jiyoon. "They've embraced the tradition of prom, but they've updated it with a new twist. That's real balance."

Oh no. She was being boring. You couldn't get elected to run Town Meetings all year if you were boring. I don't know if it was seeing the two of them from a distance or what—the crystallization of all the stuff I'd been hearing?—but I could see the problem, suddenly. The problem was that Mack didn't have anything to prove. People would think he was funny and cool just because he was a white guy. Not to mention a white guy who played sports and wasn't into academics and was related to Andy. Whereas Jiyoon, she'd walked onstage with the weight of a story on her back. She didn't have to prove she was funny; she had to prove girls were funny. She didn't have to prove she was cool; she had to prove Asian kids were cool. It was like she had graffiti on her face that said *Quiet, Smart, and Boring AF,* and we in the audience were reading it, taking it as truth.

No wonder she had worried her prep didn't matter. How could it? In the face of *that?*

"Take Hype Club," said Jiyoon. "That's a dead tradition. *Dead.*" She smacked her lectern. Mack, who'd been rolling his tie between his hands, jumped. "All Hype Club does is go to football and boys' basketball. What about other sports? What about girls' sports? What about dance team? Debate team? Art shows? Choir concerts?"

Brilliant move. Talk about a silent majority. All the people who didn't play football or basketball wanted hype too.

"So when you say you want to revitalize Hype Club"—how

generous, Ji; *revitalize* has three too many syllables for Mack—"what I'm hearing is, give more stuff to the same people who always get stuff."

"Time," said Marcela, blinking.

"Yesss," I hissed. I loved it. Jiyoon on the offensive. It was risky, but she was probably right if she'd figured she had nothing to lose.

Marcela started to tell Mack he had a one-minute rebuttal. He cut her off. "*You* try to get people to come to girls' sports. Or, what'd you say, choir shows? Girls are great"—one of his stupid-ass friends gave a *woot-woot,* and Mack paused, flustered—"but there's a reason everyone in America watches football but no one cares about female soccer."

Female soccer, lol. Like the match was laying eggs. Some guys were allergic to the word *women.* Jiyoon illegally cut in. "And what's that reason?"

"It's—it's just *better.* You want to watch athletes at the top of their game."

"Odd," said Jiyoon. "The Chawton football team went two and ten last season, but G-Soc won the league and advanced to the state semifinal."

The raucous cheers of the girls' soccer team drowned out Mack's reply. Since when did Jiyoon know sports stats? Team nicknames? She *had* prepped.

"It's Mack's turn to speak," said Marcela, not quite successful in repressing her smile.

"Okay," said Mack. His neck and cheeks were all red. "Okay.

The Hype Club does support everyone, because the football team *is* everyone. They're playing for us all. That's why people say, '*We* beat Potomac; *we* beat Sidwell.' But even so, you're a hypocrite."

Marcela winced. Given Mack's Latin skills, I doubted he knew what *ad hominem* meant.

"You say you want a Hype Club that supports everyone, but I say, what about a Triumvirate that represents everyone? We've already got Social Comm president for the girls, and the Mildred for the ner—for the smart people. So why . . ."

Mack, I realized then, would have been angry even if Jiyoon had debated like a limp noodle. He had been angry long before she'd made him look stupid. He was angry because she was running. He was angry that she'd dared.

"So why," he said, "why should *you* get to run?"

"Time," Marcela said quietly. "Jiyoon?"

The auditorium was dead still, but Jiyoon didn't jump in right away. When she spoke, her voice was firm, and she addressed not Mack nor Marcela but us, the audience. "I get to run," she said evenly, "for the same reason that *any* of you could run. Because I'm a student at Chawton."

She stopped long enough that I thought that might be it.

"I think Mack touches on a larger point, though. About tradition and innovation. About whether we want things to be the way they used to be, or the way they should be. The way they could be."

She stared us down.

"To me," she said, "Chawton is a school where anyone can be chairman. Where anyone can be Social Comm president, for that matter. Chawton is a school where it doesn't matter what you look like when it comes to people trusting you to represent them and think about them and make good decisions on their behalf. And that's why I'm running. Because I believe we're that school. Because I believe we *can* be that school. Because I love this school, and I want to work hard for it. I want to learn and grow and change, and I want Chawton to learn and grow and change too."

The applause started. It built. Paul and I stood, and Monique with us. Ms. Margolis. Mr. Peabody. Ashby, Greg, Zachary, Cilla—and it hit the tipping point, and it was everyone.

Well, not everyone. But enough of everyone that I loved this school too.

CHAPTER 18

I waited for Jiyoon at the auditorium door. She came out after everyone else, looking as calm as she'd looked onstage.

"OH MY GOD YOU WERE AMAZING!" I tackled her in a hug.

"Let go of me," she barked. *"Now,* Jem."

I set her down, and she gave me a bashful, proud smile. I had to throw my arms around her again.

"You dork-ass," she said. We both started giggling. "I can't be seen like this," she said. "I look too self-satisfied. Come to the bathroom."

The bathroom wasn't empty. Hannah Garland started clapping, and Arden Lyme, at the mirror, said, *"Thank* you."

"She slayed, right?" I said.

"Oh, stop," said Jiyoon, disappearing into a stall.

"How did it feel?" I asked.

I didn't get an answer. Jiyoon thinks it's barbaric to talk while peeing. "I discharge stuff out of only one orifice at a time," she'd told me once, and I'd said, "What about when you're on your period?" and she'd said, "I guess you hadn't noticed I'm silent for a week of every month." "And very constipated," I'd added, and she'd hit me with her Latin notebook.

We were really good friends. That's all I mean to say. Jiyoon and I had built a space for just the two of us, my favorite room in the house of my life, the sunroom with board games and a massive, misshapen begonia, and I resolved to remember that. Even if—

Even if *what*, Jemima?

She came out. "Tell me everything," I said.

"Not now," she said, washing her hands.

I went to art history. It was a class of mostly sophomores, and I always sat in the back. It felt like taking public transportation alone. I enjoyed both experiences.

Ms. Ipswich twisted shut the shades. Today was Mondrian. It reminded me how late in the year it was. What had happened to September? Slides of cave paintings and the Venus of Willendorf. New shirtdresses, a new Triumvirate, the promise of senior year. Now the bottom of my backpack was gritty with pencil shavings and the torn edges of notebook paper, and my shirtdresses had begun to go the way of all flesh, sweat stains stiffening the armpits. I missed cave art. Art before the history of art intruded. "A self-conscious rebuttal of the past," said Ms. Ipswich, gesturing toward Mondrian's primary colors, his straight lines. I hated him.

How was it already May? I would never be in high school again.

I wished I'd run for chairman.

Not this year, obviously. Last year. I hadn't even considered it. Only boys ran for chairman. I'd been pretty sure I'd get the Mildred, so I figured I'd be on Triumvirate anyway.

I wouldn't have beaten Andy. Andy was invincible. Mack, though . . .

I might have had a chance against Mack.

Was I jealous? Jealous that Jiyoon was the one to shatter glass ceilings? Jealous that Jiyoon got clapped for when she walked into the bathroom?

It was horrible and irrational and went against all my fine thoughts during the debate, and it was true. I was jealous. I set down my pencil. Ms. Ipswich's lecture was no longer getting through to me. I hadn't expected the jealousy, but the thing was, I hadn't expected this outcome, either. I wouldn't have been happy if she'd lost the debate. But I wouldn't have been surprised.

I'd been so sure the debate would go according to the unspoken rules of Chawton that I hadn't even wondered how Jiyoon's winning would affect me and Andy. Now I did. It would change things, wouldn't it? My best friend embarrassing his brother in front of the whole school?

Can I confess something?

You know "bros before hos" or whatever the female version is? "Sisters before misters"? I felt like I didn't have that impulse. Take, for instance, the teeming hotbed of epic romance more commonly known as the national Quiz Team championships: on the last night I'd told Jiyoon and Ashby and Monique and the other girls that I'd sneak out to 7-Eleven with them to buy soda and gummy worms so we could hang in a hotel room watching *Key & Peele* and stuffing our faces and playing Apples to Apples and dissecting the social dynamics of the week. It'd have been fun. But the second I had a chance to hide behind folding chairs with a guy I barely knew, well, I was *gone*.

It was a choice born of desperation. How many chances with guys was I even going to get? Girls, on the other hand, were always around.

I had to wait at school until Powderpuff practice at seven, and Ms. Edison let me hole up in her classroom. I texted my whereabouts to Jiyoon. "I've got fifteen minutes before the bus leaves," Jiyoon said as she came in. She dramatically collapsed into a chair. "Wow. It has been a weird day."

"All the postdebate stuff?"

"What I said before about plunging into the abyss—I didn't realize that it would involve everyone staring at me too."

"Staring how?"

"Like they're seeing me for the first time. John Pullman

actually said that in English. He was like, 'Oh, I didn't know *you* were in this class!' And the worst part was that I couldn't even say, *Uh, it's May—you are daft.* I want him to vote for me, so I had to smile and be like, 'Yep!'"

"John Pullman *is* daft," I said. "He never remembers free-dress days."

"I kind of want to be anonymous again. But I've blown that forever."

"But that's a good thing, right?" I said cautiously. "The debate went so well. You got a standing ovation. You might win!"

"Meh, probably not. But yeah. It went well." She ducked her head, but she couldn't hide her delighted smile. "Don't quote me on that."

"I'll maintain your modest façade," I promised, "even though I know how swollen your head's gotten. God. I can't believe you *want* to be anonymous. All this attention is totally wasted on you."

"Is that a tinge of jealousy I detect?" She was still smiling, which meant, I was pretty sure, that she hadn't detected my actual tinge of jealousy. But it felt good to give voice to the feeling. It took away its force.

"The only thing I'm worried about," I said lightly, "is that Andy's going to hate me now."

"I ended up next to him in the lunch line and he definitely ignored me on purpose," said Jiyoon. "If I equal you and he equals Mack, then yeah, he hates you. It's the transitive property of mortal enemydom."

It was like a punch to the gut. But Jiyoon had no idea. Which was my fault. I had pretended to her that this was just another of my silly crushes.

If only I'd told her what was going on.

"There goes my Last Chance Dance pick," I said.

"Because that relationship had *so* much promise," she said, rolling her eyes. "Get a new crush, Dorcas. Someone who deserves you this time."

I thought I might start crying. Because Jiyoon was so nice, but also (mostly) because my chances with Andy were really and truly destroyed. I had to change the subject before she noticed. "I was sitting next to Paul at the debate," I said. "Did he text you?"

She brightened. "Yes. And. Drumroll, please. On Saturday, we are going to—hey, where's the drumroll?—*dinner and a movie.*"

"WHAT?" I clutched my chest. "A guy of our day and age who knows what a date is?"

"He even called it a date," she said, brimming over with smiles. "We're not *chilling.* Or *hanging.* We're going on a date."

"I'll come over and take pictures as you get into his car," I said.

I walked to the football field slowly. Andy was all business, blowing his whistle, setting drills, and absolutely not making eye contact with Jemima Kincaid. I ignored him back all practice, but I couldn't resist lingering afterward, stuffing pinnies in net sacks and jogging the field to collect cones. At last it was just Andy and Tyler and Melanie, who I think was hanging around for the same reason as me except for Tyler.

"We're all set here," said Andy. "You guys got big plans tonight?"

"Might go game with Joey and them," said Tyler.

"That sounds so fun!" said Melanie. "I love watching video games!" Sure you do, Mel.

"What about you, Monroe?" said Tyler.

Andy checked his phone. "Yeah, I gotta bounce. I'm meeting up with some friends at Tysons. Nice practice."

He fist-bumped Tyler and gave Melanie a nod. He looked at me. I must have looked weird, because he said, "All good, Kincaid?"

"Oh yeah!" I said brightly. "Yep! I've got to get going too! Thursday night!"

The four of us were walking from the field, and I realized I was about to fall into the super-awkward position of having claimed an urgent need to leave and then ending up in a near-empty parking lot with no car and no ride. I veered sharply toward the front circle. I'd wait there for my mom. Or my Lyft. Whatever. "Enjoy your evenings!" I cried. I sounded like a teacher.

"See ya," said Andy. "You've got a ride?"

"Oh, well, no," I said, "not yet, but I'll just, you know, make a few calls, deploy my contacts, drag my mom out of hibernation"—I found myself waving my phone madly in front of my face—"utilize this amazing piece of communicative tech-nology. . . ." Shut up, shut up.

"Okay, cool." Tyler and Melanie looked back questioningly, and Andy said, "Go ahead, I have to ask Jemima about a Trium-virate thing. Maybe I'll see you later at Joey's."

He turned to me, and for one hopeful, desperate second, I thought we were going to talk. *I really like you, Jemima. You're really cool. Do you want to make out in my car?*

And then I remembered. The debate, the lunch line, the transitive property of mortal enemydom. The flags had been planted, and we were on opposite sides.

"Everything okay?" he said.

"Oh, sure!" I said, maybe too loudly. "I'll get a ride."

He grimaced. God, did he hate me, or did he *pity* me? Ride-less, planless, on a Thursday night in May? "Sorry I can't take you," he said. "But you could come to Tysons. I'm chilling with some buddies from my old club lax team."

"I don't need to tag along," I said in a chilly voice. "Don't worry about me."

He raised his hands in that annoying *Don't shoot* gesture. "Have it your way."

"I will, thanks."

"Sweet." He rattled his keys in his pocket. "Have a good one, then."

"You too."

I wanted to spin around so I could march away before he did, but I was fixed to the spot. He raised a hand and left.

CHAPTER 19

It was Mom's birthday Friday, and Dad made a reservation at Founding Farmers in DC. It's this sleek restaurant where everyone's a hotshot lawyer or lobbyist or congressional staffer. There are lots of ankle boots and glossy lipsticks. I always walk into places like that and instinctively suck in my stomach.

The hostess tapped around on her iPad and told us it'd be a few minutes. "We had a reservation for seven-thirty," said my dad, "and it's seven-thirty-five."

Crispin and I made a flicker of eye contact. It was comforting to know there was someone else who wanted to sink into the floor. The hostess had white-blond hair that was scraped into a very tight bun. "Aesthetic: bald with a doorknob," Crispin whispered to me. I allowed a small smile.

"We simply don't have a free table," she informed Dad. I

guess she was used to dealing with overaggressive DC types. "Would you like to wait at the bar?"

"We're not falling for the 'wait at the bar, bump up the bill' routine," Dad blustered.

Mom, either tired or embarrassed, edged over to a bench by the door. Dad paced. I sank into the morass of my mind. At school that day, I'd seen Andy across the Commons, poking a giggling Brittany in the ribs. Then we'd passed each other in the hallway and he hadn't made eye contact. I'd messed everything up. Maybe I should have taken him up on the pity invite, gone to Tysons, and fake-laughed at dumb bro jokes.

Crispin elbowed me. "Quit it," I said.

"I'm bored and my phone's at eight percent. Play a game with me." He nodded toward the three hosts huddled around the iPad: Ol' Doorknob, a rail of a white guy with emo-band bangs, and a black guy with a compact dancer's body. "Those three," said Crispin. "Marry, bury, bang?"

It took me a minute to recognize the game. It's otherwise known as Do, Die, Marry or Kiss, Marry, Kill, or a much more explicit name that had scarred me when I'd learned it at a slumber party in ninth grade. "I'm not playing that with my brother," I told Crispin.

"Yeah, because you're so dignified and prudish around me . . ."

He had a point. "Okay. Fine. I'd bury Ol' Doorknob. Marry the black guy. Look, he's smiling. Sleep with the white one really fast and get it over with."

"It's cute that you still say *sleep with*," said Crispin. "Give me a group."

I gave him a table of three guys in suits. After a grossly detailed inventory of their physical attributes, Crispin made his call. "All right, Bump," he said, leering. "Marry, bury, bang: Mack Monroe. Paul Cunningham. Andy Monroe."

My mind lurched at Andy's name. "That's unfair," I said. "For one, Jiyoon has a thing with Paul, and for two . . ." I didn't want to explain the whole Andy thing. "I didn't give *you* anyone you knew in real life."

"Too bad for you."

"Fine." I crossed my arms. "Assuming Jiyoon's out of the picture, I guess I'd marry Paul, bury Mack, and Andy, I'd definitely ba—"

"What are you two whispering about so seriously?" said Dad, popping up between us.

I jumped. "Dad! God!"

"I am your dear sire, Jemima, but ought not be confused with the Heavenly Father." He was in a good mood. I bet they'd comped him a drink. Yep, there was the bartender, catching his eye as he slid forward a tumbler of something on ice. Dad sipped. "That's more like it. Don't let me interrupt. Go on talking about whatever it was you were talking about."

"Yeah, Bump," said Crispin, "you were right in the middle of a sentence, weren't you?"

Dad turned to beckon Mom over. I hissed at Crispin, "Stop."

"Don't worry. I'll never betray you." He patted my shoulder. "But I *will* make you feel extremely uncomfortable."

I tried to glare. I ended up smiling instead. I hadn't wanted to be in a good mood tonight, but it was like Crispin had heaved up a rock inside my mind and discovered that there was actually some cheer there. We were seated in a booth upstairs. Crispin slid in after me. "What was that you were saying about Andy Monroe?" he said innocently.

"How *is* Andy Monroe?" said Mom. "Such a nice boy, I've always thought."

Her opinion might change if she knew what he'd done to me in the back of his Jeep. "He's good," I said.

"Good at what?" said Crispin.

Luckily, our parents never picked up on anything. "So!" I said, glaring at Crispin. "Jamboree's coming up. Powderpuff, prom, all that stuff."

Dad was surveying the wine list, reading glasses on his nose, but Mom said, "Prom! Is it still in the Commons? I remember that from my Parent Board days. So much decorating!"

Back when Crispin was at Chawton, she was big into school volunteer stuff. She stopped because the migraines got worse.

"Jemima's idea for the prom theme got chosen," said Crispin.

"Really!" said Mom. "Tell us about it!"

"Well, we wanted to avoid all that stupid, patriarchal, heteronormative promposal stuff."

"Promposal?" said Mom.

So *that* took a minute. Even Dad looked up from the wine list long enough to say, "Astounding. Truly astounding, the effort that today's youth plug into the silliest things."

"Oh, Rick, you don't remember how you asked me to your spring formal?" Mom looked healthier than usual: her skin didn't have its usual wan, papery look, and her eyes were sparkling. It made me realize how flat she'd gone. She used to be sparkly all the time.

"Of course I remember," said Dad. "I was a senior, your mother was a sophomore. . . ."

I'd heard this story before. Dad had borrowed his roommate's Mustang and surprised her at her sorority house so that he could ask her to the dance on a fancy joyride. That's a proto-promposal if I've ever heard one. They never got to go on the joyride, though, because a neighbor called the police about all the engine revving, and when Dad's name wasn't on the registration, they thought he'd stolen the car.

Nobody our age talked about what it was like to watch your parents get older. To know that all their hijinking teenage charm had turned into middle-aged bluster, that the dashing young buck who talked his way out of a disturbing-the-peace ticket had become an old guy raising a stink about a restaurant running five minutes late. And we imagined we were forever young, I thought, but this would happen to us, too, soon enough. Even so, I couldn't stop believing we were different. Would we really get old? It was—

"Incomprehensible," Dad growled at the menu. "Absolutely

incomprehensible. Why must they be so cutesy? *Tomato chow-chow* and *bacon lollis*. Really? Who wants to suck bacon?"

Mom let out a light sigh, her hand resting on Dad's arm. "Back to your prom, Jemima."

"Right. Yeah. So we wanted to get out of the paradigm where a girl has to wait around until a boy asks her."

"What's wrong with that?" said Dad.

I ignored him. Either he was trying to rile me up or he was too far gone to bother. "But Sadie Hawkins is just as heteronormative, and besides, it posits girls asking boys as a major reversal of roles, right? Like 'This is sooooo weird, but for one day a year—'"

I was interrupted by the waiter. Dad ordered a bottle of wine. "Four glasses for the table, sir?" said the waiter.

"Four, yes," said Dad.

I tried to be cool. His answer had always been *three* before. The waiter brought the bottle to Dad and they did the wine rigmarole while the rest of us watched in our due reverence: the knowing nod, the thoughtful swish. "Excellent," Dad pronounced. "A triumph."

The waiter poured four glasses. Dad lifted his. "To my beautiful wife."

"And our beautiful children!" chirped Mom.

"It's *your* birthday, Mom," said Crispin.

"Cheers," said Dad. We clinked. I faked nonchalance, though Crispin acted like a dork at me, widening his eyes in shock as I sipped my wine.

"Mmm," said Mom.

"Robust," said Dad. "Full-bodied."

"Full-bodied, indeed," said Crispin, lifting his glass to catch the light. "Voluptuous. Overflowing its corsets."

"So what we came up with for prom—" I said.

"Do I detect a note of strawberry?" said Dad.

"Like a pink Jolly Rancher," said Crispin.

Dad rolled his eyes. "I won't bother treating you as an adult, Crispin, if you can't take anything seriously." He returned to the menu.

"We set up this website. . . ." I stopped talking as a test. Nobody even reacted. Mom was whispering in Dad's ear, and Crispin was doing this thing he did sometimes where he stared really hard at an inanimate object. Right now it was his wineglass. So much for conversation.

The waiter came with appetizers. "Chèvre-bacon dates," he said, "and devilish eggs."

Dad snorted at *devilish*. Before the waiter was even gone, he said, "This place. The liberties they take with basic English."

Usually I was all about that discussion—you know, descriptivism vs. prescriptivism, slang, the youth, inventing words, Shakespeare, language serving a purpose, clarity, rules—but not tonight. It felt stale. The waiter must have been over it too, because he just said, "And a crab cake for the lady."

"Oh!" said Mom, pleased. "I didn't see that on the menu!"

"It wasn't there," said the waiter. "We understand it's a special day."

"Honey," said Mom once the waiter left, and kissed Dad on the cheek. "Thank you." She loved crab cakes. Dad wasn't always great at showing it, but we all knew the truth: Mom was the love of his freaking life.

Would I ever order an off-the-menu crab cake for the love of my life?

Would anyone ever order an off-the-menu crab cake for *me*?

If earlier Crispin had flipped a rock to uncover my good mood, now all the maggots of jollity were wriggling away into the earth. We ate the appetizers. Nobody asked me about the dance. I didn't bring it up again. Dad had a moist, glistening piece of glazed bacon stuck in the corner of his lips. "Jerry finally got back to me about the court costs," he said, obviously just to Mom. She nodded along at his story. Crispin had returned to staring at his wineglass.

I finished my wine. Oops. I was the first. I could feel the alcohol. It was like my head wasn't totally attached to my body anymore.

The chunk of bacon was still hanging at the corner of Dad's mouth. I poked at Crispin. "My turn," I whispered. "Those three waiters."

"What? Oh. Maybe later."

I felt trapped. I couldn't even get out of the booth. The bacon chunk quivered, reflecting the candlelight, as Dad talked.

Why hadn't I gone with Andy to Tysons? We could have talked in the car. *Look,* I would have said, *I didn't know that Jiyoon was going to be so good.*

God, I'd kill right now to feel his mouth on my neck, his back beneath my hands. I probably never would again.

Dad's story ended. "How's your apartment, Crispin?" said Mom.

"Oh, fine."

"Is your furniture still working out?"

"It's all the same as I had at the house. So, yeah."

Silence. Dad had the twitchy look of someone who wanted to check his phone but knew he shouldn't. Mom closed her eyes. The appetizer plates were empty but still on the table, and I was worried Dad would start complaining about the service.

Keeping the mood up was Crispin's job, but he was running his finger along the bottom of his wineglass. I cast around for something to talk about. "Powderpuff practices have been surprising," I said. "I'm somehow, like, *good.*"

"That's wonderful," said Mom. But I'd told her that when I'd gotten home yesterday. Dad's head ostrich-swiveled in *Where is my waiter?* indignation.

"Soccer skills help, obviously, but it's also like I have all this built-up aggression I get to use, and I *like* plowing through the other team, which makes me worse at soccer, but . . ."

Mom nodded encouragingly, but she had heard literally the same thing yesterday. I trailed off. What was the point? I tipped back my empty wineglass and licked the rim. At other tables, people were talking and laughing. Why was it *my* family that had to be weird and antisocial and moody? What kind of family were we, anyway?

"Did you see what I forwarded you about Dale?" Dad suddenly asked Mom.

"I think your response was entirely valid," she told him. "I can't imagine why he's reacting that way."

He tented his fingers. "Agreed."

Silence reigned. I realized I was doing the ostrich look for the waiter myself.

"I'm hungry," I said.

"We're all hungry," said Mom.

Crispin was texting under the table. "Real social," I told him.

"Shut up, Bump."

"You shut up."

"Children," said Mom.

"Who are you even texting?" I said. "Thomas?"

"None of your business."

"I bet it's Thomas."

"I don't think I've heard you talk about Thomas," said Mom innocently.

"I bet you haven't," I said. "Thomas is Crispin's *colleague.*"

"And he's texting you on a Friday night?" said Mom.

Crispin was like a deer on high alert, tensed at the crack of a twig. I knew I needed to shut up like a minute ago. He slid his phone under his thigh. "It's a work thing."

"Oh, a work thing," I said.

"Jemima," said Crispin. He never calls me Jemima. "Stop."

"Stop what? Stop wishing this family would actually act like a family and be honest with each other for once?"

"Lower your voice," said Dad.

"Thomas is Crispin's colleague," I said, "and also—"

"Stop talking right now," said Crispin. "For once in your fucking life."

"Children!" said Mom.

"Also," I said, "his boyfriend."

Dad frowned. "Your company policy allows that?"

Crispin started to stand. I grabbed his arm. "You need to learn to keep your goddamned mouth shut," he told me as he shook me off. "No, Dad, it doesn't. And yes, I'm aware that's a problem." He slid out of the booth. "I'm sorry, Mom, but I can't do this. Happy birthday." He slipped down the stairs.

I was frozen. "It *is* a problem," said Dad. "He could get fired. Or worse."

Neither Mom nor I responded. A waiter swooped in for our appetizer plates and another swooped in with our entrées: Mom's salad and Dad's steak and my salmon and Crispin's ravioli, six sad squares of pasta.

"That sort of promiscuity," said Dad, "is beyond inappropriate."

"He left his phone," I said. It was facedown on the bench.

"Maybe he'll be back," said Mom.

"Doubt it," said Dad.

"I'll go find him," I said.

But he wasn't downstairs at the bar, and he wasn't out on the sidewalk, and I stalked the guys' restroom for like ten minutes and he didn't seem to be in there either. I went back to the table. Dad was on his phone, and Mom was leaning her head back, looking gray. Nobody spoke.

CHAPTER 20

Can I come over? I texted Jiyoon as soon as we got home. *It's an emergency.*

Sure. Get your Dorcas over here.

I got a Lyft. I wasn't about to ask for a ride. When I got to Jiyoon's apartment complex in Annandale, she was already sitting on the concrete stoop. "Hey," she said. "You look like . . ."

She hugged me.

"What do I look like?" I mumbled into her shoulder.

"Like you need a hug. You want to go over to the swing set?"

The complex had a playground at the back by the dumpsters. A wire fence enclosed patchy grass and a rusty swing set with two crumbling wooden swings. They rasped in protest when we sat down. "Is there anything more depressing than a rusty swing set?" I said.

"Sorry it's not up to your standards."

"Aren't they worried some kid's going to get tetanus?"

"Hence the disclaimer," said Jiyoon with a nod toward a sign: PLAY AT YOUR OWN RISK.

We got up some speed, swinging in sync. There was a half-moon, though it kept being obscured by billowing gray clouds. "Want to hear something amazingly shitty I just did?" I said.

"Of course."

But then we got out of sync and I had to wait. It felt like when a teacher's futzing around instead of handing out the tests, a reprieve right when you don't want one. Finally we were next to each other again, and I told her the story.

She was quiet. She whizzed past me a few times. "Wow," she said.

"Yeah."

In my life, I've said a lot of shit I've regretted saying. When words are constantly falling out of your mouth, you're going to lose a few extra. But I'd always thought that was better than regretting what *wasn't* said. I'd thought I was being brave. Authentic. True.

Now I was starting to think that maybe the bravest thing would be to shut up every once in a while.

"Sounds like he was pretty mad," said Jiyoon. We were out of sync again, and I felt a sudden wave of nausea. I tried to breathe deeply, but I burped a heaving burp and it brought up the taste of the salmon that I had eaten with my parents, quickly and quietly, after we realized that Crispin wasn't coming back. My mouth flooded with saliva. I scraped my toes against the dirt and jolted to a halt and tried to make my inner ears figure out I wasn't moving anymore.

"I didn't know you got sick on swings," said Jiyoon after I lifted my head from between my knees.

"Only now that I'm old." I felt pathetic. "Do you think it'll be okay?"

"I don't know."

I just wanted her to say yes. "You don't know?"

"Why do you think your dad was so upset?"

I shrugged. "Professionalism. Blah, blah. He's got a thing about it."

"You think that's all?"

I considered it, lacing my fingers through the chain. "Dad's known for ten years that Crispin's gay," I said, "but it's like he doesn't believe it. When a waitress walks away, he'll watch and then nod at Crispin like, *Look, an ass, let us appraise and appreciate.*"

Jiyoon shuddered. "Gross."

It had never struck me as particularly gross. It was a guy thing, I'd always thought, and I'd seen Dad do it all my life. I'd appraised and appreciated myself, to be honest, even if I didn't get a male-bonding nod. But it *was* gross, and it made me wonder what else hadn't registered, what else seemed fine but was rotten through and through.

"After Crispin left," I said, "Dad called him promiscuous. But doesn't that mean, like, sex with lots of people?"

"Ah," said Jiyoon.

She wasn't going to say anything I wouldn't say myself. Jiyoon was careful about family. Which was smart. You don't know how loyal you are to your family until an outsider criticizes them. "So that was probably homophobic," I said slowly. "Equating being gay with being promiscuous."

"Probably," said Jiyoon.

"Damn," I said. "Why is everything always more complicated than I think it is?"

Jiyoon laughed. "You don't have to take on the world, Jem. Don't worry about your dad. Just deal with yourself. Apologize to Crispin. Mean it. Then give him some time."

Naturally, I'd come to the opposite conclusion: that I'd wait around for Crispin to approach me, and meanwhile I'd mount a crusade into Dad's office to tell him how much implicit bias he had. "I'll think about it," I said.

"I'm freezing," she said. "I'm going to get a sweatshirt. Want one?"

"Let's go inside. I'm cold too."

"We can't. My dad's home." When her dad's out of town on a job, her little brother shares a bed with her mom, but when he's back, Min has to sleep on the couch. "I'll be right back."

I moseyed around on the swing, twisting back and forth slowly so I wouldn't trigger the motion sickness. She came out and tossed me a sweatshirt that smelled like her. "Have you got a new crush yet?" said Jiyoon.

"Ha," I said gloomily. "No. And every time I see Andy, he's got a different girl flirting with him. It's so annoying. They're all over him."

"He flirts back," Jiyoon pointed out.

"They're like ants crawling over a candy bar. I just don't

see why they're willing to trade in all their self-respect for the chance to get poked in the ribs by a hot guy."

"You know, Jem," said Jiyoon, "sometimes I can handle it, and sometimes I can't. And tonight I guess I can't. How are you getting home?"

"What?"

"I'm kicking you out. You calling a Lyft? Or trying to get a ride?"

"By *can't handle it*," I said slowly, "you mean *can't handle me*."

"Not you," said Jiyoon, chewing her bottom lip, "but yeah, the things you say. I'm still your best friend, okay? I just need a weekend off."

Dumbly, I requested a Lyft. Jiyoon waited with me, but I didn't trust myself to open my mouth. *I liked you better before you ran for chairman,* I wanted to say. I won't lie: I cried on the drive home.

Prudence rasped into my driveway at 9:08 on Sunday night. *Sunday nights are depressing,* Paul had texted. *Want to distract me with some good old-fashioned fear for my life?*

I did. I obviously did. This Sunday night was worse than most. Mom had dropped off Crispin's phone at his apartment, so I knew he had it, but he hadn't picked up any of my calls or responded to any of my texts. Neither had Jiyoon.

The nice thing about Paul was that you knew he wasn't going to open the conversation with something normal and tear-inducing like "How was your weekend?" Instead, as I buckled my seat belt, he said, "Let's talk about seafood."

"Oh my God," I said. "Let's."

"Who," said Paul, "what weirdo, first tried to pry open a lobster for food?"

"A very hungry weirdo."

"And who would have first tried crayfish? They look like giant bugs."

It was calming just to sit in Paul's car. Driving it was even better. We tooled around the Home Depot lot, and after thirty minutes I'd stalled only once. "You're doing well," he said.

"Really?" For some reason a lot seemed to hang in the balance. I stopped the car. "I'm doing okay?"

There was definitely a quaver in my voice. I guess Paul heard it too. "You're doing okay, Jemima."

I burst into tears. Shit. Nothing screams *not okay* like crying when someone tells you you're okay. "I'm just stressed," I said.

"Yeah, I saw Jiyoon last night," he said.

Right. The Date, capital *D*. No wonder she wanted a weekend off from being my best friend: she had something more important to do. Weekend off, my ass. Best friends don't take weekends off. "Oh," I said coolly. "You guys have fun?"

"Sure," said Paul. "But she told me, well—"

I cut him off. "She *told* you?" I was furious. I never would have told her about Crispin if I'd known the story would shoot on to Paul like a marble in a chute. "I can't believe her."

"Relax," he said.

As usual, that word had a paradoxical effect. I could basically feel my sphincter tighten. "I told her that stuff in utter confidence, and I can't believe—"

"She didn't talk about you, okay?" he said. "She said she has a lot going on. The election, the Quiz Team tournament, exams. And I figured it must be the same for you."

"Oh," I said.

"You want to do a figure eight around those light posts?" he said.

I nodded.

"If you're ready."

"I'm ready."

I did a beautiful figure eight. I went from zero to twenty with nary a jolt, and I didn't put in the clutch in the bend of a curve, and I didn't rev the engine when I moved from second to third. I stopped. "Nice," he said.

"Always the tone of surprise," I said, but my heart wasn't in it.

"I really like her," he said. "I want you to know that. I'm not just messing around."

"Great."

"She makes me think."

"Me too," I said. "Me too. Hey, listen. Would you take me home?"

Chawton School

CHAPTER 21

When I got to school on Monday, the Quiz Team crowd was clumped, backpacks on, in our usual spot near the front hall's columns. I managed to pull Jiyoon aside. "How was the rest of your weekend?" I said.

"Fine."

"The date?"

Jiyoon glanced back at the group like she was wondering what she was missing. Not much: Greg was trying to beat his record for speed-eating a cream-cheesed bagel while Jonah kept time and Ashby and Monique acted grossed out. Paul wasn't at school yet. "Fine."

"I want to talk about what happened Friday night," I said. I was trying to be as direct as possible. "I know I was slut-shaming."

"How'd you figure it out?" said Jiyoon. I shot her a look. I was worried I'd heard sarcasm, but she seemed neutral. Maybe even curious.

"Well," I said, "neither you nor Crispin was around to help, so I turned to my next best friend."

"BuzzFeed?"

"You know me." BuzzFeed, etc. I'd done some hardcore googling. "You can learn a lot about hating women on the internet."

Jiyoon laughed. "I hope you don't mean that the way it sounds."

"And"—I paused, because God, I hate apologizing, even when I totally know it's totally necessary—"I'm sorry. That you had to hear that. Again. I want you to know that I'm really trying to do better. It might not always seem like it, but I'm trying, Ji."

"I know," said Jiyoon. "That's why I'm your best friend."

"Even though I'm a crappy feminist?"

"We're all crappy feminists," said Jiyoon. "It's hard. That's the point. You have to think all the time. And then you realize you're doing something wrong and you have to change. Of course we're all crappy."

"But I'm the crappiest."

"Jemima Kincaid," said Jiyoon to the ceiling. "Always trying to be special."

I swiped at her arm with the back of my hand. She punched me back. Just two thirteen-year-old boys, messing around. It felt good.

Andy was in a sulk, which I knew the moment I stepped into our Triumvirate meeting after school on Tuesday. He was sprawled in a desk chair, his chin wedged onto his chest, and he only put away his phone when Gennifer was like, "I have places to *be*, and we have a lot to *do*, sooo . . ."

Election logistics were handled rapidly. The Candidate Open Forum would be held after school next Monday, and we'd need to make ballots for the vote at Jamboree. "Any volunteers for that?" said Gennifer.

"I suck at anything involving scissors," said Andy.

"Convenient," said Gennifer. "I suppose you don't know how a dishwasher works either. And you're bad at folding clothes, right?"

"Whoa," said Andy. "How did laundry get into this?"

"I'll add the ballots to the List of Shit Nobody Wants to Do, which"—she eyed us—"is *not* going to become my personal to-do list."

I wasn't trying to make life harder for Gennifer by not volunteering. I was just distracted by Andy's crankiness. I wished things could go back to the way they'd been before, when his knee would be nudging mine right now, when we'd have rides upon rides ahead of us, when it actually made sense to daydream—

"Hello!" snapped Gennifer. "Are you two even part of this Triumvirate anymore?"

Andy shoved back his chair. "I'll be back," he said curtly. "Don't wait for me."

As soon as he left the room, Gennifer said, "What's *with* him?"

"Who knows," I said. "Men."

"*Men,*" Gennifer repeated darkly.

We giggled a bit. "Are you ever confused by the signals guys send?" I said.

"Psh. Only all the time."

"How do you read them?"

"Are you asking for advice? First you have to tell me what guy."

"Nope," I said. "Nope. I knew you would try to turn this into something transactional."

She rolled her eyes. "Fine. Leap into character assassination. As you do."

"I'm just saying, I ask a vague question and you're immediately all about the gossip."

"You think you know me," Gennifer said scathingly. She flipped to a new binder tab with a thwack. "He said *Don't wait,* so I don't know why we're wasting time. For Powderpuff, we need to order the fan T-shirts for the fund-raiser, but first we need the budget numbers."

"I can get those from Mrs. Pfeiff."

"Excellent." Her voice was still chilly. I didn't know why I cared. It wasn't like Gennifer was my friend. Maybe we could have been friends in an alternate high school universe, where we weren't locked into place by the things we'd chosen on day one, not to mention the things we didn't get to choose—

"I should name myself sole empress," Gennifer was saying with disgust. "I do all the work anyway. All you do is daydream, and meanwhile Andy's taking the longest piss known to man. Jamboree's the weekend after next."

"I'll concentrate," I said. "What else do we need to do?"

"I talked to Paul."

"Paul?"

"About the Last Chance Dance. Remember? That little dance we're hosting?" She waved a red folder in front of my face. "He gave me the folder with everyone's picks. All encoded." She showed me the first page of the gibberish. It looked like a bunch of really first-rate passwords.

"Ms. Edison has the key, right?"

Gennifer blushed, which got my attention. "I want to be completely open and honest about this, because it's weird, but Ms. Edison didn't understand what I was telling her—you know how she is. . . ."

She met my eyes, and we came dangerously close to giggling.

"I said I'd give her Paul's data so *she* could figure out the matches with the key, but . . ."

Gennifer pulled a sheet of paper out of the back pocket of her binder.

"She emailed the key to me instead."

I squinched my eyes. "Wait. You have everyone's encoded selections—and also who corresponds to what code?"

I sounded incredulous for a reason: I just couldn't believe that Ms. Edison was such a dingbat. I mean, OMG. But Gennifer took my tone as impugning her moral fiber. "Jemima. You think I'm the *worst*. I would *never* look at it. Never. After I printed the key, I deleted her email, and I only ever had this one hard copy of the data from Paul, and I'm putting it all in this folder and leaving the whole thing with Ms. Edison right now."

I was barely listening. I was gazing at the red folder and thinking, *I* would look at it. Not the whole thing. But if I had that folder in a room by myself, I'd figure out who Andy put.

Was it better that I was willing to admit it? Or did that make it worse, that I had the capacity for self-awareness but was still such a crappy person?

Gennifer had stopped talking. She was gazing at the folder too. I wondered whose picks *she* would look at.

What if we made a pact, right here and now, to take one peek, decode one name's worth of picks, just as a treat, a little perk for organizing the whole dang thing—

Knock, knock.

We both jumped.

"Yo," said Mack, cracking the door. "Is this sensitive Triumvirate business?" He said it satirically, nipping his consonants, as if there couldn't be such a thing.

"Yes, go away," I said at the same time as Gennifer said, "No."

He came in. "Where's Andy?"

"No clue," said Gennifer. "He stomped out."

"Ol' McCool stomped out? Let me guess, he couldn't take another minute of you, Jemima? You were ball-busting as usual?"

"Oh, shut up," I muttered.

"I need to get home," Mack told Gennifer. "Like, now. I've got conditioning in Herndon at five. And my fucking brother's run off with the car keys."

"I can take you," said Gennifer. "I'm about ready. Just wait here a sec while I go to my locker. Jemima, we're done, right?"

"Yes," I said, packing up as fast as I could. I didn't want to be stuck alone with Mack. "I'll go stop by the business office."

"Great," said Gennifer, distracted. "See you."

Chawton School

CHAPTER 22

The business office was closed, so I had to go after school the next day. It took so long to get the budget numbers from Mrs. Pfeiff that I was late to Quiz Team practice. I swarmed in all flustered, carrying a bazillion bags, everything half falling out because I'd stopped by my locker in such a rush. "Oh my God," I said as I crashed through the door, "never be an accountant—"

They were in the middle of a question. Mr. Peabody didn't stop. "This man renounced interference in the 'domestic conflicts' of postcolonial African nations in the La Baule speech—"

I shut up. The team, gripping buzzers, didn't look at me. "His eventual successor, Jacques Chirac—"

Jonah buzzed in. "Mitterrand."

"Correct for power," said Mr. Peabody.

"Sorry," I said, sliding into the seat nearest the door. "I would have been on time, but I had a meeting with the business office."

"Of course," Ashby whispered, just loud enough for me to hear.

"What do you mean, *of course?*" I said.

"Guys, we're in the middle of a round," said Mr. Peabody.

"Of course you didn't make our last practice a priority," said Ashby.

"It's not like I would have *chosen* to have this dumb meeting," I said. "I'd so much rather be here with you guys—"

"In the middle of a question, in fact," said Mr. Peabody.

"Jem," said Jiyoon. "Just, like, can we get into this later?"

I shut my mouth. "Your bonuses, Team A," said Mr. Peabody with some relief. There were only two more questions, one about cyclic compounds and one about hockey goalies, neither of which, obviously, was my thing. I sat there expectantly, thinking we'd do another round, but everyone else set down their buzzers with the half-sad, half-relaxed feeling of no longer being pummeled by trivia questions. "Let's talk logistics for the tournament on Saturday," said Mr. Peabody. "It's at Thomas Jefferson High School. Let's meet in the front circle here at ten."

"I'll be sort of late," I said. "I, er, have Powderpuff that morning."

Ashby rolled her eyes. "Yes?" I said, because why be normal when you can be super aggressive, says my brain when it's tired. "Is there something you want to say to me, Ashby?"

Jiyoon sighed, I didn't know at who.

"Just that I'm questioning your priorities," said Ashby.

Mr. Peabody shuffled papers, looking awkward. He's so

conflict-averse that if you're wearing a non-dress-code sweat-shirt, he'll cover his eyes and shout, "LA-LA-LA, DIDN'T SEE THAT" until you tell him you've taken it off. "Guys," he said.

"You're captain," said Ashby. "And you can't even get to our last tournament on time?"

"Whoa!" said Greg. "Shots *fired!*"

"I'll get my own ride," I said, "and I'll be there long before actual play starts."

"I'm sure you will," said Ashby.

"It's an active war zone!" yelped Greg.

"God," I said. "Everyone. I'm doing the best I can, okay?" Was I going to cry again? It was all too much. "I'll see you," I managed, and I shot out the door.

My mom was supposed to pick me up at four-thirty, so I daw-dled at my locker. But when I checked my phone, I saw she'd texted: *Headache. Any chance you could get a ride?*

I stomped my foot. I actually did. Toddler-style. Who did she think I was, some queen everyone wanted to haul around in their litter?

No, I typed. *No chance. It's either you or I'm sleeping at school.*

I couldn't send it. I knew the scene at home: the spring sun besieging the windows, the shades holding firm, and Mom so insubstantial she'd barely make a bump under the covers. The air purifier in the corner would be sucking all the scents from the room, one of the many, many no-good nostrums for the aches that never stopped aching no matter how much ginger tea she drank, how much fish oil she took, how many needles were painstakingly slipped into her energy centers. She'd have her eye mask on. Her phone would be next to her with Do Not Disturb turned on for everyone but Dad and Crispin and me.

No problem, I wrote. *Feel better!*

I pushed send, but the inner glow of filial piety lasted only a few steps, which was how long it took me to remember I didn't have a ride. I stomped my foot again. Sure, I could get a Lyft, but—this was my interior monologue—what kind of unloved, unlicensed Chawton senior needed a Lyft to take her home from school?

I wheeled around the corner into the stairwell.

Jiyoon and Paul dropped each other like hot potatoes.

"Oh my God," said Jiyoon. "Hi."

I was blushing like a freaking milkmaid, but they were too. Now I knew what it meant to have an image seared onto your retinas. Seeing your best friend make out with your driving pal was clearly equivalent to, if not worse than, staring at the sun during a solar eclipse.

"Er," I said, "hi. Um, I'm just leaving! So, you know, carry on!"

"We're good," said Paul. They fell into step with me, and the three of us walked silently from the school. I know what you're thinking: *You,* Jemima Kincaid? *Silently?* 'Tis not an adverb that e'er applieth to thy fecund tongue! Well, it's true. Most uncomfortable situations only make me talk more, but apparently there's a level of awkwardness that can short-circuit even me.

We were almost to the parking lot. I was following them because I wasn't capable of the speech required to split away. "You got plans for tonight?" said Jiyoon, not meeting my eyes.

"Not really. Homework. What are you two up to?" Great-Aunt Dorcas was out interacting with the youth.

"It's Official Date Number Two!" said Paul. He did this nerdy fist pump, and Jiyoon rolled her eyes and beamed. They were so cute I could barely keep my eyes open to watch it. "We're going mini-golfing."

"Did you google 'clichéd date ideas' or something?" I asked him.

"Don't be mean," said Jiyoon.

"I'm not! Mini-golfing is a great idea!" In fact, I loved mini-golfing. It was like naming your baby Evelyn: so old-fashioned that it came full circle to cool. "I haven't been mini-golfing in forever," I said.

Jiyoon shot me a worried look, like she thought I might be angling to tag along, just as Paul said, "You should come. The car has four seats."

"But it's already got a third wheel, ha, ha," I said. "Nope. Not a chance. You two have fun!" *Great-Aunt Dorcas waves a wrinkled hand at the young sweethearts, recalling fondly the long-ago spring when her fancy too had lightly turned to thoughts of love!*

"If you say so," said Paul, shrugging. "But we like company."

I had seen the look on Jiyoon's face. "No, thanks," I said firmly. They got in a car that was definitely not Paul's old Civic. "Hey," I said through the window, "where's Prudence?"

"She's in the shop," he said. "Her clutch went out."

I watched them drive away.

Once, Crispin took me hiking. He wanted to scout out the Billy Goat Trail in Great Falls before he took a date there; he was trying to impress this guy who was outdoorsy. We stopped at a rock that hung over the Potomac, a hundred feet up, and we lay down and watched the clouds sail like ships overhead. From the path behind I heard a kid screaming with laughter as his mom chased him down. I had an overwhelming rush of feeling: a wave of tenderness for the world, the whole world and everyone in it, and the tenderness came with sadness, because it was fragile, this world. It could break.

That's what I felt as I watched Paul's car make the turn onto the road.

Well, that along with a load of loneliness and jealousy that could have curdled the freshest milk around.

I opened Lyft, and then I opened the messages app instead. I started a new text to Andy Monroe. *You still at school?*

The typing dots appeared, and disappeared, and appeared again. *Yeah, at baseball game, what's up?*

I marched over to the diamond. Andy and a few other senior guys, Hype Club types, were in the bleachers. "Is this almost over?" I asked him. "I need a ride home."

His eyes flicked toward the guys beside him. "It's the bottom of the sixth."

"No clue what that means," I said, "but I'm not in a position to be picky." I plopped down at his side. It surprised him. I caught him making a little shrug-grimace at Tyler. "Yeah," I said, "don't even pretend we're not—"

"Whoa!" he said. He cut me off fast. He must have sensed my recklessness. That's what it was. The sense of the ending had come hard and fast. Everything was about to change. "Whoa!" he said again. "You don't know what *bottom of the sixth* means?"

"No."

"Take a guess."

"No."

"Come on, Kincaid." He poked me in the ribs. "You've spent years showing us all up. How about you let us be the experts for once?"

"Enlighten me," I said. "Does *bottom of the sixth* mean I'll get a ride soon?"

"Let's start with the concept of innings," said Andy. "Every inning has a top and a bottom."

"Like a bikini," Mike said helpfully.

"*Now* I get it," I said. "Thanks for translating it into a language a woman can understand."

But I stopped being snarky when I realized they weren't hearing a word I said. They tripped over each other in their earnest explanations. The information was not presented to be learned. It was presented to be presented. They argued about how much higher the pitcher's mound used to be, or maybe how much lower, and I sat back and watched the game, guys in dirt-smeared, close-fitting white trousers. Every once in a while Andy pointed out a play to me, and I said, "Wow. Cool."

After the game was over—high school games, I was informed, have only seven innings—we tromped to the parking lot. I hopped into Andy's Jeep without an invitation. He'd been talking about the Nationals with the guys and he just sort of continued the conversation all the way to my house. The whole situation made me remember something my mom had said about her pain meds. She said they made her feel like she'd been trekking along some jagged, wearisome terrain when suddenly she was yanked up by a little chain attached to her back, and she'd rise into the sky and fly over the flint, the rocks. Before, I never got why she didn't like to take those pain meds. That was because I'd always focused on the flying part. But now I remembered there was also a chain.

When he reached for me in my driveway, which I knew he would, I said, "Wait." He stiffened, but I said, "My mom's asleep and my dad's not home. You want to come in?"

I pointed him up the stairs and went down the first-floor hallway to the master bedroom, where Mom sleeps. (There's a bed in Dad's study that's supposedly for guests, but usually for him.) Mom liked me to check in with her when I got home. I opened the door. Gray light, the weird odorlessness. She was flat on her back, hands crossed gently over her chest. She had her satin eye mask on, and without moving a thing but her lips she murmured, "That you, honey?"

"It's me," I breathed.

"I'm sorry I couldn't—"

"Go back to sleep, Mom. Feel better."

I crept out. Andy was frozen halfway up the staircase. I led him to my bedroom, which was above the kitchen, thankfully nowhere near Mom's room. We began to kiss.

No, not kissing. We slammed our faces into each other. That's how I'd put it. We were going for quantity over quality; force, not accuracy. He slid his hands up my back, and before I knew it, my shirt was on the floor. His was too. None of my bras were sexy—this one was practical and beige—but Andy didn't care, not as long as it provided a convenient display case for my boobs. He said, "Damn. Damn, Kincaid."

He slid a hand down a cup and leaned in to kiss my neck. The feeling was intense. It was like falling asleep in class, when you feel your eyes rolling back, your eyelids thick and heavy. He unhooked my bra. My breasts flopped out, and he nabbed one like a shortstop with a grounder. (See? I'd learned something.) Stumbling, I pulled the Andy-Jemima unit onto the bed.

"Wait a sec," he said. He groped around in his pocket and dumped some stuff onto the bedside table, keys and shit. He unlocked his phone. "Seriously?" I said. "You're checking your phone? *Now?*"

He chuckled. "Chill, Kincaid. Putting on some tunes." Fine, but the break was weird. It was like when the lights come up for intermission at an emotional play and you don't want to look anyone in the face. I felt suddenly self-conscious, my stomach rolling over my waistband, my boobs lolling all over the place. I thought, I don't owe him anything. I can stop whenever I want. I could make him go.

But I wanted this. An acoustic playlist twanged on. He pulled me on top of him to straddle him. I could feel a protuberance— *the* protuberance, egad—under my crotch. I inadvertently slipped forward, and he groaned, and I shifted back and he put his hands on my bare back and moved me back and forth. His eyes were closed, his forehead furrowed, a groan escaping every few breaths. I liked it too. He undid his fly. His pants came down a few inches. My hand was at his hip, and, curious, I moved it to the warm, taut hollow next to his hip bone.

He tipped his head back onto the pillow. The segment scheduled for kissing was over, I guessed. I drifted my hand center, downward, under the elastic of his boxers—oh! Crap. I'd bumped it. I'd bumped it with the back of my hand. Which probably meant I needed to stop pretending it wasn't there. I rotated my hand and tentatively wrapped my fingers around it.

Now what?

Based on vulgar gestures learned on the middle school field-trip bus, I knew there was a sliding motion. But how fast? How tight? Why hadn't I googled this? What kind of negligent digital native *was* I?

Andy squirmed upright, and I jerked my hand away before I accidentally wounded him or something. I knew guys were sensitive down there. Once, I'd basically immobilized Crispin with a four-square ball. Andy was wriggling his pants down. So much for a slow, erotic disrobing: I saw a flash of gray boxer briefs, but they came down with the pants, and then, suddenly, oh God, there it was, the whole hairy, fearsome, ridiculous apparatus. Balls and all. Andy swung his legs to the floor and sat on the bed as if—pardon me, there is no other comparison—he were taking a dump. We were kissing again, but I could totally imagine my face, like in a Lichtenstein painting where the hero kisses his lady love just as she realizes the bomb's about to go off. That's what I looked like. Lips attached, but eyes wide and skittering to take a look at the imminent danger.

Slowly, but not subtly, he began to push my head down. I found myself kissing his neck, and his shoulders, and his . . . his vestigial boobs, I guess you could call them. The push downward might have bothered me if I hadn't been so relieved to be off the hook for taking the initiative. It was like a group project with a bossy partner, when you let their annoyingness go because they're doing all the hard parts. Or at least I assume that's what happens. I'm always the bossy one.

All the while I was thinking these things, my head was being nudged toward the pale, hairless thing that protruded from the thicket of dark hair, like a pink grain silo that, improbably, had sprung from the wilderness.

Can I talk about my spectrum idea again? Jemima Kincaid's Spectrum of Sex (trademark pending)? I see it like a rainbow. You can point at a particular wavelength and say it's blue, but how can you tell when blue shifts to violet? You can't. It's continuous. There are no bands.

That's how I'd teach sex ed. I wouldn't even call it sex. Stuff you want to do with someone you like. Or someone you don't like, not all the time, not even most of the time. Andy was groaning. I hadn't googled this skill either, but it wasn't hard. I seemed to be rather proficient, in fact, based on those noises. "Oh baby," he kept crooning in this stupid low voice. Really? I think I speak for all teenage girls when I say a baby is the last thing we want to think about while doing anything at all sexual.

Instead, as I gave Andy what is known in the vernacular as (awkward cough) a blow job, I thought about the spectrum. I thought of the markers we place on sex, the language we use. *First base, second base. Making out* vs. *hooking up. How far would you go?* and *She's a slut.* But I'd tell girls: Look, this is holding hands, and look, this is their parts inside you, and look, look at the vast, unmarked space between. There are no divisions. There's no border you cross between virgin and deflowered, Madonna and whore. The lines you set are in your own mind. The borders you cross, you mark yourself.

Chawton School

CHAPTER 23

"*Carpe diem,*" Mrs. Burke intoned. "'Seize the day.' Perhaps the most quoted Latin phrase, and no doubt the most inanely quoted. Used in its contemporary sense to affirm life, to encourage action, whereas in its odic context, it's a memento mori." She peered at us over her purple glasses. "Miss Kincaid, define *memento mori.*"

"A reminder of death."

"For, as Horace's line reads"—as usual, Mrs. Burke didn't bother to acknowledge the correct answer—"*carpe diem, quam minimum credula postero.* Miss Kim, translate."

"'Seize the day, trusting as little as possible in tomorrow.'"

"Discuss, class. What does that mean?"

"Do it now," said Mack, "because you never know when things are gonna go to sh—to crap."

Mrs. Burke pursed her lips and surveyed us. She wore a

shade of purple lipstick so retro I could imagine it on one of Gennifer's edgier friends.

"I give you my full attention," she said frostily, "and I expect *your* full attention."

That had to be pointed at me. I was thirty percent here, max. "Sorry," I said. "I'll—"

"Don't be so hasty to shoulder the blame for others, Miss Kincaid," said Mrs. Burke.

What?

Jiyoon seemed as calm and focused as ever, and Mack, for once, was thumbing industriously through a Latin dictionary. But there were distinct traces of an upheaval. Victoria, Tiam, and Lacey were shoving phones back into their pockets. Larchmont and Lola straightened, as if they'd been leaning over those same phones.

"Since one of the landmark odes of world literature holds so little interest for you," said Mrs. Burke, "put away all materials besides a sheet of paper and a pen."

She laboriously moved to the projector—she was the only teacher in the building who had held on to the ancient overhead projectors, with transparencies and a lightbulb—and put up the Latin ode. "Number your paper one through five," she said. "Question one. In what Aeolic meter is this poem constructed?"

You know what else tipped me off that there was something going on? That nobody seemed to care. That Mrs. Burke gave us an evil, impossible pop quiz, and they were all so distracted, so disturbed, that they sat there and took it.

* * *

Once I'd noticed the hum of agitation and excitement, it was everywhere. It felt like the afternoon before a sure-thing blizzard, when it hasn't started snowing yet but everyone knows it's going to happen. I walked past a huddle of girls, and I saw Julianna Johnson crying in the center.

Uh-oh. I checked my own phone. It was blank, but as I held it, texts floated in from Gennifer.

I assume you've seen

We need to triage

Meet in Edison's at lunch.

Seen? I responded.

Then Gennifer:

Oh god

I waited. I was in calc now, and the warning bell sounded. Sixty seconds before Mr. Ulrich would collect our phones. He had a basket where we put them when the bell rang.

A screenshot came in from Gennifer. And another. And another.

I swiped through. My mouth fell open.

Abbott, Rebekah:
Martin Chowder
Peter Li
Andy Monroe

Andrews, Lily:
Tyler Donner
Johnny Threep

Avi, Robert:
Jasmin Egbert
Gennifer Grier
Larchmont Kenney
Heather McAuliffe

Screenshots piled in. One. After. Another.

The bell rang. Mr. Ulrich pounced, shoving the basket in my face. "Exit the phone world and enter the real world!"

"It's—I can't—it's an emergency—"

"In an emergency, your parents would contact the main office." He waggled the basket.

"Mr. Ulrich . . ." I couldn't rip my eyes from my phone. They were Last Chance Dance picks. The secret crushes of the senior class. They'd been hacked, and they'd been posted.

Oh my God. How could this have happened? Who did this? Everyone would hate us. They'd think it was our fault.

And everyone would know my only pick was Andy.

Andy would know my only pick was Andy.

"Jemima!" barked Mr. Ulrich. *"Now!"*

The class was looking at me. Not sympathetically. Mr. Ulrich carried the basket of phones to his desk. I stared at it. We all stared at it. It was like he had a basket of bombs. "Parametric curves in the plane!" he said, clapping his hands vigorously. "Shall we?"

I found my homework. My scrawled graphs, the problems I'd worked, like artifacts from another world.

Why had I put only *one*?

Paul's voice echoed. *Only a moron would put information like that into a website.*

Calc class lasted approximately a decade, nine years of which were spent dreading my lunch meeting with Gennifer and the guy everyone now knew I had a weird obsessive monogamous thing for. At the bell, I was first out of my seat. I rooted through the basket to find my phone and speed-walked down the hall-way, avoiding all eye contact. My plan was to find a stairwell where I could text Paul (*How did this happen?*) and Jiyoon (*What should I do?*) and hide from the world as long as possible, but Gennifer caught me. "Jemima!" she called. "Tell Ms. Edison we need her room, okay? I'll be right there."

I was stuck. Ms. Edison was alone at her desk. "A last-minute meeting?" she said, standing and gathering her papers. "Of course, no problem. Anything wrong?"

"Nope, nope, not at all."

"You look a little frazzled, Jemima."

"Physics test later!" I squeaked.

"Take a deep breath," Ms. Edison advised.

"Oh, right. Good idea."

"That always calms me down. Just seems to make my prob-lems go away!"

I wanted *her* problems. "Nothing like a deep breath!" I said wildly. "Air in the lungs! Mm-*hmm*!"

"Don't be too hard on yourself," she said, edging to the door. "You're a second-semester senior!"

Yes, I thought, that's exactly what's caused this pile of steaming shit into which I have trodden.

"None of this *really* matters, right?" said Ms. Edison.

It was one of those moments when it becomes utterly clear that every adult, even a youngish one, has forgotten what it was like to be a teenager. Maybe they don't forget the woes, but they forget how important they are. They get all, *This too shall pass. This will seem trivial when you're a real person like me,* and all the while they're thinking, This doesn't really matter.

But it matters.

I'm telling you, it matters.

Ms. Edison left, and a second later Gennifer came in, her lips drawn. *She* got it. "Well," she said, her voice clipped, "it's a crisis. Emmie and Bryan have already broken up, and I think Julianna's going to dump Kyle during lunch. And then there's Jasmin, she's *distraught,* but did she really think the slut-shamey culture here was going to let her get away with putting fifteen guys? And—"

"Wait, wait, rewind, rewind," I said.

Gennifer swung down her backpack and looked at me impatiently. "Yes?"

"Why are Emmie and Bryan breaking up? They've been together since freshman year."

"Because Emmie put Zack. Bryan's best friend. Have you even looked at the lists?"

"I haven't had a chance," I said, unlocking my phone. "Mr. Ulrich—"

"Don't bother." She wrapped her thin, cool fingers around my wrist and dragged my phone out of my face. "I've already told you the highlights, and you'll have plenty of time to analyze the details later. We both will, given that we'll be ostracized for the rest of our high school careers."

For someone who had built a whole social life around avoiding ostracism, Gennifer had an odd serenity. Or was it odd? Maybe this was the natural serenity of the worst-case scenario, the one that you always thought might happen just because it was so bad. It was the serenity of seeing an iceberg on the *Titanic*. The serenity of being reaped in *The Hunger Games*.

"Let's discuss our plan." Gennifer arranged the pleats of her skirt and opened her Triumvirate binder. Throw a disaster at her, she'll throw an agenda back at you. "Our class morale is in shreds. As is the reputation of our Triumvirate, but that's a lost cause. Should we even *have* prom?"

"Wait," I said, taking up my phone again. I knew what it'd look like (*Kincaid, Jemima: Andy Monroe*) but I wanted to see it.

"We need to be leaders," said Gennifer. "We can't get hung up in the nasty details." She made a swipe for my phone.

"Just because you've already *looked* at the nasty details!" I snapped, pulling the phone out of her reach. "I haven't even seen my own name!"

"Weston Burgman, Tyler Donner, Bobby Flynn, Greg Hoffman, Lucas Yin," recited Gennifer.

"That's not who I put."

"That's who put you."

"What—wait—Tyler? But—Weston?" I shook my head to refocus myself. "I meant my own listing." (Wait, I thought again. Five guys put me? Including Weston Burgman, the captain of the basketball team? Was this some twisted joke?) "I meant who I put."

"You didn't hear?" said Gennifer. "God, Jemima. You truly have no idea how bad this is, do you?"

I knew it was really bad, and I knew Gennifer thought it was really bad, but I could also tell that the tiniest bit of her was enjoying it.

"We," she pronounced, "were left off."

"Left off? Who's we?"

"You. Me. Andy. The Triumvirate."

"No way," I said.

Gennifer opened up her own phone and scrolled through the list to *Greenhorn, Mitchell.*

"It's blank for him," she said. "Because he didn't submit the form. But our names aren't even there."

Andy walked in while I was still gaping at Gennifer. I gave him a giant grin—he didn't know who I'd put! No one knew!—before I realized that joyful relief was pretty much the opposite of the feeling I needed to project right now. "Welcome to ground zero," said Gennifer.

Andy sat down heavily. "We need to figure out who did this."

"Maybe Paul can trace who infiltrated the website," I said.

"Do you guys really think that's what's important right now?" said Gennifer. "We need to focus on healing wounds. Repairing morale. Not finding a culprit."

"If we don't find a culprit, we're going to get all the blame ourselves," said Andy. "Of course, maybe one of us deserves the blame."

I nodded. I'd been thinking the same thing. *Anything can be hacked,* Paul had told me. *Anything can be leaked.* We'd encouraged everyone to trust the system, but we hadn't known ourselves how the system worked.

"Start a suspect list," Andy told Gennifer.

She snapped shut the binder. "I'm not your secretary."

"Come on, you have paper right in front of you—"

She stood. "I have friends to take care of. Very upset friends. You can waste your time with detective work, but you're not wasting mine." She left the room, giving the door a tidy slam behind her.

"Whew," said Andy. "Spicy."

"Maybe it was her," I said. "That was kind of a suspicious reaction. Maybe she wanted to stir up drama." I felt instantly guilty. Gennifer was more devoted to our class than anyone. "I don't actually think it was her," I quickly added.

Andy met my eyes. My face went hot. The last time we'd been alone together, there'd been significantly less clothing involved. "Me neither," he said. "But still. It's weird that we aren't on it."

"Seriously."

"I wonder what everyone's saying," he said. "I haven't talked much yet with the hoi polloi—"

"Hoi polloi," I said automatically.

"That's what I said."

"No, you said 'the hoi polloi.' But in ancient Greek hoi means 'the.' So you have to say—"

Andy shoved his chair back. "Nope. Nope. Not doing this, Kincaid."

"Not doing what?" I knew that had been obnoxious, but, well, that was me: I was obnoxious. Andy knew that by now. "Now you won't say it wrong in a college seminar."

"You think you're so great," said Andy, and not in a nice way. Not in a teasing way.

"I do not."

"You think you're too good for me. Too good for anyone."

"Are you fucking kidding me?" This was too much. "*You? You're* saying that? I gave you—you're the one I've been—and you won't even be seen in public with me!"

Andy's cheeks went pink. "Says the girl who only talks to me when she wants a ride, and only wants rides when nobody's around. You wouldn't be seen at Tysons with me. You ignore me at Powderpuff, and you won't even make eye contact in the hallway. *I'm* not the one who wanted to keep our shit a secret."

My jaw dropped.

"I get it, Kincaid." He shook his head. "I get it. This was all a setup, right? You get us to go with the Last Chance idea, get everyone to submit their crushes to the website—and then you publish the whole fucking thing."

I couldn't believe this was happening.

"It's brilliant. I'll give you that. But then again, the revenge scheme of Jemima Kincaid *would* be brilliant."

"The revenge scheme?"

"We all know you hate us. So you set off a bomb in our class. Nothing's going to be the same. Powderpuff, prom, Jamboree. Graduation. Fuck, our reunions. Our memories of high school. You've destroyed us. And you're loving every second of it."

Chawton School

CHAPTER 24

I had two more classes and I don't know how I got through them. My mom wasn't picking me up until an hour after school let out, but I couldn't find Jiyoon anywhere. I spent the rest of the hour hiding in Ms. Edison's room, not caring that I was doing all my physics problems wrong. As soon as I finally got home and closed the door to my bedroom, I called Jiyoon.

I got voice mail. I hung up and flopped back on my bed and let tears leak out. But she texted me almost immediately: *I'm bowling with Paul but you doing okay?*

I know you're in the middle of Official Date #3 and I kind of hate myself for asking but can we talk for five min?

Walking outside just a sec

My phone rang. "The employees saw me duck out," she said. "They probably think I'm trying to steal the bowling shoes."

"But they're holding your regular shoes as collateral."

"But my regular shoes were Crocs."

"No. No. Jiyoon Kim. Tell me you didn't wear your tie-dyed Crocs on a third date."

"Um."

"Why, Jiyoon? Why?"

"I really want to continue defending my footwear, but I left Paul alone to safeguard our lane from eighteen fifth graders at a birthday party, so maybe tell me what you're calling about?"

"Right. Yeah." I'd been smiling at her Crocs ridiculousness, but already I could feel a sob rising in my chest. "You must have heard the basics."

"Yeah."

"Everyone thinks it was me. Andy, and everyone else."

"Yeah. I heard that too."

"From who?"

"Like . . . the usual rumor mills. Online, mostly. Private accounts, so I'm getting all these notifications that I've been tagged and then can't see what they're saying. But every once in a while it's someone I follow. I can get the gist."

"But it's about me?"

"Well. And me. Because I'm your best friend, so I must be involved too, right? They're saying I should quit the chairman campaign. Resign my candidacy."

"I'm so sorry," I whispered. I hadn't thought it could get any worse.

"Unless you actually did the leak, you don't have to be sorry," Jiyoon said shortly. "I want to know who did it. Because right now it feels like it was meant to sabotage my campaign, but I know it was probably just some idiot trying to start a lot of drama."

"What does Paul think?"

"Oh, he's all, 'What do people expect for posting their secrets on the internet?' Which is kind of annoying, to be honest. I changed the subject."

"I know you should get back inside."

"No, you're good. What?"

"Just . . ." I rolled toward the wall. Quietly, so quietly that I wasn't sure Jiyoon would be able to hear, I said, "Why does everyone think it's me?"

"Because you weren't on the list."

"But neither were Andy and Gennifer."

"But—I'm not saying I endorse this, obviously—if they had to pick one of the three of you, who are they going to pick? You. You argue a lot, you rock the RBF. . . ."

"I *cultivate* the RBF," I said, and Jiyoon laughed. "So," I said, "if a girl looks anything other than one hundred percent decorative at all times, she's a criminal?"

"The patriarchy is definitely a factor," said Jiyoon. "But it's also—I don't know how to say this—everyone kind of thinks you hate Chawton."

"I've been going to Chawton since kindergarten!" The tears were rolling, and I didn't know whether it was because the rest of the school thought wrong or right. Did I hate Chawton? No. Yes. "I've been working my ass off for Chawton all year."

"Everyone kind of thinks you hate *them*."

"That's because they hate me!"

"You always say that."

They had hated me in kindergarten, when I'd read books on movie day. In middle school, when they'd called me the Jeminist. In high school, when they'd rolled their eyes every time I raised my hand. I'd found my niche of friends, and nobody else wanted me to be in their group or on their team or—

Wait, I thought. I was on Triumvirate. I was the Tigers' running back. Five guys—five fairly mainstream guys—had put me as Last Chance Dance picks.

Andy had thought *I* was the one who didn't want to be seen in public with *him*.

"Damn it," I said. "They don't hate me, do they?"

"Well, now they might," said Jiyoon, giggling. I had to laugh too. It was all so messed up. All along I'd had it, the popularity I'd pretended not to want. It was a different kind of popularity—I wasn't Gennifer Grier, I wasn't Andy Monroe—but I'd been known, respected. Maybe even liked.

In the past.

"Don't worry about your campaign," I told Jiyoon. "I'll figure something out. Right now you have one goal. Beat Paul in bowling. Do me proud."

"You? Aren't you the one who needs bumpers to break into the three digits?"

"Be that as it may," I said with dignity, "you'd better win."

★　★　★

– 217 –

My phone woke me with "Build Me Up, Buttercup" on Saturday morning, but it might as well have been the Dies Irae for how much I wanted to get out of bed. But I pulled on Powderpuff practice gear and packed fresh clothes for the Quiz Team tournament. Over breakfast, I wrote out a list of the food I'd need for the post-tournament gour'mores—damn it, Greg's stupid word was *not* catching on—*s'mores* party. I didn't know how I'd get to the grocery store, but instead of prepping for the party earlier, I'd spent my time trying to think of a valid excuse to cancel it. The only idea I'd had was arson.

Mom dropped me off at school and said she'd pick me up in two hours to run me over to TJ, the school hosting the tournament. I channeled innocence and walked springily over to the seniors who'd already gathered on the field. "Hey," I said.

Nobody said anything back.

Cool.

"Team Tiger!" Andy called. "Find a partner, grab a ball, warm up your arm!"

I glanced around. Everyone had paired up suspiciously fast. "Can we do a group of three?" I asked Ruth and Melanie.

"Um," said Melanie, "I guess."

I stopped trying to talk to people. At every water break, I heard more chatter about the leak. Girls who'd listed a lot of guys were called slutty, but nobody talked about the guys who'd listed a lot of girls. Girls who'd listed only one guy were obsessive and creepy and card-carrying members of Future Cat Ladies of America, whereas a guy who'd listed one girl was romantic and sweet. Girls who hadn't listed anyone were stuck up;

guys who hadn't were playing hard to get. If you're wondering why I'm using exclusively hetero language, that's because exclusively hetero kids participated. The LGBTQ kids—the ones who were out, anyway—none of them listed anyone at all. Even Zachary hadn't ended up submitting any picks. It was like they knew it wasn't for them.

I wished I'd thought of that ahead of time. I wished I'd thought it was a problem.

Andy tugged Christina's ponytail and draped Haley's sweatshirt over the crossbar and threw back his head in laughter with Jasmin, but he ignored me.

I had a new theory.

What if it was *him*?

The leak was tanking Jiyoon's candidacy. Mack suddenly had hope again. Andy had immediately accused me, which he could have done to cast secondhand suspicion on Jiyoon. It was the transitive property of mortal enemydom, biting us in the ass yet again.

I didn't know *how* he'd done it. But that didn't mean he hadn't.

After practice, unlacing my cleats on the bleachers, I heard Jasmin and Lacey and Ruth talking. They were right behind me. I think they wanted me to hear.

"Let's be honest," said Lacey, who was fond of saying mean things in the name of honesty. "We all know who had access. *Her.*"

I could feel their glares on my back. Naturally, I couldn't help turning around. "You have something to say to me?"

Jasmin rolled her eyes, and Ruth looked pointedly away, but

Lacey sighed. "If *I* don't say it, who will? Yeah, Jemima. We think it was you. Who else could it have been?"

"Literally *anyone*," I said. "That's who else. It was a website. Anyone could have hacked it. Or hired someone to hack it."

Lacey fluttered a hand through the air. "The thing is, it doesn't matter who it was."

Typical. You prove someone's point wrong; they claim it was an irrelevant point.

"Because you're the one who forced us into this shitty idea."

"*Forced* you? I don't recall holding you at knifepoint while you typed—"

"It's your fault," said Lacey. "And nothing you say will change my mind about that."

Gennifer hadn't exactly ignored me during practice, but she'd given me a wide berth. She snagged me on my way to the locker room, where I was going to take a pro forma shower before Mom picked me up, and dragged me over to Andy. "What?" he said testily, like we'd interrupted some sacred meditation ritual rather than his pinny sorting.

"Ms. Edison emailed me," said Gennifer. "The teachers know about the leak. She thinks we should still have prom, just scrap the Last Chance theme. Call it Night at Monte Carlo, since we already have the casino decor."

"Fine," said Andy.

"And," said Gennifer, "*I* think we should decide how to apologize to the class."

"I'm not apologizing for something I didn't do," said Andy.

"That's exactly what we need to do," said Gennifer. "We didn't take security seriously enough. We didn't protect the data. So we need to apologize."

"That's stupid," said Andy. "It's one person's fault. The person who leaked it. Let's focus on proving who it was, and then *she* can apologize."

"While, in general, I appreciate the use of a default feminine pronoun," I said, enraged but trying not to show it, "I can't say I appreciate the implications of *that* statement—"

"Kincaid, cut your shit," said Andy.

"*You* cut *your* shit, Andy," said Gennifer before I could respond. "That rumor's bull. It wasn't Jemima. She's a bitch but she's honorable."

Whoa. I was not expecting backup from those quarters.

I did, however, note the possible tombstone inscription. *Here Lies Jemima Kincaid, Honorable Bitch.*

"She cares about Chawton as much as anyone," said Gennifer. "So don't even, Andy."

He raised his eyebrows in contempt, but he didn't say anything. God, he was an asshole under stress. Or maybe just an asshole.

"Well," I said. "The Right Honorable Bitch Jemima Kincaid thanks you, Gennifer."

I pronounced her name the proper way, with a *J* sound. It was a first. She smiled a little and said, "You're welcome."

We were quiet. Gennifer tightened her ponytail. I glanced at the time. Mom would be here in ten minutes, but as long as I managed to get my hair wet, people would assume I was clean, right?

"I'm not apologizing," said Andy.

"Let's just focus on making Jamboree happen," Genni-fer said wearily. "Because if we don't pull off the election and the Powderpuff game and some semblance of a prom, I don't know how we're going to walk across that graduation stage next weekend."

CHAPTER 25

I slid into my seat and grabbed my buzzer just as the moderator said, "Any questions before we begin?" Ashby's eyes skipped away from me like I wasn't even worthy of a glance, but Jiyoon smiled and mouthed hello.

We ended up with an even record in the morning's round-robin tournament, which gave us a middling seed for the afternoon's double elimination. The TJ Quiz Team was selling pizza as a fund-raiser, and we took our slices to a big table. "I'll take it upon myself to clear the air," said Greg, turning to me with an affect of huge largesse. "Did you do it?"

I'd just taken a bite. The cheese was too hot and I choked on it. Everyone waited while I coughed. "No," I finally managed.

"Convincing," said Ashby.

"You're a junior," I said. "Why do you even care?"

Jiyoon kicked me. Aggression, clearly, was not the right

move. "I mean," I said, going for conciliatory, "obviously you have a lot of friends who got burned. I get it. I do too."

"It's not that bad for the group of us," said Zachary. "I didn't submit, and Greg put everyone."

"Not everyone," said Greg. "I have standards."

"*Low* standards," said half the team in unison.

"And you know what happened to me," said Monique.

I'd tried to scroll through the data, but it had made me sick to my stomach. "No, what?"

"I put Rohan and he put me!" she said. "We matched!"

"Something good came out of this?" I said.

"He texted me minutes after the leak like, *Might as well go to prom together, that cool with you?*"

"Romantic," said Jiyoon.

"Sorry," said Monique, rolling her eyes at Jiyoon. "Not every guy can be as enlightened as yours."

"That's true," said Paul with a smirk.

As we followed the rest of the team to the first game of the afternoon, I whispered to Jiyoon, "They don't think I did it, right?"

"Did they sound like it?"

"No?"

"Of course not," she said. "They're your friends."

It helped to hear it. The weird thing about being vigorously suspected was that you started to think, Maybe I did do it. Or you started to think, Maybe I'm the kind of person who would do it. I could almost believe the story they were telling, even though the story was about me.

We lost the first game, won the second, and lost the third. That was that. Our last Quiz Team match. Zachary set down his buzzer carefully, as if placing it in its final resting place. "The end," he said.

"Farewell, O beloved buzzer!" said Greg. He gave his a kiss.

"Ew!" said Monique. "You're basically licking everyone's sweaty hands!"

Naturally, Greg responded by actually licking the buzzer. I stood. I hadn't played badly but I hadn't played well. There's a zone of preternatural anticipation you can get into with any game that requires speed, when you know where the ball's going before it gets there, when your brain makes connections you didn't know you'd seen. I'd been in that zone before with Quiz Team, but I hadn't been there that day.

I don't know what about a master's in education qualifies you to drive a short bus packed with teenagers on the Capital Beltway, but Chawton teachers do it all the time. Mr. Peabody got us back to school, and I finagled a ride home from Jonah. The house was silent. I'd made the grocery list, but how was I going to get to the grocery store? Everyone was coming over in two hours, and ten bucks said my parents were where they usually were at five-thirty p.m. on a Saturday: Mom in bed, Dad at the office.

Hey.

Hey.

The kitchen island was piled with chips, salsa, napkins, skewers, two-liters, and all the ingredients for the gour'mores: chocolate graham crackers, Nutella, Hershey's bars, peanut butter . . . everything on my list. Then I saw the list itself, marked over with neat check marks. I could see my mom, slim and stalwart behind the cart, scrutinizing the shelves for ginger snaps. Finding them. Wrapping the list around the cart's handle to make the check mark.

"Hi," said someone behind me. Crispin was leaning against the doorjamb. "How was the tournament?"

"You're here," I said. Stupidly.

"So I am. Did you kick ass?"

"We got ninth."

"Nice."

"Out of fifteen."

"Ouch."

I was quiet. He was quiet. "I don't know," I said, "why I make more mistakes than anyone else."

"You missed that many questions?"

"You know what I'm talking about."

"I'll give you this," he said. "For someone related to me, you are shockingly dumb."

Unless I was imagining it, there was a quirk to his mouth. "You have no idea," I said.

"Thomas and I broke up."

I put my hand to my mouth. "Oh my God. It's my fault. I'm sorry."

"You hastened the demise, but it's not your fault. Dad was right. We can't sneak around at work. Thomas might look for a new job next year anyway, and if so, well, then we'll see."

"But you really liked him."

"Yeah."

"What if he was your soul mate?"

"The universe is messed up if you get only one shot at your soul mate. If we're meant to be together, we won't be foiled by obeying a little company policy."

"For someone related to me," I said, shaking my head, "you are shockingly mature."

"Come here." He opened his arms and I collapsed into them. He hugged me the way he always did, lifting me off the floor and rattling me like maybe he could get a quarter to fall out if he tried hard enough. "I should probably hate you," he said. "But I'm a saint, so we're cool."

Tears sprang into my eyes. The grace of Crispin. It was a pretty sweet deal I'd gotten, I'll tell you. To be randomly allotted one brother, and to have that brother be Crispin? It was enough to make me believe that the universe wasn't messed up after all.

Crispin had come over to help me set up for the party: payback, he said. We made fancy recipe cards for each variety of gour'mores. (The name was definitely, tragically, here to stay.) *Cookies 'n' Cream Gour'mores. Nutella-Banana Gour'mores.*

Ginger-Toffee Gour'mores—with melted caramel instead of chocolate. Crispin and I both have the handwriting of an uncoordinated second grader, so the cards looked pretty shittastic. We hauled everything down to the basement and set up the food table next to the patio, where we'd have the fire pit.

I didn't know Mom was there until she said, "The thought just occurred to me . . ."

She was wearing her bathrobe and holding a box of Ritz crackers.

"What about a roasted marshmallow with Ritz and a Reese's?"

"Genius!" I cried. I hugged her. "Thanks for all this. For going to the store for me. I don't deserve you." Crispin was already beginning the Ritz-Reese's recipe card. "Either of you."

"Oh, honey, that's not how life works," said Mom. "Nobody deserves anyone. That's why we all have to be grateful."

"You sound like a greeting card, Mom," said Crispin.

"You know who I'm *not* grateful for?" she said, whacking him with the box of Ritz.

"Ow!"

Flushed and smiling, she turned back to me. "Your dad pulled out the fire pit. A few logs, too, and newspaper for kindling. Do you know how to start a fire?"

"I'm relatively confident that Quiz Team is well stocked with pyros."

"Make sure the fire stays in the pit, okay? Jemima, I trust you, but you know the rules. No alcohol. No drugs. No—"

"Do you remember the last party I hosted?" I said.

"Hmm," said Mom. "It's been a while. Would that have been your pirate birthday?"

"Yep. When I turned eight."

"I do remember. You insisted that we sing 'Yo-Ho-Ho and a Bottle of Rum' instead of 'Happy Birthday.'"

"Well," I said, "no need to worry, because this party's going to be exactly as wild as that one. This is Quiz Team."

The first difference between the pirate party and the gour'mores party, however, was that at the latter an actual bottle of rum appeared, smuggled in Ashby's backpack from her parents' liquor cabinet. Vodka showed up with Monique, and two bottles of wine with Jonah. "But my parents are home," I said, looking at the bottles strewn over the basement.

"We got it," Ashby and Monique sang out, and they put the alcohol in the closet. I shuddered. They could spike their sodas if they wanted, but not me. Not after what I'd done on one glass of wine at Founding Farmers. "Let's play a game," I suggested.

Half the team was already acting drunk, which was ludicrous because it had been like three minutes since the bottles had been popped. After a lot of shouting and non sequiturs, we decided on Pit. It's this game that's supposed to be like the market trading floor. You try to get all the corn cards, or wheat cards, or whatever crop, and basically it's a lot of yelling. I'm good at yelling, and I nearly won round one, but I was missing one soybean card when Vivek slammed down the bell. Round two was better. I got all the barley and won. "Yes!" I yelled, airplaning around the room. "Oats, peas, beans, and barley *grow*!"

"It's just a game, Jemima," said Ashby.

"I'm aware," I said. I didn't bother explaining my philosophy of games, which was that they were a lot more fun when everyone got really into them.

My mom tiptoed down the stairs after round four. She beckoned me over. "Are you guys planning to play this . . . this shouting game much longer?"

"Oh," I said. "You mean you're going to bed?"

"I can always put in earplugs."

"It's time to build the fire," I said. "I'll get them outside."

Her face cleared. "If you wouldn't mind, honey. Or stay inside, but keep it—"

"No, no, that's okay."

Our fire pit wasn't actually a pit. It was a bronze bowl with a little tripod, more Pottery Barn than L.L.Bean. The second I said *fire*, the guys sprinted outside to light newspaper with matches and feel macho. The patio was a recessed patch of cement, surrounded by a low brick wall. We sat on the wall while Jonah and Vivek fussed over kindling.

The backyard was twilit, the windows of neighbors' houses yellow against the navy sky. "I'm trying every variety of gour'mores," said Greg with his mouth full.

"And then you're going to puke in the flowerpot," said Zachary.

"Happily. I'll get to taste them again on the way up."

I scooched away. Paul made space for me by moving toward Jiyoon. Their knees bumped. I hopped up to roast another marshmallow.

Later, when everyone was stuffed full of gour'mores but still roasting marshmallows—it was hard to stop; there was something entrancing about the way they slowly browned—Monique asked, "Jiyoon, are you still getting blamed for the leak?"

"Not as much as Jem," she said, nudging my marshmallow with hers.

I winced. I hadn't opened any social-media apps since last night.

"But you're the one who's got a campaign hanging on it," said Ashby.

"I feel like we need to find out who did it," said Monique. "Everyone wants someone to blame."

"They should be blaming themselves," said Paul. "Who types their crushes into the internet and hits submit without imagining something bad might happen?"

"Me," said Greg. And me, I thought. And 118 other seniors.

"Just don't say that in public," Jiyoon told Paul. "The last thing I need is victim-blaming from my boyf—from you."

"You can call me your boyfriend," said Paul.

"AWW!" said Greg. Cilla and Monique joined in. Jiyoon flicked her eyes up, but she couldn't hold back her smile. "Fine," she said. "But keep in mind that I still haven't granted you permission to call me your girlfriend."

"Take your time," said Paul. "I'm patient." He was so busy beaming at her that he forgot to monitor his marshmallow, which burst into flames.

I was still thinking about what Monique had said: that until they knew who'd done it, no one was going to leave Jiyoon alone. Or leave me alone, for that matter, although that was less important. I owed it to Jiyoon to find out who did it. After all the times I'd been a crappy friend and a crappy feminist, I could do this one thing right.

"I have a theory," I said slowly. "The person who did it must care a lot about Mack winning. They must have been able to access the data easier than just about anyone."

"Anyone but me," said Paul, and Jiyoon said, "Do *not* say that in public!"

"I think it was Andy," I said.

In the silence, Greg said, "Accusing the big guy. Jemima, you got some balls."

"Ovaries," said Jiyoon. "Fallopian tubes. Uteri. Literally anything but balls, Greg."

"Is *uteri* really the plural of *uterus*?" said Zachary, perking up.

They were off and running, chasing the topic to its ridiculous end because that was what we did. "I believe it's *uteroose*," said Jiyoon. "Fourth declension." Firelight flickered on their faces. The neighbors had turned off their lights. Outside our circle, the sky was so black that we could have been the only living beings left on earth. Graduation was next weekend. Right now we were the most important people in the world to each other, but in the future we would be people who would catch up with one another. Who would reminisce.

"What are you going to do about it?" Ashby asked me.

"I'll talk to him," I said. "I'll text him right now."

CHAPTER 26

Most of Quiz Team had curfews, and the ones who didn't were the ones driving the ones who did. By midnight everyone was gone. I stayed out on the patio. The fire was burning out. I was eating a waxy tube of Ritz crackers, letting them sit on my tongue, salt-side down, until they disintegrated.

I checked my phone, even though I knew I hadn't gotten any messages. I'd texted Andy forty-seven minutes ago: *We should talk.* No response. I tapped around and came across a picture of Gennifer and her crew from a few minutes before. All the girls were in that pose where you pop your butt and twist your shoulder and float your arm: you know, where you look skinny but also like you've thrown out your back. Mack was in the next picture, kissing Gennifer on the cheek while she made a cute, squinty face. Then there was Andy, one arm around Melanie and the other around Lily, a goofy smile on his face. I mostly looked at the girls. Their crop tops, their dipped heads, their straight hair. Their rightness. If they ever felt like they didn't belong, they never betrayed it; they faked that feeling away. I was envious, deeply envious, and I realized I had been for a long time. I'd covered it up with disdain. "I'm not like other girls!" I'd said over and over. But I wanted to be like other girls. I did.

I texted Andy again.

I know it was you who did it

I ate another cracker.

Do you want to come over

"Is this a booty call, Kincaid?" Andy said as he got out of his Jeep. I'd gone out barefoot to meet him in the driveway.

"No!" I said. "I said we should *talk!*"

"Damn," he said. "You're breaking my heart. Well, what do you want to talk about?"

"Aren't you mad at me?" I said. Last I'd seen him, remember, he'd been passive-aggressively referring to the *she* who'd engineered the leak.

"I kind of realized that theory was ridiculous," he said.

"Oh." That took some wind out of my sails. I'd been imagining that we'd go at each other with claws out, each of us accusing the other one. Like a verbal cage match. My fantasy, I guess. "You want a Ritz?" I offered him the tube.

He took a stack. "Are we going to stand in the driveway all night?"

I led him around to the patio. "Why do you trust me all of a sudden?"

"Trust? That's going a bit far. But I know you didn't leak all that shit."

"You were pretty convinced." I affected a deep voice. " 'You set off a bomb in our class. You've destroyed us. . . . ' "

"Okay, yeah, I was upset. But I was at this party just now—"

"Yeah, I saw—"

"Stalker."

"You know what I hate? The whole 'stalking' shtick. The whole point of posting stuff is for people to look at it, but then when people actually look, everyone's all, 'You're so creepy!' "

He laughed. "Are you going to have a problem with everything I say, or are you going to let me tell my story?"

"Sorry, I forgot. Women should be seen and not heard."

He plopped down on the brick wall. I sat next to him but left a good foot between us and crossed my arms for good measure. "Your name came up at the party," he said.

"I bet."

"Yeah, at first it was . . . what you'd expect. But then all these girls started defending you. Like they couldn't believe you were getting all this shit for something you didn't do."

"Actually?"

"Gennifer started it. Then Melanie was like, 'She's the only one who speaks up when Mr. Ulrich calls girls *sweetheart*.' And Jess said something about how you always stand up to the assholes in econ who talk about welfare in a kind of racist way, and even Lacey talked about Latin, something about how you made a big thing of it when the textbook tried to say that this god who wouldn't take no for an answer was romantic and devoted, instead of creepy and toxic—"

"They were *listening*?"

"Gennifer used her honorable-bitch line again. And I was like, Okay. I'm convinced." He shrugged. "Even though I know you think it was me."

"Wow," I said. Impulsively, I put my hand on his shoulder. "I won't tell anyone, Andy, but . . . *was* it you?"

"You'd tell everyone," he said. "You wouldn't be able to shut your big mouth for a second."

I considered. "Yeah. True. But was it?"

"Kincaid," he said, gazing into my eyes, "it wasn't me."

I could have melted. The dying fire, the darkness, the two of us alone in the middle of the night. But I couldn't let him go so easily. "Convince me," I said, dropping my hand.

"Why would I have done it? I just want to have fun. It's the end of senior year. Now everyone's mad at Triumvirate."

"Mack's going to get elected chairman. That's why you'd have done it."

"If I were a junior, I'd vote for Jiyoon."

"Wh—what?"

"I love Mack, he's my brother, but come on, he'll be a shitty chairman. And he'd be perfectly happy without it. Probably happier. It's a lot of work."

I stared at the fire, barely seeing it. So much for brotherly loyalty, I thought. If it had been *my* brother—

Then again, my brother was Crispin. Andy's brother was Mack.

Andy must have seen the confusion rippling across my face. "Aren't you going to disagree with me?" he said, smirking. "Where'd you go, Kincaid?" He put an arm around my waist and pulled me toward him, and he kissed me.

I kissed him back. Of course. I felt myself collapsing, rational thought leaving the building—stop!

"Then who did it?" I said, ripping away.

"It could have been anyone." He was looking at my lips instead of my eyes. "Anyone with the money to hire a hacker. Five minutes on Reddit, a couple hundred bucks, done."

At Chawton, the casual wielding of two hundred dollars eliminated basically no one. "What about Jiyoon's campaign?" I said. "If everyone thinks it was me, they're not going to vote for my best friend."

"Gennifer's not going to let you take the blame."

"Even if it means Mack losing?"

"Kincaid," said Andy, almost gently, "you don't actually think Jiyoon could win, do you?" He kissed me. The kiss was harder this time, and I let myself fall into him. He kneaded my back, sliding his hands onto my bare skin, and my hands were under his shirt now too.

"Come inside," I said. We were barely inside the basement before he tugged off my shirt. My bra, hallelujah, was neither safety-pinned nor beige. It even had one of those interboob roses, which I usually cut off because although I may not shower as frequently as I could, if a plant actually took root between my breasts, I would consider it a capital-P Problem. Andy didn't notice the rose. I don't think he even noticed the bra. He was all about the tissue therein.

I pulled off his shirt, in part to get a break from the groping, and we stumbled over to the couch. Before he sat down, he kicked off his shoes and stepped out of his pants and boxers. Whoa. We were going there. He stood before me, unabashed as freaking Adam. I pulled off my skirt. He tugged me down to the couch. Once I was on top of him, he went to work on my bra clasp, wriggled me out of my underwear.

Naked with a guy. Maybe it'd have felt more momentous if lust hadn't taken over. We twisted. We squirmed. We kissed wherever our mouths landed. I can't describe—God, I mean, it's only biology, but it was unbelievable—the force of the urge to keep at it, to go further. We were on our sides now, and I wound a leg over him and rocked back and forth like this was a sitcom and I was a dog humping someone's leg for a cheap laugh.

He was sucking at my neck, and I was making the mewling noise that would have mortally embarrassed me under normal circumstances. He pulled back suddenly and said, "Wait. What are we doing?"

"I don't know, but keep doing it."

He chuckled. I kind of hated him for having enough mental wherewithal to chuckle. The pause de-lusted me, and I started feeling weird about being naked in the place my parents watch movies, and I started worrying about my stomach, which was usually puffy but not *this* puffy, damn those Ritz crackers. I wanted those thoughts to stop, so I started kissing *his* neck, and he groaned and flopped back and I gripped him between my legs and that was all the talking for a while.

He pulled away again. Before he could say anything, I said, "Let's do it."

"Do what?"

I knew he knew what I meant. Which was annoying. "Do I have to spell it out?"

"Spell it out, Kincaid." Teasing me. Licking my ear. "Aren't you good at spelling? Don't I recall an eighth-grade spelling-bee victory—"

"I won it on *pachyderm*," I said. Now I was nearly gasping. The ear thing. "Come on, Andy, you know what I mean."

"Do you want to?"

I thought of Crispin's advice—*Keep thinking about what you want, every minute*—but I couldn't think. That was the problem. All I could do was want. "Yes. Yes."

He hesitated.

"What's got you so worried?" I said.

"I'm kind of a douchebag, Kincaid."

"But I am too."

"Hand me my pants, would you?" There were three heart-breaking seconds of thinking he was getting dressed. Then he extracted a condom from his wallet. "You sure?"

"I'm sure."

"Because I'm not a rapist."

"Oh, good, that's what I always like to hear before I sleep with someone."

He tapped my lips with the foil-wrapped condom. "Shh, shh, don't be sarcastic, just shut this mouth, shh, shh—"

I giggled and he put a hand over my mouth. It was sexy. In a way that I wished it weren't, in a way that had to do with power and control. He did some maneuvering, ripping foil, shifting away from me, putting it on, and I looked at the weave of the couch and thought, Here it is. The big moment.

And I thought, No! There are no borders! This moment is no more important than any other moment in my sexual journey!

And I thought, Ew, please, never think the phrase *sexual journey* again.

He propped himself above me and we began to kiss again. Now I was preoccupied, though. What if I bled? Weren't women supposed to bleed the first time? I considered getting a towel, but I didn't want to explain why to Andy. Oh well, I thought. It was a dark blue couch, and I was an old pro at removing bloodstains. (A small upside to never tracking your period.)

Soon we were back to our frenzied pitch. "Give me some help, would you?" he said.

I froze.

"Like," he said, grimacing, "put it in."

So I grabbed it with one hand and opened myself up with the other. There was an inevitable flashback involving tampons. And then—

Okay.

I guessed we were having sex.

There was pressure, and it felt, well, like having something inside me, something considerably larger than even a jumbo tampon. But it didn't hurt. Probably (TMI alert) because I'd gotten so wet. He pushed in, slowly. It didn't feel particularly good or bad. Honestly, it didn't really *feel*. He moved out and back in.

It didn't take that long. He finished with a shudder and a whimper, same as before. He fell on me and breathed hard against my shoulder, hard enough that he left a patch of moisture there, like the billow of hot tea when you're wearing glasses. "That was so good," he said.

"Uh," I said, "thanks?"

"Yeah," he said, "yeah." His eyes were closed. "Let me do you. Hold on." He heaved himself up and tied up the condom like the grossest water balloon in the history of water-balloon fights. Then he twiddled his fingers between my legs. "Tell me what to do," he said, but honestly he was doing just fine, and I guess I was kind of primed for it after all that nude neck-kissing, but, well, anyway, I came so fast it surprised me, a full-body clench and release. I tried not to make any noise, but a groan escaped. He grinned into my face. "That was hot," he said. Then he lay down between me and the back of the couch, and he closed his eyes.

I stared at the ceiling. He was taking up more than his fair share of the couch, and I had to keep my body tense to avoid falling off. I felt like a shipwrecked rat clinging to a piece of driftwood. I am a person who has had sex, I thought.

"Hey, Andy?" I whispered. "You're wrong."

"Yeah?" he murmured.

"Jiyoon *could* win. She's got a chance. A good chance."

He didn't respond. I squinted at his face. His mouth was open. He was asleep.

ASLEEP!

I wanted him gone. I wanted my house and body and mind to myself. I poked him. He didn't stir. I gave him a gentle shake, and a not-so-gentle shake. He grunted. "You better go," I said.

He stretched. "Yeah."

He put on his clothes. I watched him thread his belt, stuff his wallet into his pocket. He left the condom on the floor. I put on my T-shirt and skirt, no undergarments. "I'll just go out this way," he said, nodding toward the basement door.

"Yep."

He gave me a lopsided smile. "See you around, Kincaid."

"Yeah. See you."

CHAPTER 27

The Candidate Open Forum was after school on Monday. It's usually not well attended, since almost everyone has decided who to vote for by this point, but this year it was packed. Gennifer had predicted that. "People will be looking for drama," she had said. She'd eyed me. "You sure you can handle it?" She had to deal with the delivery of the carnival games, and Andy had a lacrosse game.

"You bet," I'd said, but I was more nervous than I let on.

There was a hiss when I walked onstage. I ignored it and tried to hold my voice steady. "Welcome to the Chawton School Candidate Open Forum, your last chance"—someone booed; bad choice of words—"to hear from your candidates before you vote on Saturday." I introduced Jiyoon and Mack. Keep the focus on them, I reminded myself. I was in charge of facilitating audience questions and timing the candidate responses, and that was it.

The first question, from an earnest freshman, was on the environmental impact of our disposable lunch plates. "In the big scheme of things," said Mack, "what we do has, like, zero environmental impact. It's not even a rounding error." He had only one plank in his platform, so of course he returned to it. "We should focus on things that actually impact people," he said. "For example, I want everyone to feel supported. So I want to encourage everyone to show up to as many games as possible. And if that means a little more crap in the landfill, well—"

"Time," I said. "Jiyoon?"

"I agree with you," she said, addressing the freshman and ignoring Mack. "For a school of our resources, it's immoral to throw out five hundred paper plates a day. I've researched the cost and viability of compostable plates, and I've talked with Mr. Merman, the facilities team leader. It's something we could implement next year."

The audience started filing out halfway through. By the end of the hour, there were only about twenty people left. Jiyoon kept it super professional and thus super boring. Mack's answers were so dumb they were also boring. At the end, he unceremoniously hopped off the stage to join his friends. He didn't say anything to either of us. Jiyoon closed her notebook and said, "Thanks for running this."

"No problem. Um, Ji—"

"Can we"—she nodded at the remainder of the audience—"wait?"

I got it. She didn't want to talk to me where people could see us. Gennifer's underground machinations were working—

everyone had been a lot friendlier to me today—but even so, our Triumvirate was regarded with suspicion and animosity.

Finally the auditorium emptied. "Okay, phew," she said. "Glad that's over."

"How's everything been? With, you know. The campaign stuff."

She grinned. "You're referring to everyone hating me because of you?"

"Yeah. That."

"The online stuff has quieted down, as far as I can tell. And people are smiling at me again."

"Oh, good."

"Which doesn't mean I'm going to win. But I never was, was I?"

"All he can talk about is Hype Club."

"Yeah, I don't think the average Chawton voter really cares." She sighed. "Five days till this is over. I can't wait. I'm glad I ran, but I can't wait."

"Do you have a minute? I have something to tell you. Something big."

She grimaced and looked at her phone. "The late bus leaves in three minutes." I must have looked forlorn, because she added, "I'll call you."

I helped Gennifer with the carnival games, and afterward she gave me a ride home in her massive SUV. She looked teeny-tiny at the wheel.

"Do you tell your friends everything?" I asked her.

"Not what I had for breakfast. But lunch, yeah."

She was trolling me. Which I respected even though it was annoying. "I mean important stuff. Like if something happened with a guy."

"I love how you think I'm, like, the ultimate arbiter of social codes."

"God. I'm just taking a survey. Collecting information."

"So what happened with you and a guy?"

"Nothing."

"Jemmy. Tell your old friend."

"We're not friends."

She sighed dramatically. "Sorry. I forget you insist on that."

"You're too—"

"Too what?" she said. For the first time, she sounded actually irritated. "Too vapid? Too ditzy? Too obsessed with my appearance?"

"Um, you literally just used the word *vapid*. You're not vapid."

"I'm so pleased I've met your vocabulary standard." She gripped the wheel tensely through a turn. "I do have a brain, Jemima."

"I know that."

"Yeah? Because sometimes you seem to forget. Sometimes you seem to think pretty equals dumb. Entering a Sephora doesn't suck away brain cells, you know. Caring about clothes and guys and social stuff doesn't mean you don't care about anything else."

I sank down in my seat, exasperated. "Since *when* have I—"

"You've got this idea that all girls are competing with each other, and you automatically win because you have blue armpit hair and don't date and never wear mascara."

"I don't wear mascara because I practically Oedipus myself every time I try!"

"Because you'd *never* lower yourself to watch a tutorial."

"Gah," I said. "Not true."

"Don't say *gah*. *Gah* is for texting only."

"Oh em gee. Ugh. Asidfiklagh."

"Stop."

I straightened, feeling slightly cheered. "Honestly, I've watched the tutorials. But on the first stroke I always turn my eyelashes into one eyelash. One eyelash to rule them all."

"I could teach you in five minutes."

"I'm hopeless. Loudly crying face emoji."

She laughed despite herself. "You *are* hopeless," she said. "I'm just saying, anytime we say there's only one right way to be a woman, they've won."

"Who's *they*? The forces of the patriarchy?"

"Who else?"

"I never thought I'd live to see the day," I remarked to the ceiling, "when I'd hear Gennifer Grier spouting off about the patriarchy."

"There you go again," she said.

I watched the strip malls flash by the window, nail salons and Chinese takeout. She had a point. "I can't believe you're dating Mack," I said.

"Rule of thumb. Don't say stuff like that to people about their boyfriends."

"Do you actually like him? I'm just curious. He's kind of, um, abrasive."

"He can come across like a dick," said Gennifer. "But yeah, I like him. He's a little boy inside. That gets me."

"That's kind of cute." I shot her a sly glance. "Colon right parenthesis."

She shook her head, but I think she took it as the olive branch it was. "It's been a long day," she said.

"A long *year.*"

"No kidding."

We both looked out the windshield for a minute.

"I don't know if I'd have done it," said Gennifer, "if I'd known."

"Done what?"

"Triumvirate."

"Really?"

"You don't think about that?"

"Never."

"Never?"

"It always seemed inevitable to me. That it'd be the three of us."

"Not for me," she said. "Tons of girls could have been Social Comm pres. Jasmin, Lacey, Mackenzie, Lily. If I'd known how much Lily wanted it, I probably wouldn't have run."

"Whoa. You regret it?"

"I wouldn't go that far." Gennifer turned onto my street.

Her delicate wrists moved the tank of a car in a way that was sort of mind-blowing. "But I think about what this year would have been without Triumvirate. And sometimes I wish I'd let the alternate reality happen."

"Isn't that the definition of regret?"

"Is it?"

"I don't know. Maybe not."

That was exactly how I'd been feeling about having sex with Andy. I had been thinking about the alternate reality: the world in which I hadn't texted him on Saturday, the world in which, weeks ago, I'd moved my knee away from his. And sometimes I wished I'd let that world happen.

But I guess I didn't regret it.

Next time I had sex, I didn't want it to be like this. Next time I wanted trust. Next time I wanted a relationship. I didn't *want* to want strings but, damn it, I wanted strings.

But I didn't regret it.

I didn't regret it.

"Thanks for the ride," I said as Gennifer pulled into my driveway. "See you." I'd started to shut the door when I stopped and stuck my head back in.

"Hey? Ghen?" With a hard *G*. I couldn't help it. "Thanks for telling everyone I didn't leak the picks."

"Sure."

"You're a good friend."

She fluttered her eyes like a Victorian maiden on the verge of a swoon. "Me? Your *friend*?"

"I'm glad you're on Triumvirate." I paused, embarrassed. "That's all. Yep. Cool."

"You too, Jemmy," she said. "It's been . . . well. Not fun. Not always."

"Not often."

"But . . ."

I nodded. "Understood."

She nodded back. I knew she was mocking me, mimicking this throaty, overzealous way I nod. Whatever, Gennifer. You can mock me. As the old proverb goes, If thou dost dish it out, thou must take it.

"Understood," she said.

CHAPTER 28

I wasn't within spitting distance of Andy until Town Meeting on Tuesday. We all got there right before the bell, and I gave him a businesslike nod.

Andy called the meeting to order. "Happy Tuesday," he said, "and this *is* a happy Tuesday, because it's the last Town Meeting of the year."

There was an aggressive whoop from the senior section, and some uncomfortable laughter. Andy shifted the mike from hand to hand. The undertones were clear. They were ready to be done with us, the Triumvirate that'd screwed them over. "Um," he said, "I hope you're all excited for Jamboree!"

He did an arms-above-the-head dance move, which revealed to me this supreme truth: coolness is in the eye of the beholder. Last week everyone would have hollered and laughed, and Andy would have flushed with pleasure and said, "Okay,

okay, settle down." This week he got stolid stares. The dance move looked cheesy, like when a teacher trying to muster some enthusiasm starts raising the roof and saying, "Get excited for VECTOR MULTIPLICATION!" and you're just like, Stop.

Andy picked up on the vibe fast. His arms fell. The swagger evaporated. "Let me give you a brief overview of the Jamboree schedule," he said. I thought of that Horace line from Latin class. Andy had been all about *carpe diem*, seizing the day, heedless and bold, and now he'd learned the rest: *quam minimum credula postero*. Trusting as little as possible in tomorrow. He was just a guy. A guy whose time would pass.

"Plan to be here *all* weekend," he said. "The softball game's right after school Friday, and then we'll do the cookout and the bonfire. Be back at ten Saturday for guys' lacrosse and the awards ceremony."

They weren't responding. He glanced back at us and said, "Yeah, so Gennifer's going to tell you about the rest."

That hadn't been the plan. She took the mike. "Hi!" Andy slunk back and sat down without looking at me. "So after that, Powderpuff! It'll be fantastic. Both teams have been practicing hard, although I happen to know the Tigers are going to bury the Angels—"

She got some laughs with that, and some boos, but the good kind. "Angels forever!" someone shouted, and the senior section devolved into chants.

Gennifer, pleased, tapped the mike. "Save it for Saturday! Juniors, you'll vote for next year's chairman at halftime. After the game, we'll announce your chairman, as well as the new Social Comm pres and the new Mildred—er, the recipient of the Mildred Mustermann Award for Academic Excellence."

I turned to Andy. "What are we saying about prom?" I whispered.

"Where. When."

"What about the theme?"

He shrugged.

"We have to apologize," I whispered. Gennifer was telling them the rules for Jamboree, as Ms. Edison had reminded us to do: casual dress, no coolers or bottles, remember how many alumni come, do Chawton proud. "Now's our chance."

Andy stiffened. "No."

"We owe it to them," I said. "We're the ones who—"

"No," he said too loudly. Ms. Edison shot us a beady look from the front row. Andy's palms were gripping his thighs.

"Yes," I muttered.

"*No.*"

Ms. Edison drew her finger across her throat. "As for Saturday night—" Gennifer began, and I jumped up. She raised her eyebrows, and I nodded. "Jemima's going to tell you about that."

Good old Ghen.

"Hi," I said into the mike. My voice shook. I was thinking too much about the audience, the skeptical seniors who'd only recently stopped believing I was the one who'd leaked the data. But I remembered that Jiyoon was out there too. Last night on the phone, when I'd told her what had happened with Andy—

everything that had happened with Andy—she hadn't even thought to get mad at me for keeping it from her for so long. She had asked me questions instead, a lot of questions, some of which I didn't have answers for. Now she was listening to me, rooting for me. She was always rooting for me.

"Prom's at eight on Saturday," I said, "right here in the Commons, which Social Comm will be decorating after school on Friday. Drop by to help if you want." I paused. "Furthermore, on behalf of the entire Triumvirate . . ."

Out of the corner of my eye, I saw Andy stand.

"I want to tell you how deeply, incredibly . . ."

Andy was coming toward me. I stepped away. Thank goodness for cordless mikes.

"Sorry," I said. I hit the word too hard because I was trying to casually evade Andy. He was two steps away and getting closer. Gennifer's hand was clapped to her mouth.

"Yeah," I said, stepping away from him, "we're sorry for what happened with . . ."

It was extremely hard to deliver a sincere apology under these circumstances.

"God!" I said, my voice finally sounding like my own. "Stop chasing me, Andy! Just let me talk!"

Someone laughed, and then everyone laughed. Andy froze. I turned back to the audience. I'd found my voice again. Just let me talk! My eternal cry. Let me *talk!*

"Okay," I said. "I guess I'm not speaking for the whole Triumvirate. But I can speak for myself. And Gennifer, right?"

Gennifer nodded. "I am so, so sorry that I didn't take proper care of the secrets you entrusted to me. I didn't leak them, but I didn't do enough to ensure they weren't leaked. I don't know if you can ever forgive me, but I want you to know, I realize what I've done and I feel awful and in the future I'll be a lot better about secrets. One of these days I'm going to learn to shut my big fu—freaking mouth."

I gave several throaty nods. No one cheered. No one yelled "WE LOVE YOU, JEMIMA!" or rushed the stage for a bear hug.

And that, it turned out, was fine.

Chawton School

CHAPTER 29

Gennifer and I were wrangling with long strands of beads. It was Friday after school, and we were trying to hang bead doors. You know, the ones that make a waterfall noise? And walking through them makes you feel like you've entered a different world, the glamorous sphere of the casino, so far from the mundanity of quizzes and projects that you barely recognize your school?

Well, that was the idea.

"Fuck these beads," muttered Gennifer, teetering on the step stool, her hands full of a rat's nest. "You know what? Fuck them."

I had my own rat's nest. The beads were awful. "Don't you have underlings who could do this?" I asked Gennifer. "Isn't untangling beads the whole point of having underlings?"

The Commons was buzzing with Social Comm girls, who

had traded their coiffed everyday looks for super-cute outfits befitting physical labor, so, like, seventy-dollar sweat-wicking tank tops. I kept thinking derisive thoughts, and then I'd be like, Stop! You're not winning! But it was complicated, I thought, because in truth I felt superior and inferior, both at once. Madison Porter, e.g., was wearing work overalls with a pink sports bra underneath, exposing five inches of tanned rib cage. There was even a hammer in the hammer loop. It was a ridiculous outfit—obviously we weren't hammering in the Commons—but she looked positively winsome. If we were baked goods, she'd be a cupcake and I'd be, like, a garlic bagel. I was wearing jeans and a T-shirt I'd won during an evening activity at the Quiz Team championships for naming all twenty-eight members of Dumbledore's Army. It said ON A SCALE OF 1 TO 10, MY OBSESSION WITH HARRY POTTER COMES IN AT 9¾, and it had already developed pit stains.

How much of my girl judgment, I wondered, was the water I was swimming in? And how much had I developed to reassure myself that I was okay the way I was?

Gennifer summoned Lily and Lacey to help me with the beads. Lacey and I used Lily as a sort of human spool, winding her with the strands we'd untangled. We couldn't stop laughing. Maybe *every* girl felt unokay sometimes, I thought. Maybe it was part of the water, this core belief that being female was not okay. I looked around the Commons, alive with bright outfits and laughter. Every girl was fighting her own match, but as soon as she opened her eyes and looked at the field, she'd see the linewomen she had to block for her, the receivers who could take her passes. We were on the same team.

"Where's that ladder?" said Gennifer, fuming. "Andy's been gone for-freaking-ever."

Ms. Edison had given him the master key so he could get into the maintenance room. "I could go find him," I said, even though it was the last thing I wanted to do. If you didn't count his chasing me around the stage at Town Meeting, Andy hadn't talked to me since Saturday night. Or texted me. Or made eye contact with me. It was messing with my head.

"Would you?" said Gennifer. "Thanks."

I went upstairs. There was Andy, sauntering down the hallway. Just seeing his easy lope made my hackles rise. "Why didn't you get the ladder?" I said. "Give me the key."

"Whoa there, Kincaid," he said. "Patience, grasshopper."

"Don't call me a grasshopper."

"It's a saying."

"I'm aware it's a saying. That doesn't mean you can call me a freaking grasshopper."

I charged onward. He turned around and fell into step with me. "I'd ask what pissed you off," he said, "but what doesn't piss you off?"

"Oh, fu—" I made myself shut up. If he was trying to get a rise out of me, I wouldn't give him the pleasure. At the door to the maintenance room, I spun toward him. "Give me the key so I can get the ladder." He dangled the key a foot above my head. I swiped for it and missed. "This isn't funny. Open the door."

He opened the door.

"Now you can go away. I don't need your help."

"Are you sure?" he asked.

"Positive."

He flicked on the lights and followed me in. "You can't carry the ladder by yourself."

"Sometimes even women can—"

I heaved at the ladder.

Damn.

It was twelve feet long, even telescoped shut. I could lift an end, but there was no way I'd even get it out of the maintenance room, much less down to the Commons.

"*I* couldn't carry it by myself," he said. "That's why I was coming back for help."

I fumed.

"Please," he said, "allow me." He tried to lift my hands off the ladder, but I gripped harder.

"You can get the other end," I said.

"*You* want to be the one who goes backward down the stairs?"

He was right.

Again.

Damn. I was so mad.

"One of these days you're going to take a chill pill, Kincaid," he said, "and you won't be nearly as interesting."

"You think I'm interesting?"

I hated myself for asking.

"Sorta," he said.

I opened my mouth. I didn't even know what I was going to say. I was just mad. He leaned across the ladder and kissed me. I jerked away. "Don't think you can ignore me all week and then kiss me," I said furiously. "I'm not some game you can pull up on your phone when you're bored."

"Whoa, Kincaid," he said. "Who's ignoring who?"

"You didn't even text me after we—" I flashed a glance at the door. It was closed. "After we had *sex*," I hissed.

"You didn't text me," he pointed out.

"No, but—"

"But what? It's my job? Because I'm the guy? Look, Kincaid. I can't do this no-strings stuff. It's too weird."

That was *my* line.

"I—" I started, but that was as far as I got because he plugged my mouth with his. I thought, Is Andy offering me strings? Then I stopped thinking because apparently that was what I did when Andy Monroe kissed me. Our shins knocked into the ladder between us. I pushed my face into Andy's, tangled his hair with my hands. "Hold on," I said, and I stepped over the ladder. I clocked my shin, but I didn't mind. Andy boosted me onto the tool table and I wrapped my legs around him and we kissed like we had moments to live.

He started to pull off my shirt. I resisted. "The door automatically locks from the outside," he said. "We're safe." I gave in, and pulled off his shirt for good measure. I'm about to have sex at school, I thought. Last week I didn't have sex, and now I'm about to have sex in a maintenance room. It was tawdry, but tawdry wasn't incompatible with the people we turned into when we were together. The people we'd forced each other to be, I thought hazily as he pulled me off the table so he could jam a hand down my jeans, fingering the upper elastic of my underwear. All the assumptions we'd each made.

His head was deep in my chest now, his hands working to unclasp my bra. It fell to the dusty floor. He licked my nipple. We deserved each other. "Oh," I said.

Not an *oh* of revelation. An *oh* of whatever you're doing to my breast, it's making me grasp your shoulders and shut my eyes and wince. Whatever you are doing to my breast, oh, let it never stop. Let Gennifer despair of ever getting the ladder. Let the sun fall behind the field. Let the bonfire begin. Let the world spin on, let Powderpuff be played, let our Triumvirate cede power to the next, and let this never stop.

"Damn," said Andy, panting, craning up at me, "you're such a tiger."

I thought he was spouting a stupid compliment he'd learned from a movie. Or porn, more likely. Gross. "I've never understood that," I said, reaching to unbutton his pants.

"Understood . . ." He unbuttoned mine.

"The whole tiger-sex thing. Like, are tigers known for their sexual prowess?"

"Huh?"

"Isn't that what you were saying? About tigers?"

"I said—never mind."

"Wait. Explain."

"It's nothing, Kincaid. Don't worry about it."

"Too late. I *am* worrying about it." He started kissing me but I pulled back. "Explain."

"I thought you knew," he said.

"Knew what?"

"The Powderpuff teams," he said. "The Tigers and the Angels?"

"Yeah?"

"That's what I was referring to."

"You were saying I was good at Powderpuff? That's what came to mind as you licked my boob?"

He sighed. I felt underdressed. I *was* underdressed. My jeans unbuttoned, my shirt tossed who knows where.

"Promise you won't get mad," he said. "I seriously thought you knew. Girls aren't supposed to know, obviously, but Gennifer found out, and I guess I just figured it was impossible to be on Triumvirate without—"

"Just tell me."

"Tigers and Angels," he said. "*T* and *A*?"

"So?"

"You still don't get it?"

I was so annoyed. "Still," I said. "I still don't get it. Please spell it out for dumb old me."

"*T* and *A*. Tits and ass. That's how we divide the teams. It's all a joke, really. It's not that big of a deal. The girls with good tits go on the Tigers, and the girls with good asses are Angels."

"So the guys cheer . . ."

"For the team they're into." He shrugged. "You know. You usually like one better. It's a pretty even split. Which is interesting from an anthropological perspective, right?"

"Oh my God."

"You aren't going to go on a feminist rampage about this, are you?"

I stared at him.

"I shouldn't have told you. I thought you'd be cool about it."

"I can't believe no one's—how long has this—"

He started kissing me again, not on but around my mouth, as if homing in on the target, and he guided my hand to his crotch. He hadn't rebuttoned his pants, and his soft boxer briefs clung to his dick, and I wrapped my fingers around it. I don't know why. "That's better," he said. "Forget I said anything."

"It's *so* sexist," I said.

He had his hand down my pants. "It's harmless," he said. "It's a joke."

"Oh—"

Same kind of *oh* as before. I tried to get it together, but his hand on me, my hand on him, it was too much to handle. "It's *so* sexist," I said again.

"Come on, Kincaid," he said, kissing my breasts and my stomach, getting on his knees, kissing a trail down from my belly button, and down, and down. "Have a sense of humor." I threw my head back and grasped the table with one hand, his hair with the other, and I didn't think about anything for quite some time.

CHAPTER 30

The music was blasting. The turf field was teeming with people holding hot dogs. The grills were staffed by brusque caterers who were clearly thinking, What the hell is up with this school? By the time Andy and I had hauled the ladder from the maintenance room, Jamboree had begun.

We ditched the ladder in the deserted Commons, and Andy ditched me about as fast. I was glad to see him go. In a daze, and slightly bandy-legged, I walked to the main tent.

"Where did you *go?*" Gennifer demanded. "You abandoned us. Did something come up?"

So to speak. "Sorry. Yeah. The ladder was really heavy."

"Are you okay?" she said, squinting at me. "You look kind of pale."

"Yeah, I feel weird."

She grasped my arm and peered into my eyes. "You look horrible."

"Thanks."

"Much worse than usual."

"Your bedside manner needs work," I told her. I twisted my arm from her grasp. "Honestly, I'm just hungry, and it's hot. What's on your list for me to do?"

"Are you PMSing?"

"I don't know. Maybe."

"What do you mean, *maybe?*"

"I never figure it out until I get my period. Then I'm like, Oh, that explains why I acted so cancerous last week."

"It's got to be PMS." She dug around in her bag. "What do you want? Midol? Advil? Tylenol?"

"You run a pharmacy from your purse? Are you even allowed to do that at school?"

"Nurse Weber would be grateful if she knew how much work I've saved her," Gennifer snapped. "What's your worst symptom? Cramps? Headache?"

"Cramps." My internal organs *were* feeling off-kilter, though I had a feeling that was due more to the maintenance room than to my menstrual cycle. I glimpsed Andy across the field, high-fiving Tyler. I sat down on the grass.

"You need to go home," said Gennifer.

"But all the Triumvirate stuff—"

I'd seen her final checklist.

"It's under control," she said. "Go home. Take a bath and go to bed."

"Are you trying to get rid of me?"

"I'm being your friend," she said, disgusted. "Now, you need a ride, right? Can your brother take you?"

"Crispin's here?"

"I saw him a minute ago. You know we invited all the alums." She shaded her face and scanned the field. "Julia," she said, grabbing a minion, "fetch Crispin Kincaid, would you? Jemima is seriously ill."

"Tell him I'm fine," I shouted up from the grass.

Julia sprinted off. Gennifer got me to a folding chair. I did feel bad. A little nauseated, a little overheated, and a lot like I couldn't take one single moment more of Chawton.

"Recover tonight," Gennifer said, "because tomorrow is packed. We're meeting at nine for setup. And don't forget, the Mildred welcomes everyone before the Powderpuff game. Have your speech written, like, before you show up."

"It's not some huge speech. I can improv it."

"You need to recognize the senior class and the board. Ideally without making our Triumvirate look like a disaster."

"Like the disaster it was?"

"Jemima. Be positive. I think we've done a lot of good."

I caught her eye. We both giggled. Two-thirds of the shittiest Triumvirate ever. We sobered up pretty fast, though. That wasn't the kind of thing we should have been laughing about.

★ ★ ★

The minute Crispin and I got into the car, he said, "You aren't really sick, are you?"

I sank back into the seat. "I don't feel good."

"Because you're sick? Or sick of Chawton?"

"How'd you guess?"

"Because I feel the same way the second I set foot onto that campus."

"You? You were a star."

"Sure." He accepted it as his due. "But high school's still weird and hard. Even under the best of circumstances. When I think about the secrets I was keeping . . ."

"What about them?"

"I didn't realize that people care a lot less about secrets when they're out in the open."

"That is *not* always true," I said fervently.

"You want to come over?" he said.

"Please."

In the elevator, Crispin inhaled, tilted his head to the side, and gave me an annoying smile, the sort of smile that makes you feel extremely defensive. "All right," he said as soon as we got in his apartment. "Confess."

"You still have the global-warming decor?"

He shrugged. "The polar bear is cute. Also, I'm lazy. Don't try to change the subject. Take a seat on that there melting ice cap and tell your Bippy who it was. Was it Andy?"

"How—but—"

"You want to know how I knew?" I nodded. Duh, I wanted to know. "I smelled it."

I yelped, horrified. "No!"

"Yes."

"Oh my God. Can I take a shower?"

"If you tell me everything afterward." He handed me a towel and some clothes. "Use as much hot water as you want," he yelled in after me. "This apartment is not an environmentally friendly zone."

"Wow," he said when I was finished. "I'll think twice before I give you the silent treatment again."

"It destroyed me," I said. "One bad decision after another."

"You mean Andy?"

"Yeah. I mean. I don't know. No? I tried to follow your advice. To think about what I wanted. But I guess there's a difference between wanting it right now and wanting it long-term. And it's hard, because right now is always right now."

"Very philosophical."

"I'm not going to do it again. I'm set on that."

"Do you wish you hadn't?"

"I don't think so. No. It happened, so not much point in wishing it back."

"No regrets," said Crispin, but he sounded sad.

We were both quiet for a second. I was curled up in his too-big sweatpants, my wet hair combed straight back. It was like being a little kid after a nighttime bath. But when I was a kid, I never could have imagined that growing up would be like this.

"What should I do about the *T* and *A* thing?" When I had first told him, he'd rolled his eyes and whirled his hands like, *Get to the point*. I had a horrible thought. He was a guy, a Chawton grad, a former triumvir. "Did *you* know?"

"Nope," said Crispin. "They put me on the cheer squad for the Angels. Never asked me." He laughed. "I guess I wasn't as subtle about the gay thing as I thought."

"That's even worse!" I said.

"It was years ago. Do you know how much those guys matter to me now? Zero."

"But what should I do?" I said.

"You want to do something?"

"I want to make it stop."

"You're not going to make it stop."

"What if I told Mr. Duffey?"

"He's a Chawton alum."

Oh God. I hadn't even thought of that. The Powderpuff game, Mr. Ulrich had once told us, started in 1978 when Chawton and Ansel merged. Had the *T* and *A* tradition started then, too?

It was more than possible. It was likely.

Did all the alumni of the past forty years know? The alumni, who hewed so loyally to their teams, throwing cash at the Tigers vs. Angels fund-raising drive, never forgetting which side they supported?

They knew.

Crusty alumni, hundreds of Old White Dudes, cheering

lustily at Jamboree as they ogled the conveniently categorized wares of the Chawton girls.

"For all we know," said Crispin, "Andy's making up the whole thing."

We looked at each other. I didn't believe it for an instant, and neither did he.

"And if he's not, they can deny it. You haven't got any proof. If you tell, all you'll do is cause a lot of grief during Jamboree. You'll embarrass yourself. And, Bump . . ." He paused. "Haven't you embarrassed yourself enough already?"

Crispin took me home. Our house was dark, so he didn't come in. "See you tomorrow?" I said. "You're coming to Jamboree with Mom and Dad, right?"

"Yep. See you there."

I went inside. I had a speech to write. I pulled up my hood to keep the thoughts warm and began to type.

> It is my honor to welcome you, Chawton School's proud contingent of students, parents, alumni, trustees, and graduating seniors, to the 41st annual Jamboree

Delete.

I couldn't do it.

No matter what Crispin or anyone else thought I should do, I could not let this stand.

SMASH THE PATRIARCHY! I wrote in all caps at the top of the document.

I am enraged to report . . .

For an untold number of years . . .

It is a shocking—nay, shameful—conspiracy of privilege . . .

The objectification is nauseating . . .

You, yes, you personally, are complicit . . .

You have contributed to a culture of oppression . . .

I'd been born to write this speech. Right before the game, when the Powderpuff fervor had built to a peak, when I had the floor and no one could make me shut up, I would speak.

I printed it. Still feeling dramatic, in full orator mode, I chose a red folder: red for my rage, red for the scarlet letter with which I'd be branded after I took down Jamboree.

I didn't care.

But the red folder snagged something in my brain. I couldn't get to it, but I knew it was there, like when a stray hair brushes your arm and you reach for it and it's gone. There was something I should remember. Something . . .

It's late at night, I thought. I got into bed. But I couldn't stop trying to reel in the bite. It taunted me. You're just tired, I told myself, and maybe this is a form of mental malfunction like déjà vu, when you misfile information—

Misfile.

The red file folder.

Mack.

I sat up in bed.

It was Mack.

We had met after school for Triumvirate. Andy, cranky, had left. Gennifer had had a red folder with the encoded data from Paul and the key from dingbat Ms. Edison. Mack had come in, demanding a ride, and Gennifer had run to her locker, and I'd gone to the business office.

We had left Mack alone with the folder.

I didn't know why he'd done it, but I knew it was him.

CHAPTER 31

Before the lacrosse game the next morning, I went to the studio where Jiyoon was about to lead a tour. She was alone, arranging black velvet around the base of her sculpture.

"You look remarkably calm," I said.

"Why wouldn't I be calm?"

"The election?"

"I'm fine now that it's out of my control."

"That always makes things worse for me."

"Because you're a control freak," she said, but in a nice way. "Shouldn't you be out there hobnobbing with alumni? Putting on your greasepaint for the big game?"

"Oh my God. So . . ."

I filled her in about the Powderpuff teams. "Gross," she said, shaking her head.

"I'm going to blow it up."

"What?"

"I get the mike for the welcome speech before the game. I wrote a speech. An exposé. They won't know what's hitting them."

"Jem. Come over here." We sat on stools splattered with paint and bumpy with glue. "Swivel toward me and look me in the eyes," she said. "You can't do this."

"I'm definitely doing it."

"If it's true—"

"It's true."

"—then it's the grossest thing ever. It's got to be stopped. It *will* be stopped. But you can't stop it by giving a public speech at the biggest event of the year."

"That's the best way! It'll make the news! It'll go viral!"

"It'll ruin everything," she said firmly. "The whole Jamboree and your class's graduation, to start. Then the rest. Donations, admissions—it could destroy the whole school."

"Maybe Chawton *should* be destroyed. Think about how many people knew this was going on."

"I'm going to ask you a tough question, Jem. You can get mad at me, but promise you'll at least think about it."

"Okay."

"Are you giving the speech because you want this thing to be stopped, or because you want to be the one who stops it?"

That, ladies and gentlemen, is a best friend. She sees you for all your frailty and flaws, and she loves you, and she calls you the fuck out.

"Because this is the best way to stop it," I said.

That doesn't mean she's always right.

"Think about it," said Jiyoon. A student ambassador appeared at the door with a group of alumni. Without missing a beat, Jiyoon stood. "Hello!" she said. "Welcome to the sculpture studio! May I show you around?"

The lacrosse game was under way by the time I got back outside, and the campus was buzzing with students and parents and alumni. I recognized a few of the OWDs from the Senior Triumvirates, Past and Present reception back in April.

At halftime, I snuck away from Gennifer and her to-do list to find Mack. He was with the team on the other side of the field, and I hoped my triumvir T-shirt would give me a permissible pretense for being over there. I cornered him while he was alone at the water cooler.

"Hey," I said.

He didn't respond, either ignoring me or not hearing me.

"Hi, Mack," I said.

"Yo," he said, not looking at me.

"I know you did it."

I saw him stiffen under the lacrosse pads. "Did what?"

"Don't bother playing dumb."

He finished filling the water bottle. He took off his helmet and shoved a sheaf of sweaty hair off his forehead. He spat out his mouth guard. "Fine," he said at last. "What do you want?"

"I want to know why you did it."

"You know why."

"To make Jiyoon look bad and win the election?"

"I don't care about the election."

This did not compute. He swigged from the water bottle.

"I ran because everyone told me I should," he said. "But I'll be just as happy if Jiyoon wins and I can kick back and enjoy senior year."

"Why'd you do it, then?"

"You know."

"No, I really don't," I said. "To get at me? You knew everyone would blame me for it?"

He gave me a strange look. "Why would I want to get at you?"

Those were my only two theories. "Then why?"

"*You* know," he said for the third time.

"If it's not clear already, I—"

"Gennifer put Andy."

"She put—wait. She put Andy?"

"You didn't look at the data?"

"Of course not!"

He shrugged. "I flipped through. I wasn't going to do anything. I was waiting for Gennifer to get back from her locker. But I saw her code, so I looked her up, just for the hell of it, and, yeah, there it was. She put Andy. My girlfriend put my fucking brother."

"It was something dumb she typed into a dumb website, Mack. It doesn't mean anything."

Why was I trying to console him?

"I got so mad," he said. "And I was like, Okay, I'll fuck with their fucking Triumvirate. I'll post it."

"So that's why Gennifer's name wasn't on it. You didn't want everyone else to know."

"Pretty much."

"But what about me? And Andy? Why'd you take us off?"

"No shit," he said, squinting at me. "You seriously had that folder of data and you didn't even look."

"Nope."

"I took you and Andy off because you put each other."

"I put him—"

"And he put you. One and only, both of you. It was too fucking perfect. He always gets everything. And now, look, one more thing."

"He put me?"

"Just you."

I goggled.

"So yeah, sorry for ruining that," said Mack. "He's probably still into you. Ask him out. He'd be down."

"I had no idea," I said.

"Yeah," he said, picking up his helmet, "you're pretty clueless."

"Gennifer likes you," I said. "She likes you a lot."

"Whatever." He put on his helmet. "Also, just so you know, don't think I'm ever admitting this. It's your word against mine and I will fucking deny this shit till the day I die."

So much for the stirring of fondness I'd felt for him.

"I gotta go," he said, sticking in his mouth guard. He spoke through it, the words garbled. "This conversation never happened."

It would have looked suspicious not to change into my Powderpuff kit, so I did, even though I knew I wouldn't be playing. Nobody would be playing. I grabbed my red folder and found Gennifer on the sidelines. She said, "Your speech is right after the cheer routines—"

"—so be ready to take the mike immediately," I said. "You've told me. Several times."

"I'm just trying to make this happen, Jemmy."

With a nauseating rasp of feedback, the song started for the Male Tigers' cheer routine. We turned to the field, where a dozen senior guys had run out in tiny shorts and crop tops. "Oof," said Gennifer.

"Oof is right," I said. The mock cheerleading was a spectacle best avoided.

"All that pale, hairy leg," said Gennifer, shaking her head.

The audience was already roaring, and they kept roaring throughout the two-minute dance, which mostly consisted of hip thrusts, prancing, and kissy faces. The problems here extended far beyond the fact that the sun had never shone on most of these thighs. By the end, the guys were flushed, waggling jazz hands around the one guy who could almost do the splits.

"Did you put the ballots at our table in the tent?" Gennifer asked as the Angel Boys cavorted onto the field.

"As you commanded."

"Good," she said. "We'll distribute them to the juniors at halftime, and then we'll miss third quarter to count the votes."

We had already run through the logistics at least six times. Impulsively, I slung an arm around her shoulders. "Thanks, Gennifer. You're great at this."

"I know."

"You should be a wedding planner."

"Or a CEO," she said, rolling her eyes. "Check yourself."

The Angel Boys were twerking. The whole Tigers Powderpuff team joined Gennifer and me on the sidelines, and Andy and Tyler came over too. I was right in the middle of the group. The Angel Boys shook their booties to Beyoncé and the roar of the crowd, and I gazed at them and felt my eyes go wet. It wasn't sadness, or happiness, or nostalgia, or anger. I didn't know what it was.

"*What do you want?*" Mack had asked me.

I wanted everything. I wanted the Powderpuff scandal to be broken. I wanted to be the one to break it. And I wanted everything to stay the same. I wanted the Chawton snow globe to keep sparkling, intact. I wanted the sunshine to keep soaking the boys in problematic drag, the girls in football gear, the pastel alumni, the effed-up-ness of it all.

★　★　★

A few minutes later I said, "Welcome." I had taken the wireless mike onto the field. "It is my honor to welcome Chawton School's proud contingent of students, parents, alumni, trustees, and graduating seniors to the forty-first annual Jamboree. On behalf of Senior Triumvirate and the entire senior class, I hope you're enjoying the festivities."

I was speaking off the cuff. My prepared speech was tucked into my waistband, but I didn't need a script.

"I can't believe my experience at Chawton is about to end," I told everyone. "It's bittersweet. I'm excited for my next steps. I'm excited to find a bigger world. But my time here has taught me so much."

As I spoke, my eyes scanned the audience. I couldn't find Jiyoon. I did see Crispin, in the bleachers with our parents. He was wearing a derby hat.

Maybe they were right.

But I didn't do it because anyone had told me to do it. I didn't do it for any good reason at all. I did it because the field was green and the people were pretty. I did it because I wanted to play Powderpuff, damn it.

For once in my life, I kept my big mouth shut.

"That's all," I said. "Thank you. It's time for the game."

CHAPTER 32

Iplayed the first few minutes in a daze. The Angels got a touchdown off us, and I dropped an easy catch. "What's with you, Kincaid?" Andy barked from the sidelines. "Get your head in the game!"

Melanie hiked to Jessica. I ranged out deep and left and saw the ball spiraling through the blue sky, and I hugged it to my chest and got in three, four, five big steps before Mackenzie chased me down. "That's better!" yelled Andy. "Now do it again!"

Jessica went short to Haley on the next down. But on the following one, although Andy and Tyler had called another short play, she threw long, deep into the end zone on the right side. I didn't think I could even get close, but nobody else was near, so I sprinted with everything I had, my tight braid arcing behind me as Mackenzie tried to keep her mark. I was still ten feet away as the ball began to plummet, and I dove. I felt the ball between my chest and the grass. I knew by the screams of the crowd that I, and the ball, were in the end zone.

Brittany spotted Jessica as quarterback, and Jessica ran a long touchdown in the second quarter. But the Angels got another one too. The game was tied at halftime. "Huddle up, Tigers!" called Andy.

We all came in tight. "Some great work from Landover and Kincaid," said Tyler.

Haley interrupted him with a whoop. Andy gave me a tiny smile, and I felt a jolt of confusion. I had resolved that we were over. But he'd listed me for the dance. Only me.

"There's a lot of room for improvement, though," said Andy. "Listen up."

"Um, Tyler needs to handle this alone," said Gennifer. "We've got to run the election. Now."

"That can wait."

"No, it can't."

He turned back to the team, wordlessly dismissing her. "I want to see more focus out there," he told the huddle. "You're getting distracted by the crowd, and—"

"Come on, Gennifer," I said loudly. "We've got a job to do. Even if this asshole won't do his part."

"*What* did you call me?"

"You heard me." I met his glare. "The three of us have responsibilities, and Gennifer and I, at least, intend to see them through."

"Let's go," said Gennifer.

The two of us left and headed toward the tent. The huddle closed in behind us like we'd never been there. Andy didn't follow. "Why am I surprised?" I said.

"You shouldn't be," said Gennifer. She was right. This was a guy who'd sorted us by our breasts.

"I need to tell you something," I said.

"Now? We've got a hundred and twenty juniors swarming to get their chairman ballots."

"I can say it on the way to the tent." I told her about Mack: how he'd leaked the Last Chance Dance picks, and why. "Do you believe me?" I said.

"Yeah. I believe you. I didn't know. But I believe you."

"I know he's your boyfriend, and maybe he's not a bad guy, but—"

"But," she said.

She met my eyes. Gennifer is so cool, so collected. Her forehead remained smooth. Her eyes were dry. We were at the tent. "Juniors!" she called. "Form two orderly lines, please! After you sign your acknowledgment that you have received your ballot, you may make your vote wherever you choose." The juniors were excited for their first senior activity. They were annoyingly full of themselves, like they thought they were seniors already. Don't trust tomorrow, I thought, because tomorrow brings the people who will take your place. "Your ballot must be in the box by the beginning of the third quarter."

★ ★ ★

Andy didn't show up at the tent until the third quarter had begun. "Was that so hard?" he said, sauntering in. "It's called division of labor."

Ms. Edison shooed everyone out of the tent before leaving herself. (Chawton tradition. You know.) Gennifer got out her gel pens and binder, and I unfolded the first ballot, read it, and handed it to Andy to be read aloud. "One vote for Jiyoon," he said, his voice even.

Gennifer made a tick mark.

I handed him the next ballot.

"One for Mack," he said.

And so it went.

In the fourth quarter, we were behind by seven points. It was fourth down with less than a minute on the clock. We were at the twenty-yard line, and we needed a touchdown and a two-point conversion. Andy and Tyler called a time-out. "Kincaid, go deep," said Tyler. "Bowling, you go shallow." Jessica was quarterbacking again. "Get it to whichever one looks more open."

"This is it, girls," said Andy. "This is our chance to win it for the Tigers."

I ran deep. I darted around the Angel linewomen and sprinted down the sideline and turned for the pass, squinting against the sun.

Jessica flipped it to Brittany.

She was instantly tackled.

The clock blared, and the Angels—the team, their fans—rose up in exultation.

I didn't care at all.

After Mackenzie accepted the Powderpuff trophy on behalf of the Angels, Ms. Edison, Gennifer, Andy, and I came onto the makeshift stage. "Chawton tradition holds that the new Triumvirate is announced directly after the Powderpuff game," said Ms. Edison. "Let's have one last round of applause for the current Triumvirate."

I didn't have much trouble looking modest, given how little we deserved any applause whatsoever.

"Without further ado," said Ms. Edison, "I'll announce the rising Senior Triumvirate. The new Social Committee president will be Madison Porter."

No surprise there. Madison squealed and ran onto the field. Gennifer hugged her.

"The recipient of the Mildred Mustermann Award for Academic Excellence," said Ms. Edison, "is Ashby Fleming."

Again, no surprise. Ashby looked pleased. She got a round of polite applause. I shook her hand.

"And the senior-class chairman—" said Ms. Edison.

I was nervous even though I knew the results.

"—will be Jiyoon Kim."

A moment of shock, and then the audience erupted into claps and cheers and hollers, and Jiyoon, beaming, made her way down from the bleachers and took the field. Andy shook her hand and pulled her into a bro hug, pounding her back.

There they were, I thought, looking at the three of them. All girls. They would be the ones running Powderpuff. If they followed the advice I planned to give them, they'd cancel the whole corrupt event. If they wanted to keep the game, they could divide the teams however they wanted to. The tradition would die.

I'm not saying I did the right thing, and I'm not saying I did it for the right reasons. But I was pretty sure it'd be okay.

Crispin found me after the ceremony. "Congratulations," he said, hugging me. "You're no longer a triumvir."

"Thank God," I said.

"You decided not to do anything?"

"Do anything about what?"

"Good girl," he said, patting my head.

I'd been getting a lot of that.

Good job, Jemima.

Nice going up there.

Good work, girl.

And nice run on that last play!

Good. Nice. Good. Nice.

Everyone liked me this way.

Gennifer was crowded by admirers, getting the same sort of compliments. This wasn't unusual for her. She'd always been known as good and nice.

But here's what *I* now knew about Gennifer Grier:

I'd been sitting slightly behind her as we counted the votes in the tent. She had two columns on the sheet in her binder, one for Jiyoon and one for Mack. The system we had decided on beforehand was that I would open each ballot and read it and hand it to Andy, and he'd read the name aloud, and Gennifer would keep track of the count.

She had started with her binder flat on the table, but slowly, gradually, she had tilted it toward her.

Andy never noticed.

The count was close, but as the ballots dwindled, Mack pulled three votes ahead, and then four.

I opened one of the last ballots and handed it to Andy. "Mack," he read aloud.

Jiyoon, went Gennifer's pen.

"Jiyoon," read Andy.

Jiyoon, went Gennifer's pen.

"Mack," read Andy.

Jiyoon, went Gennifer's pen.

I fumbled around in the bottom of the box. "Two more," I said.

"Mack," read Andy.

Jiyoon, went Gennifer's pen.

"Last one," I said.

"And it's . . . Jiyoon," said Andy.

Gennifer slid the binder flat on the table and made one final tick mark in Jiyoon's column. "Okay, let's see . . ."

We all stared at the page.

"She edged him out," said Andy. "One vote."

"A girl chairman," I said.

"Poor Macky," said Gennifer, staring at the page, shaking her head in disbelief. "He ran a great campaign. He'll be so upset."

"Eh, he'll be fine," said Andy, shoving his chair back. "Let's get back to the game."

Gennifer thwacked shut the binder and scooped up the ballots. "Who's ready to get out there for one more quarter of Powderpuff?" She buried the ballots in the tent's trash can. "Tigers forever!"

CHAPTER 33

I skipped the Last Chance Dance. Instead I called Jiyoon. "Do you feel compelled to go to the dance?" I said. "Now that you're the face of Chawton?"

"Not at all," she said. "I'm doing Triumvirate my way."

"That's the best thing I've heard all day. You want to come over? We could work on our dioramas."

"Well, I have plans."

"Oh." I should have known. "Okay, cool."

"It's Official Date Number Four. We're going to an indoor trampoline park."

"Of course you are."

"You should come."

"No, that's okay—"

"Paul already invited you."

"Actually?"

"He said it'll be more fun if you come too. I agreed."

"Wow."

"We'll pick you up at 8:04."

At 8:04, when Prudence jangled into my driveway, Paul at the wheel, Jiyoon riding shotgun, I hopped into the back seat. We drove. I rolled down the windows and the evening air eddied through the car. We could go anywhere. We could go to an indoor trampoline park, or we could go to California. It was the kind of freedom I'd wanted my whole life. I could talk or sing or keep my mouth shut, whichever I chose. I sent up a bubble of hope—that I'd be better, that we'd all be better—and I watched through the sunroof as it faltered up to the sky. We drove. It might have been an illusion, but history, like us, was moving onward, forward. Toward the horizon, away from the dance.

ACKNOWLEDGMENTS

I began this book when Donald Trump was nothing but a washed-up reality-TV star, when I hadn't even started to scrape off my cruddy crust of white feminism and internalized misogyny. Needless to say, I have learned a lot, thanks in large part to the writings of Chimamanda Ngozi Adichie, Roxane Gay, Sandra Gilbert, Susan Gubar, Peggy Orenstein, Lindy West, and Naomi Wolf; to Christy Harrison's podcast and Heather Hackman's training; to the editorial genius of Erin Clarke; and to conversations with Lucy, Emma, Rebecca, Mom, Dad, Phil, Nate, Caroline, John, Howard, Woojin, Rita, Sasha, Ariel, and Sarah. I still have a cruddy crust, though. I have a lot left to learn. I'll keep reading and listening, so send good stuff my way.

Many thanks to Uwe Stender, my steadfast and funny and extraordinarily effective agent; to Ana Hard, cover artist; and to the whole team at Knopf, especially Kelly Delaney, Karen Sherman, Artie Bennett, and Casey Moses. As always, I'm deeply grateful to my people: my parents, my brothers, my sisters, my colleagues, my friends. And for you, Phil and Ramona, there are truly no words to express my love and gratitude. You make it so fun not to write.

ABOUT THE AUTHOR

Kate Hattemer is a native of Cincinnati, but now writes, reads, runs, and teaches high school Latin in the DC metro area. She is the author of *The Vigilante Poets of Selwyn Academy*, which received five starred reviews, *The Land of 10,000 Madonnas*, and *Here Comes Trouble*.

KateHattemer.com